"Fans of Dennis Lehane will revel in the settings and atmosphere . . . an absorbing read . . . a hard-charging plot . . . Boston nitty-gritty."

—Charles Kelly
Author of *Gunshots In Another Room*
a biography of crime writer Dan Marlowe

Praise for The Combat Zone

"Power's work, already cover-to-cover forceful, keeps getting better. Boston has never had a better P. I."

—John Lutz
Edgar & Shamus award-winning
author of *Single White Female*
past president of Mystery Writers of America
& Private Eye Writers of America

ALSO BY JED POWER

DAN MARLOWE SERIES

THE BOSS OF HAMPTON BEACH

HAMPTON BEACH HOMICIDE

BLOOD ON HAMPTON BEACH

HONEYMOON HOTEL

MURDER ON THE ISLAND

THE COMBAT ZONE

Jed Power

The Hampton Beach
TAPES

a Dan Marlowe/Hampton Beach Novel

Dark Jetty Publishing

Published by
Dark Jetty Publishing
4 Essex Center Drive #3906
Peabody, MA 01961

Cover Artist:
Brandon Swann

ISBN 978-0-9971758-2-0

10 9 8 7 6 5 4 3 2 1

Acknowledgements

I would like to thank my editor, Louisa Swann, for her fine work on this, the sixth novel in the Dan Marlowe/Hampton Beach series. In addition, thank you to Amy Ray and Bonnar Spring, two excellent writers, who critiqued the manuscript and offered many valuable suggestions.

Chapter 1

THE FIST HIT a glancing blow on the right side of my jaw, hard enough that I staggered back a couple of steps. My hands flew to my face. Standing in front of me in the doorway, his other hand holding the screen door open, was Lieutenant Richard Gant of the Hampton Police Department. He wore a short-sleeved white shirt, dark pants, and a red flushed face. His gray eyes were wild and I could smell booze on his breath.

Less than a minute ago, I had been in bed sleeping off the night's overindulgence when my unpleasant dreams had been interrupted by a pounding on my front door. I'd crawled from my bed, thrown on a pair of jeans, and staggered to the front room to see who it was. Dawn hadn't broken yet, so I turned on a light and opened the door. I hadn't been expecting trouble, but I'd sure found it.

"Are you fuckin' out of your mind, Gant?"

He was wearing his gun in a holster on his hip and he looked like he'd partaken in the same activity I had that night, except he hadn't slept yet.

Gant stepped into the room, letting the screen door close behind him. "I oughta beat you fuckin' bloody, Marlowe."

He looked at my hands; I had my fists balled at my sides. I glanced at the gun on his hip, then toward my bedroom. I had a shotgun under the bed and a .38 in my nightstand. Only a few short steps, same as the distance between Gant and myself. Even though he was drunk, he was perceptive. "You'll never make it," he said.

He was right. I'd have to stand firm and hope this didn't escalate beyond fists. In a hand-to-hand fight I knew I'd stand a good chance. Between his weapon and his mental condition—which wasn't too solid where I was concerned even when he was sober—I decided to swallow my pride and not return the punch.

"What do you want, Gant?"

Gant's lips curled, showing his teeth. "What I want, I can't do. What I want you to do, you're going to do. And now."

I'd had run-ins with Gant before. I knew the man hated me; he'd been convinced for years that I was a major criminal player on the beach. He was wrong; my bank account proved that. But Gant believed the way I lived was a cunning front, not the sad outcome of my years-long cocaine romance.

I could have demanded he get out. But it wouldn't have done any good, considering his condition and what he thought of me. Besides, I wanted to know what had brought this attack on. It was a little over the top, even for Gant.

So I said again, "What do you want, Gant?"

Gant's face turned a darker shade of red, like a booze-hound's with high blood pressure. "I want you to get your filthy business off my beach, Marlowe. If you think you're gonna peddle kiddie porn on Hampton Beach, it'll be over my dead body!"

I couldn't have been more stunned if I'd found out my neighbor was tossing around hand grenades instead of fireworks on the Fourth of July. There were a lot of things I'd thought he might accuse me of, but being tied up with kiddie porn wasn't one of them. My gut reaction was to call him crazy and every other word that fit that definition. But I didn't like the way Gant was breathing through his nose or the way he seemed to be struggling to hold himself back instead of tearing me limb from limb.

I had no choice but to handle him as I would an escaped mental patient, so I chose my words carefully. "I don't know what you're talking about, Gant. I wouldn't have anything to do with stuff like that. I've got kids."

Gant would have made a good ventriloquist—his mouth barely moved as he spoke. "And thank god they're not living here with a sleazebag like you. I'd have them outta here in a heartbeat."

My voice quivered when I spoke and it wasn't from fear, it was from anger. "I told you I've got nothing to do with any porn."

"*Kiddie* porn," Gant roared. "I want those dirty tapes out of every store on the beach that you got 'em in. I'm not waiting to build a case against you to get that shit out of my town. I want it out, *now!*"

I could've denied my involvement until summer was over, but Gant wouldn't have believed me. So I didn't try. Instead I spoke as if I was talking to a strong-arm collector for the local bookie. "The tapes aren't mine, Gant, but I'll get them off the beach. I don't want that kind of stuff in Hampton either."

"Not when you can't make any money at it, you don't." Spit flew from his mouth as he talked. "And you *will* get them off the beach. As far as them being your tapes, I'll prove that later. You'll be in Concord for a nice long stay when this is over. I hope you get slammed up the ass every night, you dirty scumbag."

Gant glared at me with bloodshot eyes that had more hate in them than a Ku Klux Klan member's at a lynching. His fists opened and closed.

After a short minute during which I felt like I was waiting for a bomb to detonate, Gant spoke. "Get that shit outta every freakin' place you got it in, Marlowe. And *quick*. If you don't, I'll . . . I'll . . ."

Gant didn't finish his sentence. I detected a flicker of fear in his eyes. Somehow I knew it wasn't fear of me but fear of what he was contemplating doing to me. He'd scared himself. He was that close to going off the deep end.

He turned, shoved the screen door open, and marched out. I didn't move, just listened to him stomp down the porch stairs. It sounded like he missed one but didn't fall.

I didn't wait to hear his car start up. I stepped over, closed the wooden door, and pressed the button lock.

Back in the middle of the room, I just stood there. With Gant gone, I started to notice the things that had taken a back seat to my efforts to get him out with me still alive. Things like my heart beating as hard as the waves hitting the shore during a nor'easter. Hands that shook but not enough to throw off the sweat that covered my palms. The feeling that some unknown disaster was about to take place at any moment. All that and more.

I walked to my bedroom on a floor that felt like it was covered in deep seaweed. I slid open a small drawer in the top of my dresser and pulled out a lone white sock tossed in with the rest of the mess. I took a prescription bottle of Xanax out of the sock. I fumbled with the cap. Tossed two of the orange pills under my tongue to let them dissolve. My mouth was so dry I had to suck to pull out some saliva. Finally, the unique medicinal taste I knew so well filled my mouth.

In my easy chair in the front room, I drank beer but otherwise I sat like I was comatose, waiting for the pills to put out the fire. Waiting for my brain to slow down enough that I could figure out what madman Gant had been talking about, and more importantly, what the hell I was going to do about it.

It was a longer than usual wait until the anxiety symptoms subsided. But they did. Finally.

Chapter 2

I SLEPT FITFULLY for what was left of the night. The beer and pills knocked me out, but couldn't keep me that way. I kept waking up, thinking about what Gant had accused me of and where the hell it was going to lead.

When I woke for the last time, I showered, shaved, ate, flicked off the big window air conditioner, and headed out for work. The second I opened the front door, a wave of heat hit me harder than the smack I'd gotten from Gant the previous night. It was July, but this was an unusual July. We'd been trapped in a weather system with temperatures in the nineties, along with sky-high humidity, for about a week now. People were starting to get ugly, in both temperament and looks. Usually our little area of New Hampshire's seacoast was spared the hottest days of summer with the wind off the water—Mother Nature's air conditioner. Not this year. We'd had nothing but hot wind rolling in from the interior ever since the heat wave had started. And there was no change predicted in the long-range forecast.

I'd walked less than a hundred yards before perspiration stuck my shirt to my body. Even the sun wasn't inclined to give the beach a break. It was a hot orange ball in the sky that seemed to move closer every day. Clouds didn't exist anymore. Still traffic was heavy. People flocked to the beach on these oven-like days. I couldn't understand it. Lie on the beach and sweat like a pig? That wasn't my idea of relief. Unless you decided to stay in the water. Still you'd be a sweat ball within seconds of stepping out.

No, there was only one thing during a blistering spell like this that could keep a person, at least a person like me, from flipping out and running along Ocean Boulevard with a roaring chainsaw—air conditioning. And I had it! Two window models at my cottage, a rarity on the beach. At work too, thank god. Two monster built-in wall units that I'd had installed back when I'd owned the High Tide Restaurant and Saloon. If they weren't pumping freezing cold air by the time I got there, they would be soon after my arrival.

I entered the Tide through the back door as I did most every day. It was still hot inside. Not as bad as outside, but not a lot better either. The wall A/C units did a good job in the dining room and bar area but the kitchen and back office weren't air conditioned. It wouldn't have been practical in the kitchen, not with the fryolators and ovens and burners going all day. The office, which was off to my left just inside the door, was solid concrete with no windows. Not practical, or even possible, there either. Today I was glad I was a bartender and not an owner or kitchen help who had to toil in an ungodly hellhole.

"Hi, Dan," came from the office.

I took the few steps over and walked inside. Dianne Dennison, the owner, was seated behind a metal office desk. She had on a white kitchen shirt with the sleeves rolled up.

Her full black hair was tied up in one of those head scarves. Dianne was my significant other. She had been ever since my divorce. She knew everything about me. The cocaine abuse, the anxiety disorder, everything. And still she loved me. And I loved her. I'd do anything for her and I knew she would for me too.

Dianne twisted back and forth a bit in her swivel chair. A revolving fan plunked on top of a green file cabinet blew a black curl of hair across her forehead on each pass. I positioned myself so the breeze from the fan would give me a pasting every so often, too.

"What's up?" I said, not expecting an answer.

She tossed the pen she'd been holding on the desk. "You look hot," she said. Then added, smiling, "Temperature-wise, I mean."

I didn't return the smile, instead I cleared my throat.

"Why aren't you out in the A/C?" I asked, already knowing the answer.

"Because I've got to get this stuff done." She waved her hand over papers on her desk. "And besides, I work in the kitchen and it's even worse out there. How would you like to swap jobs just for today?"

"No thanks." I was still trying to get my body temperature back to normal from my walk in the scorching heat. Get my breathing under control, too. I felt anxious again all of a sudden.

"Aren't you going to sit a minute?" Dianne nodded toward one of the two folding chairs in front of her desk.

I shook my head. With my shirt and shorts still sticking to my body the idea seemed as attractive as becoming a roofer for the day. "I don't plan to stay in here long."

"I don't blame you."

I toyed with the idea of telling her about Gant's visit the previous night. The more I thought about it, the more my anxiety increased and that wasn't helping my efforts to cool down. My hand dropped to the pocket of my walking shorts. I'd left the vial at home.

"Dan, are you all right?" It wasn't the first time Dianne had asked me that and it wasn't the first time I answered with a lie.

"Sure, I'm fine." I wondered if she could hear the little quiver I feared was in my voice.

She furrowed her brows. "What is that?" she asked.

She put her hands on the desk, pushed herself up from the chair. The white kitchen shirt was loose over black cotton shorts that hung just above her knees. She came around the desk and walked right up to me. I'm six feet, Dianne only a few inches shorter. She looked at my face. Her hand came up and touched my jaw. I winced. I hadn't even noticed it before, but Gant's glancing blow must have made a bruise.

"How'd you get that?"

Her deep green eyes studied me like a teacher waiting for a wrong answer. It would be tough to fool those knowing eyes. Especially today with the heat and the way I felt and with what happened with Gant last night. Still, I tried.

"I bumped the bathroom cabinet in the dark last night." It sounded lame the second I said it.

She looked down for a moment. My heart was beating so hard I wondered if she could see my shirt move. After a moment she raised her head and put her soft full lips on my jaw. I didn't wince this time. Instead I wrapped my arms around her waist and pulled her in tight. She tried to pull away. I wouldn't let her. She pulled her head back and we stared at each other.

She didn't have any makeup on; she didn't need any. I looked into her green eyes. I loved to look into her green eyes. Always. I was flush against her and she was ass to the desk. I knew she could feel me; she must've known I wasn't going to stop even with the unpleasant heat. And she was right. I wouldn't; I couldn't.

Whether I'd finally snapped because of the heat, the encounter with Gant, the beer and pills the night before, or my anxiety that was now like a jolt of meth, I didn't know. Probably all of it. But mix all that with a woman I could hardly keep my hands off in my most rational of times and we both knew what was about to happen.

"Jesus, Dan, please. At least close the door."

I couldn't tell if she was angry, wanted to help me, or was as out of control as I was. Whatever it was, I didn't let go of her. Without separating, we shuffled to the door. With one hand I closed it and moved the slide lock into place. I used the same hand to fumble with the buttons on her white work shirt. When I had them all undone, I pushed her shirt back over her shoulders and she shrugged it off. She came against me then and our lips met. Hers were soft, full, and moist and when I tried to force my tongue between them she opened them teasingly slow. I pushed my tongue harder; finally, it slipped inside and our tongues rolled around each other. Hers tasted of mint. I pushed her back against the desk again. I was ready to reach around and unclasp her black bra when her hands did the job for me.

I could feel her breasts pressed against my chest. I wanted to kiss them. But I couldn't pull my tongue out of Dianne's beautiful mouth. I opened my eyes and hers were partially open, too. Green with gold flecks. I couldn't take it anymore. I reached down and pulled her shorts down. I could feel her trying to wiggle them lower. I tugged at her panties but they fought me. Her hands came from around my neck to help.

My hands shook as I unbuckled my belt, let my shorts fall, and then got my underpants out of the way. I grabbed Dianne's forearms, squeezed. She threw her head back. Her eyes and lips were all half closed. I moved right in, probed. Her thighs opened. Our bodies were covered in sweat. I rubbed both our abdomens with one hand before I positioned myself and slid slowly and tightly inside Dianne. She groaned, closed her thighs on me as she did. I grabbed her head, pulled it forward, the silk of her head scarf soft on my fingers. Her green eyes opened. She knew what she liked and did what she liked. And I did what I liked, all the time looking into those green eyes that were looking right back at me. Right until the end. The very end.

Chapter 3

A LITTLE LATER, out front at the bar, I had a smile on my face as I scurried around getting the area ready for my regulars and the lunch crowd that wouldn't be far behind. I lugged ice for the sinks at either end of the L-shaped mahogany bar. Chopped fruit, stocked beer chests and liquor storage cabinets, and made banks for the waitresses, along with a series of other tasks I did every morning before I opened the bar. I was on automatic pilot; I could have done it all in my sleep.

My abnormal anxiety was gone now. I had Dianne to thank for that. And it wasn't like I ravished her in her business office every day. Matter of fact, I don't think I ever had. At least not like that. Although most everyone knew we had something going, Dianne had always been adamant about keeping our relationship on a low setting at work. Not only did she think it would be inappropriate to do otherwise, she also didn't want my fellow employees to get the idea she was showing me any favoritism, which, at least as far as work went, she wasn't.

When Dianne and I made love, either at my cottage or at her Ocean Boulevard condo, it was usually a slow, gentle lovemaking. What had just happened had been about as gentle as a male gorilla taking his mate. And Dianne had let it happen—she'd known I was suffering the minute she'd looked at my face. It was almost impossible to hide major anxiety symptoms, especially from someone who knew me as well as Dianne did. So I guess it was a charity lay. Or at least that's how it started out. But it didn't end that way. Her reactions had told me that. It had been something new and exciting for her. For me it changed my world. At least for today.

I was placing ashtrays along the length of the bar when the banging on the front door started. I didn't need Madame Stella, the beach psychic, to tell me who it was. The Budweiser Clydesdale clock over the back bar did that. Eleven o'clock. I came around the bar, grabbing the key from the cash register on the way, and walked to the door. Unlocking it, I swung the heavy ancient wooden door open and held it. Standing in the little foyer, inside the screen door which was kept unlocked, was Eli, my first customer of the day. And every day for that matter.

He wore his usual attire—a splotched painter's outfit including dirty white cap. He barely came up to my shoulders as he elbowed by me, muttering under his breath and gifting me with a face full of smoke from the Camel bobbing between his lips. He was one of those people who could've been anywhere between sixty and eighty. He would never say.

Right behind Eli was my usual second regular of the day—Paulie. He wore a blue post office shirt, the only thing that gave away his occupation. Certainly not his thick brown hair with a touch of gray, parted in the middle and worn down to his shoulders. He was a sorter, not a delivery mailman. That, and his twenty-plus year seniority, allowed him to wear his hair any damn way he pleased. He'd told me that himself. Many times. Jeans and sneakers completed the rest of his garb.

More personable than Eli (which wasn't saying much), he gave me a smile and a "Morning, Dan."

"Paulie."

I followed them back to the bar. Paulie sat on a stool at the L-shaped end. Behind him was a large plate glass window that looked out onto Ocean Boulevard. If you were to cross that street and walk forty feet across the municipal parking lot, you'd be at the beach and have the Atlantic Ocean spread out in front of you. It was a pleasant place to work—having the ocean right there, every day, just across the street.

By the time I got behind the bar, Eli was seated in his usual seat halfway down the bar, directly in front of our four draft beer spigots. He'd already snatched a pilsner glass from one of the columns I had lined up on both sides of the spigots. He was holding the glass up in his left hand and making it shimmy.

"How long I gotta wait for a beer around here?" he asked. "Bad enough you don't open 'til eleven, but half the time you're late."

I chuckled. This was pretty close to the way my shifts started every day.

"Not today," I said, pointing my thumb over my shoulder toward the beer clock.

Eli cleared a phlegmy throat. "Well, try to keep it up."

I took the pilsner glass, and poured a beer from the Budweiser spigot. Topped it with a nice small foamy head if I do say so myself. Eli didn't like wasting beer with a lot of foam. I placed the glass on a cocktail napkin in front of him.

While he began to make love to his first beer of the day with little slurps and sighs, I grabbed a Miller Light bottle from the beer chest and plunked it down in front of Paulie. He never used a glass. He had a Winston going and was blowing large perfect smoke rings. I watched as a couple hit the ceiling, spread and disappeared.

"Thanks," Paulie said. He didn't go for the beer, wasn't in a hurry like Eli. But when he did take that first sip, the beer would be gone in under a minute. After all, he had a daily ritual, a quota of beer to fill, and it never changed. It never did for Eli either. Or any of my other regulars.

I bantered a bit with Paulie, not so much with Eli. He didn't come alive until he was halfway through his second beer. And when he did perk up, he wasn't much friendlier but that was just Eli.

"You forgot the damn TVs, for Chrissake," Eli said, pointing up at the television on a counter protruding from the wall at Paulie's end of the bar. He looked disgusted as he said it but he was only partially right. Yes, they were both off, that TV and the one over the other end of the bar, but I hadn't forgotten to turn them on. Instead, I'd left them off intentionally, knowing that once Eli and Paulie got into the game show they watched daily, I wouldn't be able to interrupt them. If I did, I'd be lucky to get more than a "Shh" out of them, especially from Eli. And even if Clinton was holding another of his press conferences, Eli would piss and moan the entire time. I couldn't have any of that because there was something I wanted to pick their brains about before they became zombified by the game show, infuriated at the president preempting it, or we were interrupted by the next set of regulars.

Even so, I had to pick my words carefully. Eli was known to read a lot more into what people said than they sometimes meant, and Paulie, for his part, was a very bright and perceptive man. So I had to walk on eggshells with my questions. I glanced at the well-stocked aquarium that ran the length of the shoulder-high wood partition separating the bar area from the dining room. I heard a high-pitched voice from the other side. It was Ruthie, Dianne's close friend and a waitress who had been here since I'd owned the Tide. There was laughter from the other two waitresses who I knew were sitting with Ruthie, waiting for the lunch mob to parade through the front door.

"Hey wake up, will ya?" Eli was leaning over the bar pointing a nicotine-stained finger toward one of the overhead TVs. Paulie snickered down at the other end of the bar. They both were on their second beers and the time was right. It was the only time I had.

I lifted my arms, rested my hands on two spigots in front of Eli, and said, just loudly enough so Paulie, who had sharp ears, could hear me too. "I wanted to ask you guys something."

Eli raised an eyebrow and slowly leaned back onto his stool. Paulie wasn't snickering anymore. Except for Ruthie telling jokes and the waitresses' laughter, it was so quiet you could have heard a single drop of beer fall from a spigot.

I cleared my throat. "Have you guys heard of anything being sold in stores around here that shouldn't be?"

Eli furrowed his gray brows. "Whatcha mean? Them funny cigarettes?"

Paulie snickered again. I don't know why but I said, "Some stores are selling those?"

"I wouldn't know nothin' about it," Eli huffed. "He might." He tipped his head in Paulie's direction. A smoke ring drifted toward the ceiling as Paulie said, "Never heard anything like that, Dan."

I'd let my own curiosity get me off track. I didn't have time for this. I had to cut to the chase. There'd be a stampede through the front door very soon. I didn't like saying it but I did. "No, I meant porn." I left out the kiddie part that Gant had mentioned. This was tough enough to talk about as it was.

"What did you say?" Paulie said.

I'd subconsciously lowered my voice. I adjusted it and glanced at Paulie. "Porn. You heard of anybody on the beach selling it?"

"What kind a porn? Dirty books?" Eli looked at me like I'd asked him a tough algebra question.

"More like tapes, I guess."

"Tapes, tapes? What's them, movies? I wouldn't know nothin' about that either. I ain't even got anything to play them on."

"I believe that," Paulie said. "You haven't even got cable."

"Bet your ass I don't," Eli said, stubbing out a Camel in an ashtray like he was mad at it. "That's the stupidest idea I ever heard of. I ain't payin' for what I can get free."

Paulie chuckled. "Sure but what do you get? Three or four stations?"

Eli raised his shoulders. "That's right. What's the point of having more? You can only watch one station at a time, smart guy." Then he screwed up his face, shook his finger at Paulie. "You wait. They'll be outta business before ya know it. Just a damn fad."

Paulie began what I could tell would be one of his lectures on modern technology. "You're missing a lot of good stuff. There's—"

I didn't like interrupting him but I had to. The first diners of the day, a group of construction workers, had just come through the front door. To my relief they turned left and filed into the dining room. I only had minutes before the stools at the bar would be taken by people I didn't want to discuss this in front of.

"The tapes, you guys. Have you heard of anyone selling them on the beach?"

Eli snorted. "Of course I ain't." He lifted his beer, sipped.

I believed him. I got a visual of Eli with a porn tape. It wasn't pretty but more to the point, I didn't believe it possible.

I looked toward Paulie. He motioned for me to come over to him by curling his index finger a few times. I walked to his end of the bar. He was looking down. When he looked up at me, there was a very light tinge of red in his face. He almost whispered when he spoke. "Don't say I told you, but you know the jewelry joint up the street?" He pointed off to one side, in a northerly direction.

Eli shouted, "Hey, what are ya saying? Speak up, I can't hear ya. It ain't polite to whisper."

Still, I whispered too. "Which one?"

There was a string of jewelry stores along Ocean Boulevard.

"I don't know the name," Paulie answered softly. "But it's the one with the big American flag out in front of it."

I didn't know the name either but I knew which one he meant. It was the only store, jewelry store at least, that hung a large red, white, and blue flag over the store entrance every day.

"They sell them?" I asked.

Paulie turned a deeper shade of red. I guessed why.

"Yeah, they sell them. Rent them too."

I didn't want to embarrass Paulie further. There was no point. I had all I needed for now. And just in time, because a boisterous group of plumbers and electricians jostled through the doorway and made a beeline for the bar, taking up half the stools between Eli and Paulie and demanding my attention.

So that was the end of our conversation. I had work to do. The next step on the trail of the porn tapes would have to wait until later.

Chapter 4

MY SHIFT ENDED at five o'clock. At 5:01 I was out the front door, trudging north on Ocean Boulevard in the opposite direction of my cottage. The heat hadn't let up any and humidity hung in the air like a wet towel. The people I passed all wore as little as they could legally get away with. They resembled zombies—the walking dead—wasted, pale, and drained.

In front of the Casino a horn blared at a pedestrian in the crosswalk. The pedestrian, a grizzled old man, banged his fist on the hood. The driver peeled around the old man, tossing the finger and expletives out the window. There's never a cop around when you need them.

Finally, drenched in sweat, I reached my destination—Joclean's Jewelry. It was midway on one of the more rundown blocks that ran along Ocean Boulevard. It had been here for a long time, but I knew little about it. Generally, I had no need to know anything about beach jewelry stores, which I'd always assumed were little more than tourist traps loaded with trinkets.

The door was open; I stepped inside. As I expected there was no air conditioning. The High Tide was the exception, not the rule, on the beach as far as air conditioning went. The short ten-week summer discouraged business owners from shelling out for the cooling equipment and the electricity expense. Besides, usually there were only a handful of unbearably hot days on the beach. A sea breeze made sure of that. Except now, an anomaly—a hot wind off the land that wouldn't quit. I wondered if this spell would open the wallets of some business owners in regards to installing a cooling system for next year. I doubted it. I knew the beach and its business people well.

I rubbed my eyes to get the sweat out and walked between two rows of glass display cases that ran the length of the store. They didn't go back more than thirty or forty feet. The cases were filled with rings, bracelets, necklaces, and other baubles I knew nothing about. One case held smoking accessories—pipes, hookahs, and rolling papers. Besides myself there was one other person in the shop, a woman behind the counter who looked as happy as a vampire without a victim. She had short, dyed-blonde hair, a T-shirt with the name of the store emblazoned across her flat chest, and the face of someone who would never go much further in life. She looked about my age and I could tell she wasn't the owner. But in her case, unlike my past relationship with the Tide, I was sure she never had been.

One more thing—she was cranky. "Can I help you?" she said as if the words hurt coming out.

I was cranky, too. But I'd been socialized early in life, so I tried to be civil. "Just lookin' around." Then I stupidly said, for the umpteenth time in the past week, "Hot, huh?"

She rolled her eyes. A drop of sweat fell from one of her brows and landed on the display case. That made me feel even hotter. I reached behind my back and pulled my shirt free from my skin. She bent down below the counter, looking for something. Behind her on the wall was a small display of VHS tapes. Maybe five or six, all in a line, with a few others hiding behind the front ones. A small handmade sign written in crayon read: "Adult Movies For Sale."

When the woman came up from behind the counter she had a coffee in her hand. It didn't look iced. I wondered how she could drink hot coffee in this heat. She noticed immediately that the tapes had caught my eye. She didn't say anything but looked uncomfortable.

I felt plenty uncomfortable too. If it hadn't been for the heat, which was about to make me bolt out the door and head for the first air-conditioned joint I could find, I would've played an embarrassing game of footsie with her for a while. But the heat trumped embarrassment. I wanted out of that hot box.

"You rent those, too?" I pointed toward the adult movies.

She shook her head. Another drop of sweat went flying. I don't know where it went; I just knew it didn't hit me. "We used to rent. Until some of the tapes never came back and the credit cards turned out to be phony, so now we just sell."

I nodded. That made sense. What didn't make sense was how I was supposed to examine the tapes which were behind both the counter and the woman.

"Wanna see one?" she asked in a voice that sounded like I must've been wearing a trench coat,

I felt like a teenager buying his first box of Trojans when I nodded and stuttered, "Ahh . . . yeah . . . sure."

She turned and took down all five of the tapes that were face out, placed them on the display case in front of me, and hurried down to the front of the store so fast she must have thought the images on the boxes might turn me into a raving sex maniac.

There was no fear of that, from what I could see. Sure they were X-rated, but they looked rather amateurish and run-of-the-mill to me. Until I glanced at the last one. *School Girls Gone Wild!* I had to do a double take. I glanced at the store clerk. She was staring out the window at Ocean Boulevard. I pulled a pair of cheap glasses out of my pocket and studied the figures on the cover and back. The text hinted at the sexual shenanigans of young girls. High school age, or so I assumed by the way the actresses were dressed. Not nude but with parochial school skirts pulled high and tongues licking lollypops. The text also implied that they wouldn't be wearing their skirts for long and would be licking more than lollipops in the film.

I glanced at the woman again. She was looking at me now and I didn't like what I thought she was thinking. Still, I had to swallow what little pride I had left and get another look at this trash. Something like this could easily set someone like Gant off and I couldn't blame him. I cleared my throat.

The woman marched down the aisle toward me. "All set?" she asked. Her face was tinted red and she seemed as embarrassed as I felt.

I slid the tape I wanted on the counter with the front cover face down. She gathered the other four tapes, put them to one side. She didn't even look at the tape I wanted. I knew she probably didn't have to. She slid it into a plain brown bag.

"Twenty dollars," she said, holding out her hand.

She looked away as I fumbled with my wallet. That was okay; I didn't want to look at her either. And I didn't want to say another word but I knew I had to. I hoped never to come back here again so I wouldn't get another chance.

I handed her the twenty. "Do you get new ones very often?" My voice shook just a tiny bit and I wondered what she thought it meant.

Her answer told me. "You a cop? 'Cause if you are, this is all protected by the fifth amendment. That's what my boss said."

I didn't argue with her incorrect constitutional knowledge. I was too intent on assuring her I wasn't a cop. "No, I'm not a cop. I just might want some more if this one is good."

"Oh," she said, stepping back a bit. "We get 'em. But the good ones go fast."

"When do you get them?" Like I said, I didn't plan on coming back. Still, there was a reason behind my question.

She narrowed her eyes. "You sure you ain't a cop?"

"I just want to make sure I get here before the good ones are gone." I removed my wallet, fumbled with it again until I had a ten spot on the counter.

She looked at the money like it was a piece of bad meat, then shrugged. Her hand snaked out and the ten disappeared. "A kid brings them every Friday. Drops off new ones, collects on what we sold."

A kid. Probably just makes the deliveries.

"What's he drive?"

Her eyes narrowed for the second time. "Why?"

"I work right up the beach, and if I see his car go by, I can get right down here," I half lied.

Luckily, she didn't ask me where I worked. She hesitated for a few seconds and said, "He brings 'em in a white van."

"Does it have any logo on it?"

"No! And I wouldn't tell you if it did." She was getting more suspicious.

That was okay. I'd gotten enough information. And besides, between the heat and the embarrassment, I wanted to get out of that place.

"Thanks," I said.

She started to snicker then stifled it. Another drop of sweat fell from her brow as I turned to leave. I hurried out the door and plowed through the humidity. I felt like I was swimming against a riptide. It took me forever to reach my cottage. On the porch, I fumbled with the key, dreaming of the A/C I was going to blast and the ice cold beer I was going to chug.

Chapter 5

I TOOK ONE step inside my cottage and realized I had a new worry, a much more serious worry than how fast I could get the place cooled down—my cottage had been ransacked. The stand that held my television had its doors open and VHS tapes lay scattered on the floor. My couch stood away from the wall as if someone had been searching behind it. Even the large metal screen in front of my fireplace had been tipped over, exposing the inside of the fireplace.

I stood there for a minute, surveying the room and listening for any sounds. When I was fairly sure I was alone, I took the few steps to my bedroom, looked inside. Same deal. My bureau drawers had been pulled out and dumped on the floor along with their contents, mostly clothes. My closet, which had no door, had items pulled from it and strewn about. I went to my bed, which was almost pushed against the wall on the other side, and leaned over to peer inside the little drawer in my nightstand. The drawer was open, but the only thing I kept in it, a .38 black revolver, was still there. I retrieved the gun, stood back up, held it at my side. The storage box I kept under my bed had been pulled out and winter clothes removed. I bent, looked under the bed. Betsy, my double-barreled shotgun, was still there, too.

I walked to the kitchen. Cabinets were opened, their contents disturbed. Even the wastebasket and breadbox had been rifled through, judging by the litter on the floor. The doors on the other two bedrooms off the kitchen were wide open. Not how I'd left them. I didn't bother going in. I could see from here that they'd been tossed similar to my bedroom. I peeked into the tiny bathroom. Medicine and towel cabinets were in disarray.

I returned to my bedroom and placed the .38 back in the nightstand drawer. I looked at the small brown bag still in my hand. I'd forgotten about it. I went into the living room, dropped the bag on my couch, picked up the phone, dialed.

"Are you busy?" I said into the mouthpiece. "How would you like to watch a movie?"

I listened for a moment. "No, I'm not kidding. It's important. I've got trouble."

I knew those last three words would bring the person on the other end quickly and I was right. It couldn't have been more than ten minutes before my best friend, High Tide dishwasher and handyman, Shamrock Kelly, opened the screen door and walked right in. He was wearing restaurant whites. There was nothing different about his freckled Irish face except that it was a bit redder than usual and he was breathing heavily through his nose as if he'd fast-walked all the way here, which he probably had.

He took one look around and said, "Sweet Mother of Mary, what the hell happened here, Danny?"

I was sitting in my easy chair, facing the door and Shamrock. "That's what I'd like to know."

Shamrock's head turned back and forth like he was watching a tennis match. "They steal anything?"

"Nothing that I can see. The other rooms are a mess too."

"Kids?"

"That's what you'd think . . . except . . ."

Shamrock's red brows furrowed and he cocked his head suspiciously. "Except what?"

I sighed. "Have a seat and I'll tell you. Beer?"

"Is the Pope Catholic?" He didn't sound as jovial saying that as he usually did.

Shamrock plunked himself down on the end of the couch near the door, still looking around the room. I got up, went to the kitchen, and returned with two cold Heinekens. I didn't bother with glasses. Shamrock wouldn't have used one anyway. I usually did. I handed one of the green bottles to Shamrock. He drained half in one tip. His Adam's apple bobbed as he swallowed. When he was done with that first drink, I told him what I knew, beginning with the sucker punch I'd been gifted from Lieutenant Gant. Shamrock didn't interrupt except once to ask for a fresh beer. I got it; the same for myself.

When I was done with the tale, Shamrock shook his head slowly, as if he'd just heard a friend had died. "Gant. That's bad, Danny. He doesn't like you. We all know that."

That was an understatement. Gant and I had had more than one run-in on the beach. Each time, I'd come out of it with my skin intact. Barely. Each time, things easily could've gone the other way. Shamrock had been around during each of them. Like I said, he's my best friend. Still, he looked awfully uncomfortable sitting across from me. I imagined he was worried about going another round with Gant.

"Do you think this . . ." Shamrock waved his hand toward the debris on the floor, "has something to do with *that*?" He pointed at the VHS tape that was now sitting on my lap.

I glanced at it. "I don't know."

And I didn't. I didn't see what the tie-in could be. "Coincidence maybe. Just kids or junkies."

Shamrock leaned forward, his hands on his knees. "Aye, but they would've taken stuff."

He rattled off a short list. "The TV, stereo, tape player . . . and Betsy." He glanced toward my bedroom.

"I guess. Unless they got scared away by something."

"Mmm, maybe," Shamrock said, doubtfully. "Anyway, let's see what Gant's got his knickers in a twist about." He nodded toward the tape in my lap.

I handed it to him. Watched his Irish face grow redder as he studied both the front and back covers. When he spoke his voice was hushed, as if someone might be listening out on the porch.

"This looks like it might *be* goddamn kiddie porn." He passed the tape back to me like it was a hot coal.

"Maybe. But there's something about those girls."

"Yeah, they do look kinda fake. Put it in, Danny," Shamrock said, straightening his back as if he were facing a firing squad. "We're gonna have to see exactly what Gant thinks you're mixed up in."

I agreed, grudgingly. I got up, put the tape in the machine, started the playback, and returned to my chair.

The tape was cheap and amateurish right from the start. Subpar even for a skin flick. The credits, with all the names sounding phony, were held up in front of the camera, written in magic marker on white poster board. There was no sound.

We were back in the days of silent films. The plot was minimal with a quartet of what I was happy to see were probably older actresses dressed up to look young. They were portraying high school girls and were sitting on the floor along with four older seedy-looking guys. They were playing spin-the-bottle. Except in this game every time the bottle stopped, and it always seemed to stop on one of the girls, she'd stand and strip for the camera. Little girl skirt and blouse. Ponytail shaking.

I couldn't believe they were really fooling anyone. You'd need a lot of imagination to believe these women weren't at least eighteen.

One of the seedy guys would then stand and have his way with her. The girl would act as if she didn't like it. But not too much. The camera would shift jerkily back and forth between that scene and the remaining spin-the-bottle players. It went on like that until all four couples were either standing or lying on the floor and doing what you do in a porn film. The camera bumped from couple to couple. The whole thing was about as erotic as those postcards of bathing suit models beach arcade machines used to sell decades ago. Of course, to a kid back then, those postcards had been quite titillating. But this film? A grown man could do a lot better with his twenty dollars.

When Shamrock broke the silence with, "Holy shit!" I thought maybe the cheap flick had aroused my friend. I needn't have worried though.

"I know that girl!" He sure wasn't worried if anyone was eavesdropping out on the porch now. He was leaning forward again, hands on his knees, staring at the TV screen and nodding rapidly. "She's no kid, for the love a Jaysus. I seen her over at—" he hesitated, glanced at me. His face reddened quite a bit more than usual. He cleared his throat and finished, "The Midnight Reader." And before I could ask when he'd been at what I knew to be a dirty bookstore off of Route 1 in Salisbury, he hurriedly added, "These aren't underage girls, Danny. They're all of age."

It was good to get confirmation of what I'd suspected and I suddenly felt a little less dirty. "You're sure?"

Shamrock hung his head. "I'm sure about that one with the blonde hair at least. She has to be at least eighteen, probably a lot older. You got to be eighteen to work at Midnight. The cops keep a close eye on them."

That made sense. How could a store like that not be watched closely by the authorities, being out in the open and licensed as they had to be. If Shamrock was right about the girl he recognized, that was also good news. The blonde he'd identified was the youngest looking of the girls involved. And the best looking. If she was of age, it was a cinch the others were too.

"So that's why Gant took a poke at you," Shamrock said. "He thinks it's kiddie porn. And you're selling it. Can't really blame him, I guess."

Shamrock started to backtrack, corrected himself. "I wasn't talking about him striking you, Danny. That was uncalled for. I meant the kiddie porn. No one wants that on the beach."

Shamrock was obviously right about residents not wanting kiddie porn being sold locally. And neither would a drunken police detective named Gant. Still, it didn't answer my main question—why did he think I was involved?

Shamrock answered my question without me having to ask it. "Maybe it's nothing. Maybe your name just popped into his head. You know what he thinks about you. And you said he had a wagon load on."

I ran my tongue over my lips. "You might be right. But whatever his reason is, I don't want even *him* thinking I'm involved with something like that." I hesitated for a moment. "And what if he tells his cockamamie idea to someone else. You know how rumors spread on the beach."

"Like a fire at the Casino during a high wind," Shamrock said ominously.

We sat in silence for a couple of minutes. Until I finally settled on the only thing I could do.

"Why don't you run it by Steve Moore? See what he knows," Shamrock said before I could mention what I'd been thinking. He'd read my mind. Again.

Steve Moore, Hampton detective and Gant underling. Better still, a personal friend of mine. It was the only way to go. I nodded and put the whole thing to bed. For tonight anyway.

Chapter 6

SHAMROCK LEFT AROUND ten o'clock. He had to be to work early at the Tide and he decided to be good tonight. I didn't. I got up and headed for the closest watering hole—the Crooked Shillelagh—after I locked the door. The Shillelagh was just up the street from my cottage.

I didn't stay long; the A/C wasn't great. And besides, it was a week night and there wasn't much action. I didn't know what I was looking for. Or maybe I did but it wasn't there. So I had one beer, left and marched up Ocean Boulevard, down side streets, and along Ashworth Avenue, stopping at bars along the way. I had one beer at each stop. Three hours later, I ended back on Ocean Boulevard for the third time. I was a few blocks north of the Casino at the Ashworth Hotel and made last call.

The place was deader than dead. I didn't care. Something else had taken over my thoughts. Even with all the beer, I was worried about Gant and the dirty movies, not to mention the ransacking of my cottage, which I still wasn't sure had anything to do with the other two. I stewed on the puzzle a bit but wasn't too drunk to realize I'd never come to any conclusions in the condition I was in.

That's when I drained the last of my beer, tried to look sober sliding off the stool, made a pit stop in the bathroom, and left.

Outside the heat hadn't broken. As a matter of fact, it felt even more oppressive. Maybe my blood pressure was up from the beer. The street was quiet, at least for a July night. I could see people scattered along the boulevard, probably coming from the closing bars. I decided to walk home on the beach, close to the water. It might be a little cooler.

I passed a cement statue of a woman looking toward the ocean. The statue honored New Hampshire servicemen killed at sea. It meant something else to me, though. When my kids had lived with me and they were a lot younger, there had hardly been a summer night when we hadn't stopped on our nightly arcade jaunts to say hi to the Statue Lady, as we had called her.

Those were some of the best times of my life. They were . . .

Even half in the wrapper, I realized where that train of thought would end—with me making a boozed-up telephone call to my ex-wife and making a fool out of myself. Or I'd do something worse. It had happened before.

I trudged over the sand, only stopping when I drew close to the incoming tide. There was no relief from the heat, but the light of the moon shining across the water directly at me distracted my thoughts from my children. And that was good. At least when I was in this condition.

I walked on the hard sand, occasionally stepping to my right to avoid an incoming wave on my walk south. The beach was almost deserted although I could see a few figures further down. This part of the beach, on the sand, was closed after one a.m., but I'd never been bothered any of the times I'd walked on it at night. I marched along, hot wind still blowing off the land. I was sweating and planned to have a cold beer the minute I reached my cottage.

That's what I was thinking about, that ice cold beer, when a voice behind me shouted, "Hey, Marlowe."

I turned and noticed a person heading in my direction, maybe a hundred feet away. I couldn't make out who it was in the dark. The moon didn't help. I waited. I wasn't far from home now, just past the municipal parking lot.

And that's where I saw another figure coming from now. That person headed onto the sand, toward me on a diagonal slant.

Didn't think anything of that either

When the first person got closer, I didn't recognize him. He was a big man, taller than me and overweight but not in a pudgy way. He wasn't dressed for the weather. He wore a long-sleeved, button-down shirt and dark pants. I couldn't see his shoes but I knew right away they weren't sneakers. His face alarmed me. It was the kind of face you didn't want to see when you were alone on a beach late at night. When he spoke, his voice sounded like he'd been billy clubbed in the throat.

"Marlowe," he said. It wasn't a question, so I didn't answer. I did sober up fast though. My trouble radar was going off gangbusters, especially when the second figure walked up and joined us.

He was a lot shorter than figure number one. A lot shorter than me, too. A compact little runt who had dressed for the weather. He wore a tight white T-shirt that showed off a well-developed physique. Cutoff jeans, sneakers with no socks. His brown hair was thin and wispy. He had a hawk-like nose and small eyes. He was grinning. If we'd met in another situation, I might've taken a liking to him.

"We want to talk to you," Big Man said.

"What about," I asked, even though I had a gnawing feeling I knew the answer.

Big Man must've thought I did too. "Don't fuck with us, Marlowe. We want the tapes."

Those damn tapes again. "I don't have any tapes except a porn tape I bought up at Joclean's today."

Big Man licked some sweat from his upper lip. Little Guy just watched, grinned some more.

"I guess you're going to make us sweat more than we already are, huh, tough guy," Big Man said. I could tell he didn't have much patience.

"I don't know what you're talking about." Not only did I feel sober now, I think I would have blown zero on a breathalyzer.

Big Man looked at me with eyes that said he had a lot of anger to release. And he was going to release it on me. "Let's see if we can help you with your memory."

He took one step toward me. I balled my fists. I didn't plan to just stand there and take a beating. He stopped and a large caliber automatic appeared in his hand from somewhere. All of a sudden it looked like I *was* going to just stand there and take a beating after all. If I was lucky. And it wouldn't be pleasant from a man of his size either. That's why I was surprised when Big Man, holding the gun, stepped behind me. He must have returned his gun to wherever it had come from because he grabbed my arms, pinned them behind me.

That's when Little Guy stepped in front of me. He was still grinning and the moonlight bouncing off the water reflected in his tiny eyes. He looked like the type who liked his work and I had a sickening feeling what that work was. He stood in a boxer's stance. Four jabs hit me in the stomach so fast I was still thinking of the first one when the last one was all over. Little Guy stepped quickly backwards. He must have known what would happen next.

I bent and that night's beer squirted out of my mouth onto the sand. Big Man held me away from his body. I didn't blame him. The vomit just missed splashing his shoes as it was.

When I was done, Big Man pulled me back into a straight position. "How do you feel now, tough guy? You want to tell us where those tapes are?"

Little Guy was still standing in a boxer's pose, his balled fists chest high. He wasn't grinning now. He was studying my face as if I were an opponent he was trying to figure out. Maybe that's what he was doing—figuring out how to use his skills in the best way possible to get the information they wanted.

I ran my tongue around the inside of my mouth. All I tasted was puke. My stomach felt like I'd been hit by a cannonball, not the fists of a relatively small man.

"I . . . can't tell . . . you what . . . I don't know."

Big Man pulled his face closer to my ear. I felt a drop of sweat fall from his face onto my neck. "We're not going to waste more time on you, Marlowe. Here's the deal. You get those tapes together and *quick*. You'll hear from us soon and we'll make arrangements to get them. Understand?"

I nodded. Probably better not to antagonize them unless I wanted the night to end with a ruptured spleen.

More sweat hit my neck. "Good. And in case you're thinking of forgetting what I said the minute you get outta here, I think my friend wants to give you another little sample of his form. He likes the practice. And remember Marlowe, this is my buddy's way, it ain't mine. If you don't come through, next time it'll be me and I won't be using my fists on you. I'll be using my gun."

I thought about the big automatic hiding somewhere on his person.

"Good night, Marlowe," Big Man said.

I started to breathe a sigh of relief. I thought he was going to let me go and skip the just-mentioned encore beating from Little Guy. Unfortunately for me, "Good Night" wasn't said in the traditional sense.

Little Guy stepped closer again and hit my gut with a series of blows that were faster than bullets from an automatic rifle. I'd barely started to buckle over when his right fist shot out and clocked me dead center on the jaw. I straightened up. Big Man released me. I did a little pirouette on the sand. My head must have been tilted up because I could see the moon and stars and they looked awful big. And then they all began to fly deeper into space, and I hit sand that was hard as a concrete sidewalk.

Somewhere a thousand miles away a gravelly voice said, "I hope you didn't kill him. The old man wouldn't like that."

Chapter 7

I WOKE WITH a start. My eyes strained to focus and I found myself staring up at a black sky littered with stars. I was on my back, soaked in what I knew instantly was Hampton Beach's famous ice-cold ocean water. It took another small wave lapping up to my neck before I struggled to my feet. I stumbled a few feet backwards to avoid being hit by another splash of cold salt water.

I couldn't have been out long. I'd been near the water line when Little Guy clocked me. It wouldn't have taken long for the tide to come up the short distance it had. I was just glad I'd come to. If I hadn't . . . well, I didn't want to think about that, couldn't think about that. Not with my scrambled brains.

I stood there for a couple of minutes, waiting for my head to clear. When I thought I could walk without falling down, I turned and headed south toward my cottage. I was walking on dry sand, sand the rising tide hadn't reached yet, and the soft sand made my unsteady gait even more plodding.

I rubbed my jaw, moved it around. It was sore but not broken. I'd been hit by an expert. But I'd known that when Little Guy had given those rat-tat-tats to my midsection. Just like he'd probably done thousands of times before—on a heavy bag in some dingy gym and on other unprotected stomachs. He was a professional strong-arm man. Big Man too. Him maybe worse.

They wanted tapes. What tapes?

They hadn't said. Whatever the tapes were, they'd seemed to believe I had them. It wasn't that fake kiddie porn tape I'd purchased at Joclean's. That hadn't interested them. Whatever tapes they wanted, Big Man said he wanted them back quick. I hadn't been knocked senseless enough not to remember that demand.

The thought of Little Guy using his fists like they were drumsticks and my stomach was a snare drum again wasn't pleasant. Neither was the thought that he might put my lights out again. He was a knockout expert that was for sure.

I shuddered from the thought or maybe it was the wet clothes or both. I didn't know. But my shivering increased even more when I recalled Big Man's threat of taking over the heavy lifting from his little partner. I could still see the big automatic in his fist.

Suddenly getting knocked out by a punch-out artist didn't seem so bad. Not compared to the alternative.

I'd barely slogged half the short distance to my cottage. I wasn't drunk anymore. In fact, I couldn't remember even being drunk. Going through something like what I'd just experienced sobers you up real fast, believe me.

I oddly felt more comfortable though in regards to the heat, better than I had in past days. Between the hot wind drying the outside of my clothes, what was left on me of the cold ocean water, and the sweat seeping from my pores, the climate almost felt temperate.

I stumbled, kicked up sand, and headed across the beach toward the oceanfront cottages. My cottage was situated not far behind. The same cottage where Gant had assaulted me twenty-four hours earlier. Next time I ran into him, I'd have to suggest he take sucker-punching lessons from Little Guy. On second thought, maybe that wasn't such a great idea. Anything Gant learned he'd probably use on me sooner or later.

Now there were two parties interested in porn tapes and me—the two thugs and Gant. And the thugs seemed like the type who worked for someone else. It suddenly dawned on me that maybe someone besides the thugs had tossed my cottage. I hadn't asked and they hadn't said. I'd just assumed. But maybe my assumption was wrong. Even more jokers could be in the slug-Dan-Marlowe mix.

Again my mind glommed onto the same things—why did the thugs want the tapes, whatever they were, and why did they think I had them? And what exactly were the tapes? They couldn't be regular triple-X tapes. No one would have reason to use professional muscle for that. Would they? And was Gant's obsession with me and porn tapes on Hampton Beach tied in with the Big Man/Little Guy tapes?

My rattled brain told me I had only two choices. *And* I had to act fast. Both the thugs and Gant had cut me no slack on time, Gant demanding that I get tapes I had nothing to do with out of *his* town, and the thugs demanding that I return tapes I didn't have or know anything about. So I either got out of town fast and stayed away for who knew how long or I tried to find out what the story was on these tapes, how they were related to me, and how I could get myself unrelated—and quickly.

The first option was no good. I had a job. I might not have concerned myself with that obligation too much except for Dianne. She was my boss and a lot more. I couldn't leave her high and dry in more ways than one.

But just as important, maybe even more, I'd be damned if I'd let Gant—or anyone else for that matter—see me put my tail between my legs and run. There was an old promise I'd made to myself when I'd first decided to stand up to my anxiety attacks, the attacks that were my payback for years of cocaine abuse. That promise had been to never back down in any situation if there was any chance I was deciding on a course of action because of my anxiety condition. My heart, thudding in my chest right now, told me there was a chance I'd do just that if I wasn't careful.

The heartbeat and other sensations bubbling up inside were different from those a normal person would feel from the heat, the beer, the march in the sand, and the beating. Anyone who's experienced an anxiety condition knows what I'm talking about. They also know you can't lie to yourself about it.

At least I couldn't. I'd tried before. Didn't work. The anxiety is too strong. You have to face it as best you can.

So running away was out. The only other option was to face this situation straight on, anxiety or no anxiety. Find out what the hell it was all about. Deal with it like a man. But keep my eyes open, wide open. Hope that I could derail whatever danger I was in before I ended up in the hospital, jail, or worse. It wouldn't be easy.

It seemed like I walked for hours, but I finally reached the oceanfront cottages, dragged myself between a few of them. There were no lights on and the only sounds were those of loud voices and music from parties a few blocks away. I made it up the porch stairs and, after a long struggle in the dark with my keys, finally let myself in. I had the sense to lock both the screen door and the main door behind me. Flicked on the light near my easy chair.

In my bedroom, I stripped off my wet clothes, almost tipping over twice in the process. It was mostly sweat that soaked them now, the hot wind having taken care of the ocean water. I threw on underpants, shorts, and a T-shirt. Grabbed the Xanax bottle from my bureau drawer. Tossed one orange pill under my tongue.

I went to the kitchen, grabbed two Heinekens from the fridge along with a frosted mug, and set myself down in my chair. The pill dissolved under my tongue as I poured the beer into the mug. My timing was perfect. By the time I had the mug up to my lips the last of the pill had been absorbed. The beer felt very cold going down.

It was always the pill that hit me first. They'd have to invent beer that dissolved under your tongue to change that. Still, I hurried with the beer, hoping to shorten the difference in time it took them both to do their work. Finished the first bottle, opened and poured the second.

Yes, I'd promised to face this like a man. And that's just what I was going to do—tomorrow. Tonight I was going to face it like a man, too. But not a damn saint.

Chapter 8

I DIDN'T FEEL so great getting up for work the next morning. Still, I was lucky. All I had to remind me of my encounter with the two thugs on the beach was a sore jaw and a just-as-sore stomach. The additional bruise—so light I could barely see it—on my jaw and not too much more on my stomach, proved I'd been right about Little Guy being a professional strong-arm man. He did his work without leaving any more evidence than if I'd fallen out of bed.

The walk to work didn't help with the discomfort I felt. It was still hot, hazy, and humid. One more day in our beach heat wave. One more day to test even a sane man's patience. And after what had happened to me recently, I wasn't sure I could be listed in the sane column.

I'd meant to bring a bottle of water with me for the walk, but I'd forgotten. I stopped at Beverages Unlimited, a convenience store on the corner of M Street, and bought a quart. It was half gone before I'd traveled the next block. Over to my right, the municipal parking lot was already sold out of parking spaces. The faces of drivers in the snail-like traffic on the Boulevard told me that I wouldn't want to be the parking attendant in one of the private lots today asking for the exorbitant fee.

I kept my head down, plowing through the wall of humidity, dodging pedestrians as I walked. The faces that passed me looked stark white in the hot sun, as uncomfortable as a condemned man being led to "Old Sparky." Even the faces with tans looked like they'd lost a shade or two. I just kept on, taking an occasional slug on the water bottle and dreaming of the relief I'd feel when the Tide's two behemoth air conditioners were fired up and cranking out that cool, blessed air. I wondered how anyone could work without A/C, even knowing that ninety-five percent of the workers on the beach had none. I didn't need a federal jobs report to tell me a lot of workers, especially among the summer help, wouldn't be showing up for work today. And many probably hadn't been coming in since this scorching hot weather had started.

I neared the Tide, sweat dripping out of every pore in my body, and was just about to bang a left down the side street which led to the rear door of the restaurant when I noticed an unmarked Hampton police car pulled up close to the sidewalk near the restaurant's front door. Parking wasn't allowed on this side of the street except for business deliveries and official cars. There was also a small knot of people standing around the front of the restaurant.

Ruthie, our senior waitress, was chattering away with Shamrock and another waitress.

They all turned as I approached.

"What's going on?" I asked.

Shamrock started to speak but Ruthie beat him to it.

"Somebody broke in last night." Smoke from a cigarette drifted from her mouth as she spoke. Her red hair, a true red, not like Shamrock's more orange shade, was short. Still, there were strands stuck to her cheeks and forehead by the mugginess.

I was sure the break-in had been in the dead of night but still I had to ask. "Anyone here when it happened?"

Shamrock ran his hands through his damp hair. "Nah. I found it when I opened up. They must've used a crow bar on the back door."

That's when I noticed a locksmith's van parked in front of the police car. Probably to repair the lock on the door. "What'd they take?"

"Don't know," Ruthie said. There were beads of sweat on her upper lip. "Whatever they took I hope they figure it out soon, so we can get out of this heat. This is freakin' awful."

I had no argument there. "Dianne inside?"

"With Steve Moore," Ruthie answered, "but they want us to wait out here."

I don't know if it was concern for Dianne or just my desire to get out of the heat but I turned, walked to the front door. I could feel Shamrock's and the waitresses' jealous eyes on my back. Inside I was hit by a blast of cold air that felt as good as an expensive massage. Dianne and Steve Moore were seated side by side at the bar. I walked over, took a stool beside Dianne, and leaned back so I could see Steve.

Dianne did a double take when she saw the new bruise on my face. She didn't say anything though. Probably figured I'd blame it on the bathroom cabinet again. She figured right.

"What'd they take?" I asked.

"Nothing that I can see so far," Dianne answered. She had on a white kitchen shirt and blue shorts and her hair was pulled tight behind her head. She looked tired. "They helped themselves to a little booze while they were here."

She pointed to a shelf on the back bar where a half-empty bottle of Seagram's whiskey sat out of place with two rock glasses on either side of it. One had a puddle of the brown liquor still in it.

Steve leaned back on his stool. "They seemed to be interested in just the office and bar." He then added "*Your* bar, Dan."

I gave him a quizzical look but he didn't add anything.

"The door?" I asked Dianne.

"They pried it open. The locksmith's working on it now. My insurance won't cover that. Not with my deductible."

"How bad's the office?" I asked.

Dianne shook her head. "Nothing ruined, but it's going to take me the whole day to get everything straightened out. My desk drawers and the file cabinets were all dumped out."

"Probably trying to find any money you keep to open up." Steve pointed toward the Seagram's bottle and two used glasses. "That's why *they* only tore up the office and bar area. You wouldn't hide the money in the dining room or kitchen. Too many prying eyes in the morning."

Steve was right. Someone might see you retrieve it. You rarely got any privacy in those areas. So we kept the opening-up money in a small strong box in one of the beer coolers. I looked at Dianne. She nodded her head. "They found it. And my insurance won't cover that either. There was less than $200 in there though."

There was a silence, a silence during which I had some thoughts I didn't like, thoughts about a punch in the face from Gant, my cottage being searched, and my body being used as a punching bag down on the beach. I tried to suppress the idea that there might be some connection between those incidents and what had happened here at the Tide, but the idea kept resurfacing.

"Probably just kids," Steve said. "Beach urchins. Junkies maybe."

"Drinking whiskey?" I said.

Steve shrugged.

"You going to do prints?"

Steve gave me a disapproving look after he made sure Dianne wasn't watching. "The chief says there's no time for that in the summer unless it's a major burglary. This is more like larceny and vandalism. We'll get on it, but it's got to be something a little bigger for a full court press at this time of the year."

Dianne glared at Steve's reflection in the bar mirror. "It's big to me."

"I know, I know," Steve said. He picked up the glass of Coke in front of him on the bar, took a long sip. "But less than two hundred cash and a broken door lock wouldn't qualify with the chief. Not now. Not in the summer. He's runnin' around like a five-year old on a sugar overdose as it is. No sense in even asking him." He hesitated, looked back at Dianne in the mirror. "Besides, Dianne, if it was kids, prints wouldn't do any good."

It was all lame but true. The police didn't have much time to spend on a $200 nonviolent crime. Not in the summer on Hampton Beach. Especially not this summer when the sweltering days and nights were filled with even more sirens than usual. People overindulging, trying to escape just one night of the oppressive heat. A lot of them amateur drinkers. That meant plenty of fights and vandalism and sometimes worse. Often the perpetrators were young men, roaming Ocean Boulevard after midnight. Pity anyone that got in their way. And pity the police if those groups became a mob. A mob of drunken, heat-mad crazies. They'd probably try to burn down the Casino. It had been tried before.

Dianne didn't object, just sighed, probably resigned to losing a few hundred bucks and some of her time cleaning up the mess and consoling herself with the idea that it could've been worse.

The ugly thought of a possible tie-in between what had happened to me and this incident at the Tide surfaced again. I decided not to mention my suspicions to Dianne. It would only worry her and she had enough to deal with right now. I did want to run things by Steve Moore though; I'd been planning to anyway. I needed help and maybe he could give me some.

Steve pushed himself off his stool. "Sorry I can't do more, Dianne, but I'll do the best I can. If you find anything else missing, let me know."

"I will, Steve." She stood up and turned to me. "You better see if you can get this bar back together in time to open."

"I can. At least enough to open. I'll pick at the rest of it during my shift."

Steve turned for the door. Dianne called after him. "Can you please tell Ruthie and the others they can come in now."

She hurried off toward the kitchen; I hurried off after Steve. Caught him just as he was about to pull open the heavy wooden front door.

"Steve, can I talk to you?"

"Now?"

"No. I got to get this place cleaned up and opened. Later?"

"Yeah, okay." He half turned back to the door, hesitated. "Not at the station. That might not be a good idea. The White Cap?"

Did Steve know about my encounter with Gant or was he just remembering how unhappy Gant had been in the past when I'd dropped by the station to see Steve for one reason or another? Either way, it was a good idea for me to stay clear of the station, especially now.

"That'll be fine. I get out of here at five. That work for you?"

"I'll see you at the Cap a bit after five."

He left, letting the big door creak shut behind him. I walked behind the bar and looked at the mess on the floor. Nothing broken. The perpetrators, whoever they were, had at least been considerate in that way. It would take me a while to put back everything they'd dumped from the drawer under the cash register, the cabinets below that, and the back bar. They'd even removed bottles and jars from the beer barrel chests located under the spigots. I put my hands on my hips and stood there, wondering where to start.

Ruthie, followed by Shamrock and the younger waitress, paraded in and headed into the dining room. No one spoke to me. I couldn't blame them. Standing out in that heat would sour anybody's mood.

I'd just bent over and started to pick up the first piece of scattered debris from the floor, when there was a pounding on the wooden door. I stood. The Budweiser Clydesdale clock over the back bar read 11:00 on the dot.

Eli and Paulie. They didn't realize the door was unlocked. I sighed and headed for it. It was going to be a long day. A very long day.

Chapter 9

IT WAS SHORTLY after five when I wrapped up my shift and left the Tide. I marched down Ocean Boulevard a couple of blocks in the heat, took a right and hurried inside the White Cap restaurant. They, too, had air conditioning, thank god. Not as good as the Tide, hardly anyone on the beach could beat the Tide, but it was enough to break the humidity.

Steve was seated alone at a table for four, one of many tables lined up along the street-side windows. We nodded to each other and I took a seat opposite him. He was wearing a tan short-sleeve shirt, no tie. A dark brown lightweight sport coat hung over his chair. He had a soda, a straw sprouting out of it, on the table in front of him.

"Hot enough for you?" I asked.

"Hot enough that if this place didn't have A/C, I would've cancelled our appointment." Steve twirled the straw in his drink. "I forgot about that when I mentioned coming here."

I smiled. "I didn't. And I would've said something if it hadn't been air-conditioned." I looked at the unopened menus on the table. "You eating?"

Steve stuck his lower lip out. "Nah. Just the Coke."

I didn't like that. Being in the restaurant business, I was well aware of what were no-no's with the staff at most places. And because I had already had my supper at the Tide where workers paid half price, it looked like we were about to take up a choice table just as the dinner rush started up. Tip-dependent waitstaff wouldn't appreciate that. And who could blame them? I was just about to suggest to Steve that we move to the bar when a waitress came up to the table.

She had her order book open and held it up in one hand in front of her. A pen in her other hand hung suspended over the book. I was surprised by her age. Most waitresses in the summer were high school or college age. This server looked like she could be the grandmother of one of those waitresses. A very tired, worn-out grandmother at that.

"What can I get you, gentlemen?" she asked in a voice that sounded as tired as she looked.

Before I could suggest we move to the bar, Steve piped up. A big smile on his face, he said, "Just the coke and this nice view here."

He nodded toward the windows beside us that ran the length of the room and looked out onto the side street. It wasn't much of a view but the way he said it told me he didn't see anything wrong with tying up a table at rush hour with one lousy coke. Come to think of it, I'd been through this with him before—exactly where we were sitting now. I gave up the idea of asking him to head to the bar. I had a feeling he didn't like being seen sitting at one anyhow, whether on or off duty. With the gun on his hip, people who didn't already know him would guess he was a cop. It might start some gossip that would get back to the chief.

I let out a small sigh. The waitress let out a loud one, blowing a curl of gray hair off her forehead.

"Anything for you?" she asked, turning her head in my direction. She looked like she didn't expect much.

"Baked haddock, coleslaw, and french fries. And a *cold* Heineken please."

The waitress brightened up a bit, as much as someone as tired as she was could. She scribbled away and left.

"I thought you could eat half price at the Tide," Steve said. He was looking at me with a little smirk.

"I was in a hurry to get out of there," I lied. I'd spend a few extra bucks to ease my conscious and not be labeled a *jerk* which is what the Tide waitresses christened someone who pulled the same non-ordering routine in their dining room.

"I bet you would've found time if you could still get it for free." Steve still had that little smirk on his face.

He wasn't just referring to when I owned the High Tide. About a year ago Dianne had been forced to change the one-free-meal-per-shift for each worker to half price. That had been the fault of a couple of hammerheads who had taken advantage of the previous system and ordered a prime steak almost every shift. The inconsiderate ones had been around a while and Dianne hadn't had the heart to fire them. Besides, they were good workers otherwise and good workers were hard to find, even more so on the beach. So now even I paid half price. But I didn't blame Dianne; she'd had no choice. Still, I would have fired the greedy employees. I'd actually done it more than once back in the day for the same selfish actions. I didn't like being taken advantage of.

Steve leaned forward, placed both elbows on the table. "If you want to know about the break-in, it's just what I told

Dianne. Kids or junkies. No big deal and not much I can do, Dan."

All the while he'd been saying that, I'd been slowly shaking my head.

Steve sat back a bit, looked at me warily. "What then?"

Just then the waitress brought my Heineken with a beer mug. I thanked her, poured, and took a sip. Cold, barely, but adequate. Steve stared at me with the same suspicious look on his face. He was waiting for my answer,

"I've got a little problem," I said, emphasizing the word little.

I looked at Steve. He didn't say anything and I knew he wasn't going to. At least not yet. Not until I told him my story. He knew too well how big my *little* problems could sometimes turn out to be.

"And this is just between you and me," I added.

Steve pursed his lips and cocked one eyebrow. "Unless, of course, you've got some bodies buried under your cottage. Then I'd have to tell somebody."

"Ha, ha." I hesitated. This wasn't going to be easy. "I had a visitor the other night," I began. "Gant."

Steve leaned back with a groan. Held his hands up, palms out. "Wait one second. I'm not sure I even want to hear this."

I put my elbows on the table, rubbed my hands together in front of my face. "I wouldn't have come to you if I didn't need some help, Steve. You know that."

All of a sudden he looked as worn out as our waitress. I knew he wouldn't refuse to listen. Steve and I had a bond. A bond that had been strong even before I'd introduced him to Kelsey, the boy who was now his adopted son. I'd saved the boy's life too, but I would never mention it. Not even in this situation. I'd walk out the door first.

Steve shrugged, leaned forward a bit. "Oh, go ahead. What'd he accuse you of this time?"

"Selling kiddie porn on the beach."

Steve leaned back in his seat again. "What? You're joking, right?"

I shook my head. "No, I'm not. And there's something else."

"Oh, Jesus." Steve groaned.

I ignored that, plowed on. "When I opened the cottage door he slugged me in the face."

"Slugged you in the face?" Steve looked at me like I'd told him they were going to pave the sand down to the water.

"He was drunk."

Steve just looked at me. He had a look of shock on his face, but even still, I could tell he wasn't really surprised. His expression gradually changed to one of resignation. Finally, he said, "Did you hit him back?"

"No. I felt like it. But seeing he was bombed and armed," I gestured toward Steve's sidearm on his right hip, "I figured that wouldn't be wise."

"You figured right. Jesus Christ, how the hell do you get involved in these things?"

"There's more."

Steve wiped his face, forehead to chin, with one hand.

"I was grabbed by two leg-breakers last night on the beach. They gave me a working over and one was a tough little lightweight. He knocked me out with one punch. The rising tide woke me up."

Steve looked irritated when he said, "You been fooling around with someone's wife?"

I knew Steve didn't really think that. "They wanted me to turn over some tapes I supposedly have."

"Do you?"

"Do I what?"

"Have the tapes they want?"

I was indignant. "No, I don't have any tapes and I don't know what the hell they were talking about. Gant either."

Steve sighed. "Anything else?"

He didn't look surprised when I said, "Just that my cottage was ransacked, searched. With nothing taken. And I'm worried—"

Steve interrupted. "You're worried the break-in at the Tide might be connected in some way with what's happened to you."

I nodded, waited for Steve to speak. I thought he'd ask me why Gant thought I was tied up with porn tapes or why the thugs thought I was in possession of some mysterious tapes. He didn't. I could tell he already knew something, but was hesitant to share.

The waitress showed up with a casserole dish of baked haddock and my sides of coleslaw and fries. She also brought another beer I hadn't asked for. I didn't refuse it. I hurried her along, bordering on being rude, but I was anxious to find out what Steve knew. The first thing he said when she'd left didn't surprise me at all.

"You've got to keep your trap shut about where you heard this."

We'd been through this dance before. Steve knew my lips were tight. But he still had to say it. I nodded.

"All right." Steve leaned back into the table, his elbows on it again. He came as close to me as he could without sitting beside me. He lowered his voice. "I guess you already know, but a few stores on the beach have been selling triple X movies."

"Why don't you shut them down?"

Steve gave his head a little tilt. "Not that easy. First Amendment rights and all that shit. Town lawyer says we might get sued and it might not be worth it. Still, we're watching them. Sent some people in to buy some tapes and we actually found a couple that looked like they could've been kiddie porn. We could've busted them right away for that. But we looked into it and it turned out the actresses in the films might not be underage. Maybe over eighteen, but made up to look a lot younger. Gant doesn't care, says it's just as bad as the real thing. But the chief says we got to hold off seizing them 'til we're sure we're on solid ground. And we're also trying to find out where the tapes are coming from."

"That makes sense, but, except for his dislike for me, why the hell would Gant think I'd be involved in something like that? And the thugs on the beach? That's got to be tied in with this. It's too coincidental otherwise."

Steve diverted his eyes. A light tint of red crept into his cheeks. "Well, I guess you should know. But *remember*, you didn't hear it from me."

"Yeah, yeah, yeah."

Steve sucked some coke through the straw. When he spoke he kept his voice low. "I'm not involved in this investigation. Somebody else is handling it, but word on the street is that the distributor of the dirty movies on the beach is someone called the *Bartender*."

My stomach rode the elevator down to the first floor. Steve didn't go on and he didn't have to. Hearing that moniker, Gant would naturally think of me. And if he thought kiddie porn was involved, his already low opinion of me combined with the booze he'd obviously consumed before his visit, I was lucky the maniac hadn't pulled out his service pistol and emptied it into me.

So that accounted for Gant's actions. What about the tough guys on the beach?

I came up with the same answer. They must've picked up on the Bartender identity, too. But why had they latched onto me? Yes, I was a bartender, but there were a hundred other bartenders on the beach. The answer to that was simple too. What had probably convinced them I was said Bartender was my less-than-stellar reputation. I was well known in Hampton and a lot of what people knew about me had to do with some fairly shady incidents I had been involved in years ago, incidents bad enough that I'd lost my family and my business. Held on to the cottage by the skin of my teeth. I'd been paying for that period of my life for a long time now. This looked like a new bill just being delivered.

"Why didn't you give me a heads-up about this Bartender thing?" I asked. Steve looked everywhere but at me. "You didn't think it might've been me?"

I was surprised. Steve was a good friend. If he believed the rumor, half the beach probably would as well.

"No, no." He was adamant. "I just didn't want to embarrass you. Especially with the damn kiddie porn stuff. I didn't know that was probably a false alarm then. I did know you wouldn't be involved in something like that. That's ridiculous." He cleared his throat. "You didn't have anything to do with the other movies, did you?"

I must have looked like I was going to come over the table at him because he held his hands up, palms out again. "Okay, okay, I knew that. I just had to ask."

One other thing had been troubling me. What I'd heard just before I'd lost consciousness after being slugged on the beach. The gravelly voice of the Big Man, saying, 'I hope you didn't kill him. The Old Man wouldn't like that.'

"Have you heard of anyone being called the Old Man."

Steve gave me a quizzical look. "Yeah, me—by the rookies."

I smiled. "How about someone shady who might use that nickname?"

"What's this about?"

I told him.

"Never heard of anyone in particular being referred to around here as that. You said you thought you heard it just before you went under. Probably a dream. You just think you heard it before you went out cold."

Maybe. Maybe not.

We spent the next fifteen minutes in mostly idle chatter. Steve didn't know anything more about the tapes or where they'd come from. He did offer to help in any way he could with my trying to extricate myself from the predicament I was in. I think he felt guilty for having doubts. But I couldn't blame him and I was grateful for the offer of help.

I picked at my meal, managing to down no more than a few mouthfuls. When we'd exhausted all the small talk we could come up with, I paid the bill, left a generous tip, and we left, stepping out into what felt like an overheated steam room.

We shook hands and went our separate ways. I headed south along Ocean Boulevard. But instead of going directly to my cottage, I stopped at a pay phone outside of Patriot's Corner Grocery. I dropped in some coins, called Shamrock, who I knew could and would be willing to help me. When I heard his brogue on the line, I told him I was only minutes away. He said he'd have a cold one ready when I got there. That was good. We'd both need it.

Chapter 10

SHAMROCK PUT A mug of Heineken in my hand as soon as I stepped through his front door. The living room was noisy with an old clunky A/C he had in the window. But I didn't care about the noise. The room was cool and that's all I cared about. Shamrock, dressed in his usual white, flopped down on his recliner. I sat opposite him in an easy chair. It was a comfortable but messy room. A large Irish tricolor flag of green, white, and orange hung over the fireplace.

I didn't waste any time. "After you left last night, I took a walk uptown."

Shamrock smiled. "Made the rounds, eh, Danny Boy?"

I didn't return the smile. "Yeah, and on my way back I got the crap kicked out of me by two jokers down on the beach. One of them knocked me out."

"Sweet Mother of Mary!" Shamrock took a quick gulp from his beer bottle. "What did they want?"

"They wanted to know where the tapes were."

Shamrock's face took on an expression that reminded me of a second-banana character in a murder mystery. "Tapes again?"

"Yeah, and when I told them I didn't know what they were talking about, they did a number on me."

Shamrock pointed his beer bottle in my direction. "Why didn't you tell me this at the Tide, Danny?"

"There was too much going on. Dianne was upset. I thought it was better to tell you when she wasn't around. Besides, you had your hands full cleaning up."

Shamrock rubbed the red stubble on his chin with his free hand. "That was probably a good idea. Poor Dianne. I wouldn't want to see the lass get any more upset than she already was. But why did the blackguards think you had these tapes? And what's on these things anyway?"

I set my mug down on a coffee table in front of us. The table had a glass top with a small crack. Probably had been a nice piece of furniture in its day. Shamrock had found it at a yard sale.

"I can't answer the last part but I know why they think I might be involved." I proceeded to tell Shamrock what Steve Moore had told me about the porn investigation and that the police believed one of those involved in the racket was called the Bartender.

Shamrock listened patiently, unusual for him. When I mentioned the Bartender, his red eyebrows shot up and he nodded his head rapidly.

When I was done, I said, "So now you know everything I do." I hesitated. "I can't have my name associated with that kind of stuff, Shamrock. And that punch-out artist and his friend want me to give them tapes I don't have. I told you what they plan to do if I don't hand them over. They didn't sound like they were going to wait long either."

Shamrock nodded a few times, rubbed at the scruff on his chin again. "Ahh, Danny boy, you've really done it this time."

"I didn't do anything!" I said more loudly than I'd meant to.

Shamrock took his hand from his chin and waved at me. "Just a figure of speech, Danny. I know you didn't do anything. But you do have to clear your name. You have a very good . . . ahh . . . reputation on the beach."

Shamrock was somewhat right. I'd worked hard to get back the good name I had before I'd gone off the deep end with cocaine. And I'd made some progress. So I wasn't about to let any idiot with the nickname *Bartender* screw it up. I also wanted to short circuit any plans Gant might have for me. And I had an idea where to start. But it would be a two-man job.

I cleared my throat. "I hate to ask you, Shamrock, but I might need some backup on this. It could be—"

Shamrock interrupted, waving his hands like he was trying to stop a speeding train. "I'd be glad to do whatever I can to help. You're my best friend. And with Michael Kelly watching your back, you'll be as safe as a precious infant in its mother's arms."

I didn't know if I'd go that far, but Shamrock was my best friend and I knew he'd do anything for me. I hated dragging him into something that might turn out to be more dangerous than it already had been. But Shamrock had played Watson to my Holmes more than once during other predicaments I'd found myself caught up in. And they'd all turned out okay. Barely. But I knew Shamrock, and if he ever found out I was in a pickle and hadn't asked for his help, he'd be disappointed. For an Irishman like Shamrock that was disappointed with a capital D.

All I could say was, "Thanks, Shamrock."

He smiled. "Have you any ideas, Danny?"

Before I could answer, he said, "Of course, you've got ideas." He thumbed his chest. "You wouldn't have asked for Michael Kelly's assistance if you hadn't."

Now it was my turn to smile. If anyone could get a smile out of me, it was Shamrock. And Dianne. Even back when I'd hit rock bottom and they were about the only ones who'd stuck with me, they'd been able to drag a smile out of me. Along with my kids, Davey and Jess, they were the only reasons I'd struggled—and was still struggling—to overcome my inner demons. And they're nasty demons, let me tell you.

"You know someone can't have a good bowel movement on this beach without me knowing about it, Danny. Is that what you want me to do? Check out someone who's not acting regular?"

That made me smile even more. "I don't know if that's a pun or not but no. Not right now anyway. I've got something else in mind that might lead somewhere."

Shamrock looked excited, just as Sherlock Holmes' Watson always did *before* any trouble started. "Tell me what it is."

"Tomorrow morning," I began, "can you get out of the Tide by nine?"

"That's no problem. I'll work like a one-armed paperhanger. What about you though?" A little wariness snuck into Shamrock's voice and his red brows furrowed again. "Or am I going on this assignment alone?"

I reassured my friend that I'd be going along with him. "I'll get someone to cover my shift."

"What are we going to be doing, Danny?"

Shamrock listened and drank his Heineken as I told him what I had planned.

Chapter 11

I TRUDGED HOME from Shamrock's, made a phone call to arrange work coverage for the next day, and fell asleep at a decent time. I didn't stay asleep, unfortunately. The phone woke me a little after 1:00 a.m. I stubbed my toe on something trying to get to the phone in the dark. I swore.

"Hello."

"Dan, can you drive?" It was Dianne's voice.

My heart sped up. "Of course I can drive. What's the matter?"

"I meant have you been drinking?"

"No, I've been sleeping," I half lied as horrible visions of what might have happened to Dianne danced around in my head. "Are you all right?"

"Yes, but come up here," she said. "And take your time. I'm fine but I have to see you . . . now."

"The condo?"

"Yes."

"I'm on my way."

I didn't have time to dwell on how badly I felt with a slight hangover and only a couple of hours of sleep. I was worried about Dianne. Something was up. I changed quickly, headed for the door. Just before I reached it, I turned and walked to the bathroom. I ran a comb through my hair, brushed my teeth, and gargled with mouthwash twice. I didn't want Dianne to get a whiff of unpleasant breath. People, especially significant others, remember that.

It didn't take me long to reach Dianne's condo. It was north on Ocean Boulevard just before the Boar's Head peninsula which marked the end of Hampton Beach proper. I parked across the street in the municipal lot, jumped a knee-high guardrail, and jogged across Ocean. I took the half-dozen steps two at a time, opened the outer door, and entered the foyer. I pressed the button for Dianne's unit. The metallic click allowed me to open the inner door and I bounded up to the second floor. Dianne had her door open and was standing there waiting for me. Her long black hair was down and she had on a denim shirt with the sleeves rolled up, along with a pair of maroon shorts. Her feet were bare. I squeezed past her into the room. She closed the door behind us.

Dianne kept her condo neat as a pin, so right away I could see why she'd wanted me to come—her condo had been searched too. The perpetrators, if they were the same ones who'd redecorated my cottage and the Tide, had been a lot neater here. In the living room, where we stood now, the pillows and cushions on the sofa and chairs had been rearranged like someone had checked under them and then set them sloppily back into place. Books in a small bookcase had been removed and replaced every which way. The drawers to an antique writing desk in the corner were all ajar. Nothing had been dumped on the floor as it had been at my house and the Tide.

Off to the side, beyond the small dining room, was the kitchen. A few of the cabinets were open, but again, nothing had been thrown about. The oven door was open.

"Same thing in the bedrooms," Dianne said. Then, with a stern face, she said, "Now you tell me what's going on."

I hesitated. It wasn't that I didn't want to tell her. I did. But it was embarrassing.

Her hard expression tightened. "Don't try to lie to me, Dan. You haven't been yourself lately. And . . ." She stepped closer, reached up with one hand to my face. I thought she was going to touch the spot where Gant had slugged me. Instead, her soft fingers landed gently on my chin, the exact spot where Little Guy's knockout fist had connected. I thought that bruise was even less noticeable than Gant's handiwork. Apparently not to Dianne's green eyes.

"Did they take anything?" I asked.

"No."

"How'd they get in?"

"They must have jimmied the lock somehow. At least they didn't wreck it like they did at the Tide. And stop trying to change the subject!"

I wasn't really. I was just trying to figure out where to start. I walked over, sat on the expensive couch. Dianne followed, sat on the other end, and turned toward me. I began the story at the beginning with Gant's visit. And ended with my talk with Steve Moore. It didn't take long. And it *was* embarrassing.

"Kiddie Porn? On Hampton Beach?" Dianne said it as if she'd just learned there was a tribe of practicing cannibals living on the beach. "And they think you're involved?"

I cleared my throat. Wondered if I should ask for a beer. Decided against it. "It isn't real kiddie porn. We think the girls are of age and dressed to look young."

"We?"

"Me and Shamrock."

Dianne made a face like she'd just regurgitated. "That's still awful. And how would you know their ages anyway?"

I immediately threw Shamrock under the bus. "Shamrock saw one of the girls at the Midnight Reader. They have to be at least eighteen to work there."

Dianne wouldn't get upset with Shamrock; she liked him a lot. On the other hand, if it had been me visiting a dirty book store, she might not look too favorably on it.

Dianne didn't look at me as she spoke. Apparently the floor was more interesting. "So because of the Bartender connection, both Gant and these criminals think you're involved with pornography? Or maybe child pornography?"

I winced. Even though I wasn't involved with any of it, I didn't even like to hear it mentioned. It gave me a sour feeling in my stomach. "There's no child pornography," I said adamantly. "Otherwise, I guess that's it."

Dianne looked at me now, her eyes hard and piercing. "And of course, you're not."

I rolled my eyes, stopped when I saw she didn't appreciate it. "No, Dianne. Jesus Christ, what the hell do you think I am?"

Her look softened. "I didn't mean that you had anything to do with selling that stuff or anything. It's just that you do have a tendency to put your nose where it doesn't belong. Maybe that's what you did. *Again.*"

I leaned back in the couch. "No, I've only been dragged into it because of this idiot Bartender, whoever the hell he is."

Diane shook her head in disgust. "There's hundreds of bartenders on Hampton Beach and they automatically assumed the name referred to you." It wasn't a question. She hesitated for a moment as if she were debating whether to continue. "You can't blame them, Dan. You brought this on yourself."

I got a little fiery. "That was all a long time ago."

She was just as fiery. "Not that long ago."

I threw up my hands. "What? Do I have to carry that baggage around forever?"

"Apparently you do. And you've got to figure a way to get yourself out of whatever this turns out to be. You know how fast rumors go around the beach. It's a little Peyton Place. And I certainly don't want everyone thinking my boyfriend is a pedophile."

"Dianne. Come on, please." I hoped she was kidding but the mixture of anger and embarrassment on her face told me she wasn't.

"So how do you propose to clear this whole thing up?" she asked.

Usually Dianne was dead set against me getting mixed up in questionable situations on the beach even though I was always on the side of the good guys. Now she was encouraging me.

I quickly told her what Shamrock and I had planned.

She looked doubtful. "Aren't you working?"

"Rick's going to cover for me," I said.

We sat there on either end of the couch for a bit. Finally, I slid down close to her, put my arm around her shoulder, and tried to pull her close. She wasn't having any of it. I tried again. I wanted so much to look into those green eyes while I was making nice slow love to her. I'd forget for a little while about all the other troubling shit I seemed to be tangled up in. She wasn't feeling charitable though, and I couldn't blame her.

She pushed me away. "Is that all you think of, Dan? All I can think about is child pornography on the beach and your name mixed up in it. No wonder Lieutenant Gant punched you. If I didn't know you like I do, I'd hit you too."

She hesitated for a moment, furrowed her light brows as if she just realized something. "Hey, my name and business are involved in this thing now, too."

I held my hands up, palms out. "Maybe not, Dianne."

She harrumphed. "You work at my business and you are my boyfriend and what's happened here and at the Tide tells me I'm caught up in it." The stern face again. "You better clear our names and fast, Dan."

"Okay, I will, I will."

She waved like she was dismissing a lackey. "Now will you go, please. I'm tired but I'm not sure I can sleep, thank you."

"Are you going to call the cops?" I asked.

"What for? Nothing's missing here. There was money missing and damage done at the Tide and the police didn't do anything. I'm not going to waste my time."

I didn't argue; she wouldn't have changed her mind anyway.

I got up to go. Before I opened the door that led to the outer hallway, Dianne said something from the couch that gave me little lift. A very little lift. But I'd take what I could get.

"If you and Shamrock need any help, let me know. I've got a big stake in this and I want it squashed as quickly as possible."

My usual tendency would be to say, "Thanks, but no thanks." Not this time, though. And for more than one reason. "Thanks, Dianne. I appreciate it and I'll let you know if we do."

"You'd better." She hesitated, then added, "And drive carefully, will you please?"

~ * ~

A FEW MINUTES later I pulled into my driveway in one piece. I couldn't even remember the drive. My thoughts had been a jumble, thinking about what had happened, why it'd happened, who was behind it, what if anything else was going to happen, and how fast could I get Dianne and myself in the clear.

I took a Xanax and went to bed. Slept, if that's what you could call it. I certainly couldn't. It was more a half sleep full of dreams of pornographers, punch-out artists, and crazy cops all chasing me. For some reason, I had to decide which one I'd let catch me first. When it was Gant—who resembled a horned demon—who grabbed me first, I awoke with a start. Not only was I covered in sweat, I realized how bad my options must really be if my best out was Lieutenant Richard Gant. *That* was frightening.

Chapter 12

"SO WHEN THEY didn't find the tapes at your home or work," Shamrock said, between sips of ice coffee, "they thought you might have them hidden at Dianne's condo."

We were across Ocean Boulevard from Joclean's Jewelry, leaning back against the railing that separated the boardwalk from the sand. We'd been here since nine a.m., when the store had opened. Less than twelve hours ago I'd been at Dianne's condo in regards to the break-in there. Now it was late morning. Except for Shamrock taking a quick jaunt for coffees, we hadn't left.

"That's what I figure." I'd finished my coffee. I sat against the railing, one hand to either side, holding the top posts of the railing. The sky was cloudy but the heat was still over the top. I was dressed in walking shorts, T-shirt. Shamrock had on a similar outfit, no restaurant whites for a change. People passed us as if they'd lost the enjoyment of life. The heat had taken the starch right out of them.

Shamrock didn't say it but I knew that he realized that Dianne was in danger now too.

"I hope we can get this solved quickly, Danny. You know . . . the heat." He ran his palm across his sweating forehead. Just then he pointed toward Joclean's. "Look, is that it?"

I looked. A white van had pulled up in front of the store in the delivery lane close to the sidewalk. It had no identifying lettering. At least not on this side. I couldn't get a good look at the man who emerged from the driver's seat and hurried into the store.

"Now, Danny? Should we go over now?"

"Let's hold on a minute. But be ready, just in case he doesn't get an order." I figured that's what he was doing—checking out what new sex tapes the owner would need. If I was right, he'd be back to get the tapes from the van.

We didn't have to wait long. The man—a very young man—came out of the store and walked to the back of the van where I could see him clearly. He opened the van's rear doors and rummaged through the merchandise inside. Within a minute, he removed a cardboard box, slammed the van door closed, and marched back into the store.

I pushed myself away from the railing. "Come on, let's go."

Shamrock and I hurried across Ocean Boulevard. We planted ourselves in front of the store, backs to the facade. When the man, maybe eighteen or nineteen, came out, I cut him off just as he reached the driver's side door of the van.

"Hey, can I speak to you for a minute?" I said in what I thought was a non-threatening voice.

The kid must have thought different. He jumped like I'd said, "Stick 'em up."

"Jesus, you scared me. Whattaya want?" He looked nervously at me and then at Shamrock who stood behind me.

The kid was wearing baggy knee-length shorts and an even baggier T-shirt. His white sneakers were filthy. His medium-length brown hair was shiny and plastered to his head. It either needed a wash *or* was sweat drenched from the heat. He was a chubby kid, out of shape. And he *was* nervous. He definitely wasn't the Bartender. I felt more confident.

"We want to talk to you for just a minute," I said.

The kid had one hand on the door handle. He had a key in the other hand and was trying to unlock the van door. Both his hand and his voice shook. "Are you guys cops?" he asked, looking from us to the key he was struggling with and back again.

I forced what I hoped would appear to be a genuine smile. I didn't want this kid so nervous he'd jump in the van— if he ever got the door open—and peal out down Ocean Boulevard. Right now it looked like he was considering it.

"No, no," I said, smiling and shaking my head slowly. I pointed my thumb hitchhiker-style back toward Shamrock. "My associate and I are just interested in doing some business."

"Business?" the kid said as if I wanted to inject him with a toxin.

He was panicking; I had to calm him down. I had to convince this kid I was legit. And quick. Under the circumstances I didn't think Dianne would mind. At least that's what I hoped. "I'm part owner of the High Tide. I'm thinking of getting some of your tapes to sell to my regulars. Under the bar, of course. We do a big business. I think we could sell a lot of your tapes."

The kid hesitated. Looked from me to Shamrock and back again. I could almost hear what he was thinking. He knew the High Tide. Everyone who'd spent more than one day on Hampton Beach knew the Tide. And he also knew we were a big business. But could we sell porn tapes? He wasn't smart enough to know. I was hoping he was smart enough to know he didn't want to do the wrong thing and blow off a potentially big customer. He couldn't be sure the Bartender wouldn't get mad.

The kid took his hand from the van door. "How many would you want?"

Shamrock and I had gone over this already. Neither of us knew anything about the porn business except as very occasional consumers of the product through the years. We'd come up with something we hoped wouldn't scare the kid away but would be enough that he'd be interested.

"About fifty to start," I said, trying to sound nonchalant. "But we've got the biggest bar on the beach so I'm sure we'll be able to build that amount right up."

The kid looked doubtful. "Jeez, that's a lot. And we don't really sell to bars. Mostly convenience stores."

I threw out an ace. "We can pay cash, C.O.D." I knew a lot about seasonal businesses and vendors loved businesses that paid up front. I hoped the porn tape business was no different.

Apparently it wasn't. The kid looked at me like I'd just told him where pirate treasure was buried. "You'd pay for all the tapes on delivery?"

"Of course," I said, feeling like a beach big shot.

The kid shifted his dirty sneakers around on the street. "I just do the deliveries, so I couldn't decide on any of that, of course. I'd have to talk to my boss."

I threw out another high card. "I'll give you a hundred bucks if you can set up a meeting between me and your boss."

The kid raised his eyebrows, thought for a second. "Okay, I'll try. Should he call you at the bar if he wants to set it up?"

I'd been ready for that too. "No. I don't want any of my employees to know what's going on. At least not yet. Here's my home phone number. He can call me there."

I pulled a piece of paper from my back pocket, handed it to the kid. He studied it. "Like I said, I don't know what he'll say. What's your name anyhow?"

Shamrock and I had discussed that too. We'd decided not to use fake names. After all the Bartender had as much time as he wanted to check us out and a false name would have been too easy to uncover. We decided that my name—with its legitimate ties to the High Tide, combined with the suspicions of some people on the beach that I still held an ownership stake in the place, and my well-known unsavory past—might be of use for once. If the Bartender was familiar at all with the beach, he'd know all these things about me. Or he'd find out from someone who did. In this situation, those particular *quirks* might be selling points for a business relationship. A very shady business relationship.

"Dan Marlowe," I said.

The kid nodded, got the door open, and slid in behind the wheel. He rolled the window down. "I'll tell him. Maybe he'll call you."

"Don't forget the hundred for you if he does."

The kid smiled. Sweat glistened on his forehead. "I don't forget anything." He started the van, dropped it into drive, hesitated, and said, "What's your name again? Dan Farlowe?"

I tried not to show any emotion. "Marlowe. Marlowe. Dan Marlowe."

"Yeah, sure, that's it," the kid said. He pulled out into a break in the Ocean Boulevard traffic.

I turned around and almost bumped into Shamrock who was standing right behind me. I'd almost forgotten he was there. He hadn't said one word, which must have been some kind of record for him. Of course, I'd told him to let me do the talking but that had never stopped him before. Studying his beet-red face and the sweat glistening on his red brows, I realized that the heat wave we were suffering through was so debilitating that it was even slowing down the speech of a talker like Shamrock. Amazing.

Shamrock brushed the back of a freckled hand across his forehead. "Well, that sounds promising, Danny. But what now?"

I certainly wasn't going to sit around waiting for the Bartender to call, that was for sure. If this little ploy clicked, great, but in case it didn't, I had to keep moving. I'd noticed that there was an address for a film production company on the porn tape's box, a post office box in Newburyport, Massachusetts, just a few cities away. The address and the amateur quality of the production told me the tapes were probably made locally. Very unusual but it gave me another lead to explore while I was waiting for the Bartender to get back to me, if he did.

I looked at a washed-out Shamrock and knew I must look the same. I certainly felt like how he looked. "The dirty bookstore you thought you recognized the girl in the porn flick from. Is it air conditioned?"

"Yes, it's . . ." Shamrock began, hesitated, blushed. "Well, I'm assuming it is. You couldn't get anyone in there if it wasn't. Especially in those little booths they got."

"What little booths?"

Shamrock put on an embarrassed grin.

"Let's get my car," I said. "You can tell me on the way there."

Chapter 13

BY THE TIME we reached our destination, Shamrock had told me what he knew about the bookstore. It was a lot, especially since he claimed to have been there only once and that was only to satisfy his curiosity. So I knew what to expect.

The Midnight Reader bookstore was located on Route One across the state line in Salisbury, Massachusetts. It was situated in the middle of a small strip mall with the store's name emblazoned across the top of the building in blinking neon lights. There was a small entrance door and what had probably been plate glass windows at one time that were now covered in cheap plywood—probably to keep out prying eyes. Or maybe a zoning requirement, although I remembered reading somewhere that Massachusetts towns and cities had to have one area where these types of businesses were allowed. By designating industrial areas or spots adjacent to the city dump as the only places sex stores could open, most municipalities had been able to keep X-rated businesses out of their jurisdictions. Salisbury had obviously failed. Either the owner of the store had deep pockets and a stable of high-priced lawyers, or he had connections and someone's pockets were getting lined that shouldn't have been. Probably both.

Across the plywood, professionally spray painted in various bright colors, read: "XXX—Magazines—Movies—Nude Models." I pulled the car nose flush to the building a few spots from the entrance. There were only a few other cars. For all I knew, their owners were at the laundromat, convenience store, or one of the few other businesses that made up the strip mall. It really didn't matter.

It was cloudy, hot, and humid outside but when Shamrock opened the door to the establishment and we stepped inside, it was very bright and cool. I would have assumed the opposite on the lighting but I guess it might be good to see what magazines and movies you were buying.

The interior of the business was divided by several aisles that ran from the front to the back of the store. Shelving along both sides of the aisles were lined with either paperbacks, magazines, or VHS tapes. I headed directly for the aisle in front of me. I didn't make it more than a few steps before a hand shot out and grabbed my arm. I stopped. Shamrock barreled into the back of me.

"Hi, honey. What are you looking for? Can I do *anything* for you?"

I don't know how I hadn't noticed her before; I must have had blinders on. Or maybe she came from the adjacent aisle. Where ever she'd come from, I was dumbstruck. And not because I thought she was the blonde from the porn movie. It was what she was wearing that caused my speech paralysis. A black bikini that might have been underwear. And she had breasts that even I knew must have been surgically enhanced.

The bikini top, or bra, or whatever the hell it was, appeared to be a couple of sizes too small.

That was the extent of her wardrobe except for stiletto heels and gold chains around her neck and waist. The chains contrasted nicely with her dark tan. I liked that. I didn't like what I thought I detected on the inside of her left forearm. I couldn't be sure though. The area was heavy with makeup. Her blonde hair was cut in a short attractive bob style. And her face was nicely made up, although it couldn't hide the slight trace of hardness underneath. I was happy to see that, although young, she was at least twenty.

I cleared my throat. Still it cracked when I spoke. "We're . . . ahh . . . just looking around." I turned toward Shamrock.

She did too and her eyes grew two sizes. "Michael," she squealed, "you're back."

I've never seen Shamrock turn so red and I've seen him in some very embarrassing situations. Some I'm sworn to secrecy on.

"Ahh . . . yeah . . . hi," he stuttered.

"Hi who, Michael?" she said, as if giving him a lesson in manners. "Don't tell me you don't remember my name?"

I stood there listening, feeling a bit uncomfortable for my friend. But it was a little humorous too, I have to admit.

After a bit of foot shuffling and realizing he wasn't going to get out of this one, Shamrock mumbled something I couldn't quite catch.

"Michael?" she said, dragging his name out.

"Hello, Skye," he said loudly enough we could both hear it.

"Are you interested in a repeat, Michael?" she purred.

Now this was an answer I was very interested in hearing. But, unfortunately, we were rudely interrupted.

"Hey, it's my turn." The words came from a brunette who'd just walked up, dressed the same as Skye except her attire was red. And she was far from good looking. Big boobs, yes, but a pasty face with a pinched nose and years of wear and tear even the thick makeup couldn't cover up. What was even worse was an odd odor, mixed in with the scent of cheap perfume, coming from her pores. Meth maybe. It was an unappealing combination.

"Like hell it's your turn," Skye spit out. "You were in the damn bathroom and missed your turn. You know the rules."

The brunette came in closer. "Whattaya gonna take two customers?" Her breath was foul and dead. Maybe coming from dying organs inside. I backed away.

"This is one of my regulars," Skye said loudly, tilting her pretty head toward Shamrock. Then added, as if to prove it, "Michael."

The brunette turned even uglier with rage and I thought a cat fight was about to break out when a man who resembled a refrigerator hurried over from somewhere. I didn't need to be told he was the bouncer. I wondered who he bounced though—customers or employees? Probably both on occasion. He spoke in a voice that sounded like it came from a cancer victim's voice box, and there was no doubt who he was there for—this time.

"Get your fuckin' buns over there, Misty," he said, pointing toward a display case against a far wall that held sex toys inside and a cash register on top. Another sex worker leaned against it, lazily watching the confrontation as if she saw this type of blowup every day. "I heard the whole fuckin' thing. Now git! Wait your turn."

We all stared up at him. Misty didn't say a word, although she kept glaring at Skye. She slithered away on her high heels toward the display case. Her ass jiggled unappealingly.

The Refrigerator said, "Sorry for the problem, gents." He was looking at Shamrock and me.

We both nodded stupidly.

"Skye'll take good care of you." He turned to leave, hesitated, and then said over his big shoulder, "Be generous, boys. These girls work hard." To Skye he added, "And don't you forget any rules either."

The Refrigerator went one way and Shamrock and I followed Skye down the center of the nearest aisle. I felt ridiculous walking along behind a woman who had stiletto heels on and what I could now see was a thong bikini. She walked like she was leading us to a front table at an exclusive supper club. Sex magazines were stacked on racks to either side. I didn't have time to notice what specific category they were in.

"What did he mean about the rules?'" I asked.

Skye spoke over her shoulder as she walked. "Oh, just that if I'm going to have two clients, I have to collect for two," she singsonged. "You know . . . money."

Yes, I knew and it sounded expensive. Because of that I was just about ready to cut to the chase. I'd recognized that Skye was most definitely the young school girl Shamrock had pointed out in the VHS tape we'd perused. Of course, she was dressed and made up more than a bit differently. Still, I had no doubt it was her.

I was just ready to speak when she stopped and said, "Here we are again, Michael."

Michael looked embarrassed. He looked like that a lot lately. We'd reached the end of the aisle and in front of us were a series of wooden doors marked from 1 to 6.

"Want number three again, Michael?" she asked.

"I guess." He looked at me as if I could somehow get him out of this.

So I tried. "We'd really just like to ask you a few questions."

Skye put her hands on her hips, spread her legs farther than I thought possible considering her footwear, and gave me a little smirk. "You can ask me any kind of questions you want, honey. In there."

She pointed toward the numbered doors with a finger that ended in a long manicured nail. "Unless you want me to get a thumping." She meant a thumping given by The Refrigerator and from what I'd already seen, I could believe he was capable of it.

I decided our best bet was to get into a booth and ask her the questions. And quickly. I was sure she charged by the hour with a high minimum. So I nodded.

"Okay, doll," she said, smiling. "Just take any two booths. They're all open." She hesitated, then added, "Unless you want to use . . ."

Now I was embarrassed, so I quickly interrupted. "No, we'll take two."

As Shamrock and I opened the doors to booths 3 and 4, Skye slipped around behind a booth on the end. I found my-self in a very small space about the size of a broom closet. It took a short minute for my eyes to become adjusted to the dark. When they did, I saw that I was surrounded by wood paneling except for a metal piece about one foot by one foot on the wall directly in front of me. Turning around I noticed something on the back of the closed door. I pulled at it gently and found it was a small round vinyl seat, like a bar stool. I pulled it down until I heard it snap into place. I sat on it, my back to the door, facing the front of the booth.

Within a half minute, I was startled when the metal sheet on the wall in front of me slid open and exposed a plexiglass window. The bottom was peppered with tiny round holes like it had been hit with birdshot. On the other side was Skye. She was dressed as before, sitting on a small stage no bigger than a large scatter rug and only feet from me. The lighting was kind to her but still adequate and I could immediately see Shamrock's attraction to this . . . hmm . . . artist. She was sitting down, her legs spread wide. Her hands were behind her, resting on the floor and she had her upper body arched and her breasts thrust out. The black top barely contained them.

I heard the window in the booth beside me slide open. I imagined Shamrock sitting in there, looking at this like I was. Skye moved various parts of her body in an oh-so-slow undulating motion. If I hadn't been male, I might not have even noticed. She ran one hand slowly along her inner thigh and I swore she was looking directly into my eyes. Suddenly, I wondered if she could see me. I looked to see where my hands were.

When she spoke, I could hear her easily enough. That was what the small holes in the plexiglass were for.

"Come on now, honey," she breathed, and she *was* looking at me. Although maybe Shamrock thought the same thing. "Tell me what you'd like me to do and I'll tell you how much to put in the slot."

The slot? I looked around and saw just that—a little slot immediately below the window. It was open, apparently leading to the other side of the partition. Someone could get carried away with this thing, I realized. Before I did, I decided to repeat our real reason for being there.

But just then a bill fluttered onto the little stage. It had obviously come from the slot on Shamrock's side. I couldn't make out what denomination it was but I heard him mutter something. The money he slid through must have been enough for his request because Skye looked at the bill, then at Shamrock's window, and smiled.

I glanced at the wooden wall between Shamrock and I, tapped on it, and whispered, "Don't get carried away. Remember what we came for."

I have no idea whether he heard me or not. My eyes were drawn back to Skye. And not reluctantly either, I have to admit. She reached behind her and with the deftness that comes with a lot of practice, removed her bra in one quick motion. Her breasts were as large as I'd guessed, but not too large. Firm with beautiful pink nipples that she slowly began to rub with her palms. Within seconds those nipples were protruding like erasers on a pencil.

Her body had yet to show any negative effects from her addiction.

She made the standard erotic faces and sounds while she played gently with her breasts. Her jeweled fingers on her body seemed anything but standard for some reason. And she was looking directly into my eyes again. Or was that an illusion and Shamrock was seeing the same eye contact I thought I was seeing?

Whatever. It didn't matter; it was working. I could feel it. If I didn't speak up soon and change the course of this, I knew Shamrock and I would be in a race to see who could slip the biggest bill the fastest through the magic slots. We'd end up broke and without the info we came for. I couldn't have that.

Skye suddenly stopped acting like she was making love to a camera and said, "Okay, guys. What would you like me to do now and don't be shy?"

I shifted around on my little seat and almost choked when I talked. Still, I got the words out before Shamrock got a bigger bill onto the stage.

"We've got some questions we'd like to ask you." And a little louder to my friend behind the wall, "Remember why we came here, Shamrock." I heard him mumble something, which was good—at least he'd heard me.

"Questions?" she asked, her eyes narrowing. "You were serious? What kind of questions?"

I felt foolish interrogating a semi-nude woman through plexiglass but I soldiered on. "We're wondering about some . . . ahh . . . movies you've made."

Skye straightened her back, pulled her legs under her Indian-style. "What movies? What do you want to know? You a cop?"

I waved my hand. "No, no, no. We just want some information on a tape you made where you were dressed as a . . . hmm . . . young girl."

She pulled her arms around her breasts, covering them. "Nothing illegal about that."

"I know," I said. "We're just trying to get in touch with whoever made those films. We want to buy some wholesale."

She looked at me doubtfully.

"A lot of them," I said, hoping I was convincing.

She was silent for a long time. Finally, "Well, I don't know."

"Can you tell us who made the movies and where they might be?"

"I might," she said as she rubbed her thumb and forefinger together fast enough to spark. "It'll cost you. And I can't tell you now." She lowered her voice and leaned toward my window. "The management watches us here sometimes."

That gave me the creeps. I glanced around the little booth, wondering if there was a hidden camera in here that might be used to watch the patrons, too. Suddenly, I didn't want to discuss the matter here any more than Skye did.

"How about paying me for the information now?" she said, keeping her voice quiet.

I might be naive but I wasn't born yesterday. Still, I couldn't blame her—she was taking a shot.

"We'll pay when we get the info."

She scowled, then shrugged her shoulders. "All right, I guess." She uncrossed her arms, exposing her breasts again. "You guys want to continue where we left off?"

I heard Shamrock shifting around in the next booth. I could imagine that he was pulling bills from his battered wallet.

"No, we're done," I said, loud enough that Shamrock could hear me too.

"Up to you," she said. "But you got to give me enough so I won't get in trouble with my boss for keeping myself tied up with two guys for this long."

I figured *boss* meant The Refrigerator. Whether he'd be pissed that she hadn't gotten more money from us or not, I didn't want to take the chance. I didn't want what might happen to this young lady on my conscience. I took a twenty from my wallet, dropped it through the slot. It floated down to the little stage.

"How about you, Shamrock?" She nodded in Shamrock's direction but looked at me.

A bill fluttered to the stage from Shamrock's side. It was a ten-dollar bill.

Without even looking at it, or so it appeared, she said, "Double that please, Michael."

"I'm broke, Danny," Shamrock said from next door.

I didn't like that and I didn't like him using my name. I grudgingly shoved a ten through the slot.

Skye scooped up all the bills we'd deposited in one swift move of her hand. "Give me a number and I'll call you," she said. "It won't be today though. I got a date after work."

I wondered how to handle this. I didn't like giving out my phone number. I'd been doing it too much lately and to people I wasn't thrilled had it.

"How about giving me yours?" I said.

She shook her head. "That ain't gonna happen."

Considering her line of work and the people she probably met, that sounded wise. Shamrock and I were most likely high-class clientele for this establishment. Think of it. The two of us sitting here in a couple of booths, with plexiglass windows, pumping money through slots, with a half-naked woman on the other side who would probably do acrobatics if the price were right. Yeah, we were high-class all right. What a joke.

I didn't want Skye to know where I worked or my name, even though Shamrock had let my first name slip. But there were lots of Dans in the world so that didn't really mean much. I'd already taken a chance giving my name to the

Bartender's delivery boy and I didn't think it wise to do it again. But I couldn't come up with any other way of following up with Skye and what she knew about the porn tape business. And clearing my name from any involvement with that racket trumped my caution. So I had to do what I had to do. Fortunately, I'd jammed a pencil stub and pocket notebook in my back pocket in case I needed to jot down any information. I used those and slid a paper with my phone number through the same place my money had gone. She scooped it up like lightning. Maybe she didn't want The Refrigerator to know. I wondered what the business's rules were regarding a worker setting up an after-work liaison. Probably not too liberal, especially if the owner wasn't getting a piece of any action a stripper might get for an after-hours activity.

"I'll call," she mouthed silently in my direction. Then glancing toward Shamrock's window, she said, "Bye, Michael." Looking back at me, she said, "See you later, Dan." I'm sure it was just me and the situation I was in, but I could've sworn there was extra meaning in her words when she spoke to me.

I didn't have time to ponder it because one of Skye's hands brushed the stage floor behind her and the metal sheet dropped back into place, blocking my view. I could hear the one in Shamrock's booth closing, too.

I couldn't get out of that dark booth fast enough. I stood, spun around, slapped the stool back up against the door, opened the door, and stepped out into the light. Shamrock was coming out of his booth just as I did.

"Come on," I said.

He followed me as we retraced our steps the way we'd come. The joint had a few customers floating around the premises now. We'd just about reached the front door with no sign of The Refrigerator, which I'd been worried about, when Shamrock said, "Danny, look at this."

I turned. I didn't even bother to look at the magazine he was holding up for me to see. "I never seen anything like this, it—"

I didn't let him finish. I grabbed his other arm and pulled him along. He tossed the magazine back toward the rack as I did. The magazine bounced off and fell to the floor.

All the way back to the beach, Shamrock jabbered on about the Midnight Reader and Skye's charms. I tried to keep the conversation on what we'd learned, difficult because we hadn't learned much. Finally, just before we crossed the bridge, I said, "You know she's a junkie. Right, Shamrock?"

"Aye, Danny. I saw those marks, too. Poor lass. But she's a very good-looking junkie. And I'm not planning on taking her across the water to meet my ma."

I smiled. But still I knew those tracks meant trouble. "If she calls, we'll get the information from her and that's it."

"Maybe we could help her, Danny."

Maybe we could help her. But not likely. Not when it was often a struggle to even help myself. The last thing I needed was to get mixed up with a junkie stripper. It was bad enough my best friend was already infatuated with her. I shuddered. But I was careful how I spoke to Shamrock. He had a heart of gold and was the type of person who really would give the shirt off his back to someone in need. And his intentions were always good. Even though sometimes it could lead to unpleasantness.

"Maybe, Shamrock, maybe. Let's see what happens."

"All right, Danny," he said, his face beaming as we drove across the bridge and back into Hampton.

Chapter 14

I TOOK IT easy that night and got decent sleep for a change. I'd been up only a few minutes when the phone rang. I answered and heard a male voice. He didn't identify himself, just said he was the man I wanted to talk to about purchasing *items* as he called them. The Bartender. I agreed to meet him after my shift and he gave me an address.

My time at the High Tide dragged. It didn't help that business was unusually slow. I spent a lot of the time chatting with Eli and Paulie. That, and mulling over in my head how I was going to handle my meeting with the Bartender, kept me occupied. When five o'clock came, I handed over the bar to my relief.

I'd brought my car to work and parked it across the street in the municipal lot. I'd had to jog across Ocean Boulevard a couple of times during my shift to feed the meter. But I needed a car to get to where I was going now.

I pulled out of the lot and sat in traffic on Ocean in a sweltering car, praying the A/C would power up quickly. The heat and humidity were still unbearable. And again the beach was packed. Why, I didn't know. If I didn't live here, it would be the last place I'd head to. I'd stay wherever I lived, seated in front of the air conditioning or a fan if that was all I had, certainly not lying on sand like I was a slab of roast beef cooking in an oven. That's what the people walking by looked like now—cooked meat. Barely human and suffering. I shuddered and felt a shiver of relief as the air from the car's vents went from hot to cool.

When I reached the Casino, I broke free of traffic and headed north. I didn't have far to go. I took Winnacunnet Road and, after a very short distance, pulled into a large apartment complex. I checked the address the Bartender had given me, located the correct building, and parked as close to it as I could, in an area marked "Guest Parking." I got the only open spot. Walking to the building I noticed a white van also parked there. I was fairly sure this was the van the kid had used to deliver the tapes. That didn't concern me. He'd been the nonthreatening type.

My plan was open and vague as to what I was actually going to do when I met the Bartender. Of course, I was hoping I could get him to stop distributing his porn tapes on Hampton Beach. Maybe that would appease Gant. How I was going to convince the Bartender to do this, I had no idea. Maybe I'd try to reason with him. Tell him he'd end up in trouble. Or that I'd initiate some local pressure on the store owners not to carry his merchandise.

If neither of those arguments worked, I could always threaten to turn him in to the cops. I didn't know if that would scare him or not. After all, I wasn't even sure if anything he was doing was illegal, especially now that I was convinced the actresses in the flicks had been of age and just made up to look younger. And even if he called my bluff, I wouldn't have turned him in. What good would it have done? Steve had said the cops were already on to the nickname; maybe now they knew his identity. Besides, going to the cops went against part of my moral code—to never rat. Except where child exploitation was concerned and that appeared to no longer be an issue.

All this ran through my mind as I walked up the front steps of the brick building, opened the door, and stepped into the foyer. Inside there was a long series of black buttons on my right. Beside each button was an apartment number along with a paper label with the resident's name, except for a couple of labels that were blank. One blank label was beside the apartment number I wanted and it was on the third floor. The fact that some residents wanted anonymity didn't surprise me. I was somewhat familiar with this complex.

I pressed the Bartender's button and waited to be buzzed through the inner door. Nothing. I buzzed two more times before I gave something else a try. I went down the entire row of buttons, pushing one or two at a time. It took only seconds to hit all of them. And only a bit longer for at least two occupants to buzz the door. I walked in and headed up a staircase with worn beige carpeting and a chipped wrought iron railing. I went directly to the third floor, leaving the door buzzer in the foyer still chirping occasionally.

The Bartender's apartment was on the right, halfway down a long corridor. I gave a light tap on the door. Nothing. I tried again. The same. On my third try, I was a little more forceful, although I didn't overdo it. I had no desire to have a nosy neighbor peek out. I still had no idea how this was all going to turn out and thought it wise not to attract any attention.

When there was no answer to my third knock, and no sound that I could hear from inside, I almost left. But before I did, I reached for the doorknob and turned it. Unlocked. I opened the door a bit. I couldn't see much. It was semi-dark inside. Not knowing the Bartender's name, I said only, "Hello."

No answer.

"Hello?" I repeated several times, just like the knocks on the door, the third time being a bit louder. Still nothing.

I'd already decided I wasn't going to go in. My eyes must have adjusted to the dimness inside because, just as I was about to close the door, I caught a glimpse of a sneakered foot.

My heart shifted into overdrive and I wanted to leave. But I'd come this far. And also there was that promise I'd made to myself about overcoming anxiety. So I was stuck.

I gently pushed the door and as it opened, I realized the sneakered foot was connected to a seated man. I could see his entire body along with his face. What was left of it anyway. I knew instantly he wouldn't be coming down for breakfast tomorrow.

I stepped inside and glanced around. I had no interest in the decor; I *was* interested in finding out if there was anyone else around. I listened, heard nothing, debated whether to back out the door, leave, and pretend I'd never been there. Believe me, I was tempted.

But then I remembered all those buttons I'd pushed in the foyer and all the buzzing I'd gotten in response. At least one of those residents had probably already peeked out their door or peephole and seen me, or would see me on my way out. So it wasn't bravery or civic duty that compelled me to stay. It was just that the odds were too great I'd be identified as a visitor to this apartment. And if I bolted under these circumstances, I'd look like the guilty party in regards to whatever had happened here.

I closed the apartment door behind me. The room was dark for this time of day. No lights were on and heavy floor-length drapes were drawn tight against what I assumed were sliding glass doors that led to a balcony. I flicked on a wall switch beside me. A cheap overhead chandelier light illuminated a living room. Again, I didn't care about the decor. I did care about the man seated in an armchair in front of me. I stepped closer. An odor of shit hit my nostrils along with that of burned flesh. My stomach rolled like the tide.

The man's head lolled over the back of the armchair. I stepped close to see the face better. From what was left of it, I knew the police would have to take fingerprints to make a positive ID. Still, I had no doubt it was the Bartender. Both sides of his face were horribly burned, the skin black and curdled, liquid oozing from the burns. A clothes iron stood on the floor beside him. An extension cord ran from the iron to a wall socket. Balled white socks were on the floor in front of him. Probably jammed in his mouth to stifle the screams. There was a small hole in the center of the man's forehead.

I stood there like a cigar store Indian, not moving, trying to hold my lunch down. He'd been tortured. A dunce could see that. Maybe for information? But what information? The same information I had come for?

Whatever his killer or killers had wanted, I was sure they'd gotten it. No one could stand that kind of physical abuse.

I hoped they hadn't let him suffer long before they'd put him out of his misery.

My anxiety was a raging locomotive by now but whose wouldn't have been? I debated with myself again whether to get out of there or not. I wanted to leave but I couldn't do it. I glanced around for a phone. That's when I saw another pair of sneakered feet.

I'd forgotten about the white van.

I stepped around the couch as if I were walking on a floor covered in superglue, terrified at what I might see next.

It was the delivery kid all right. He was lying on his back behind the couch. He had two small bullet holes in his chest about the same size as the one the Bartender's forehead displayed. The little holes oozed blood thorough a white T-shirt. Small pools of red puddled on the light-colored carpet. He was nice and clean compared to the Bartender's condition.

The kid's eyelids fluttered. He was alive!

I ran to the kitchen, grabbed a dishtowel off a rack to stop the blood. I knelt down beside the kid and tried to do just that. Didn't last long. I was a day late and a dollar short. The kid looked at me with eyes that told me he knew his life was over way too soon. He said, "The . . . old man . . . old man," and then he died right there in front of me.

It was a shock seeing a young kid like that die from gunshot wounds. Even more so than finding the tortured body of the Bartender behind me. I tried to pull myself together.

There were no signs of physical abuse on the kid. Maybe he had walked in as the Bartender was having the wrinkles removed from his face. I figured the Bartender was probably the only one who had the information the killer or killers wanted. That's why he'd been tortured and not the kid. The kid had probably just been in the wrong place at the wrong time and had to be eliminated as a witness. Whoever shot him had most likely thought he was dead.

They'd been wrong. By a little while anyway.

And the kid's last words—*The . . . old man . . . old man.* What had he meant? That the killer was an older guy? Christ almost anyone could be considered old to someone around twenty. Even me, for sure. Then I remembered the words I thought I'd heard down on the beach the night I'd been knocked unconscious. *I hope you didn't kill him. The old man wouldn't like that.*

Could there be a connection? I didn't ponder that for more than a few seconds. I had a lot more to worry about. Namely being alone here with two murdered corpses.

There was a phone on a table at the other end of the couch. I used it.

"This is Dan Marlowe," I said. I was surprised I could talk, although my voice did shake noticeably. "There's been a murder. Two." I gave the address and hung up.

I waited a minute, standing there, not doing anything. Just waiting. Finally, I picked up the phone and this time I called the police.

Chapter 15

"YOU'LL BE ASKING him questions only in my presence, Lieutenant Gant." Attorney James Connolly stood in the open doorway of the Bartender's apartment. His curly black hair was as wild as ever. He wore a checked sport coat with a tie loosened and crooked at the throat, a battered briefcase in his right hand at his side.

I'd called him before I'd called the police. If ever I was going to need a lawyer, I figured this was the time. Connolly and I had had dealings before and I knew his phone number well. He was the only criminal lawyer I knew that I could afford. And, I had to admit, he had been very helpful in the not-too-distant past.

Lieutenant Gant spun around at the interruption. "Connolly! You again." Turning back to me, Gant said, "What, have you got this guy on retainer, Marlowe?"

I didn't answer. I moved toward my attorney as he moved toward me.

"I'm representing Mr. Marlowe in this case." Connolly looked around the room. "Whatever this case is."

I noticed sweat dripping from his forehead. He was sweating bullets. But then everyone in the room was. The M. E. had asked that the air conditioning not be turned on. Something about screwing with the time of death. Which meant the inside of the apartment was like the inside of a sauna. And the odor from the corpses caused some of the younger uniformed cops to hold handkerchiefs to their mouths and leave the apartment every so often.

In addition to myself, Gant, and Connolly, Steve Moore, a few uniforms, people from the M. E.'s office, a couple of plainclothes state police detectives, and what appeared to be a state forensic expert roamed through the apartment. Gant had been browbeating me for the past fifteen minutes and I was more than happy to see Connolly show up.

Nevertheless, Gant continued on his obsessive tack and lasered in on me. "So you claim you just showed up here and found two dead bodies?"

"One was alive for a couple of minutes. And it's not a claim, it's the truth," I answered.

Attorney Connolly jumped in. "You don't have to answer any of these questions, Mr. Marlowe."

"I don't mind," I said quickly and probably foolishly. "I've got nothing to hide."

Gant smirked. "*Mr.* Marlowe? Why the formality, Connolly? You're probably on his payroll."

Connolly lifted his briefcase, shook it in Gant's direction. "Watch what you say, Lieutenant, unless you want to face a libel suit."

Gant didn't like that but he said nothing. Instead he turned to me. "And what exactly did you want to ask Mr. Early?"

Because a couple of the cops had been able to recognize the Bartender, even with his disfigured face, we all knew he was just that—an ex-beach bartender named Thomas Early. I'd heard of him through the years. Didn't remember ever seeing him, though. He'd worked at a handful of beach bars, never at the Tide. He'd always left his jobs under a cloud of suspicion when the tills were discovered to be light. Everyone in the business had heard the scuttlebutt about Early. The beach was really just a village. And beach business owners were the worst village gossips, but in a self-defense sort of way. So, it hadn't been a surprise when the first cops on the scene had identified Early even before Gant arrived.

No one knew who the kid was. Except for his family, I doubted it was going to be important.

"I wanted to clear my name in regards to porn tapes that are being sold on the beach," I said, looking at Gant. "The ones you accused me of being involved with."

Gant's eyes narrowed. He couldn't be sure if I was going to mention his assault on me or not. He needn't have worried. What good would it have done? It was his word against mine.

Apparently convinced I wasn't going to mention the incident, Gant smirked. "Is that why you were here?" he began haughtily, "in regards to the *kiddie* porn tape racket? Maybe you and Mr. Early here had a difference of opinion over dividing the filthy profits." He kicked his foot out toward Early still on the chair.

I wasn't going to be pushed around by Gant, not with my attorney at my side. And especially in regard to me being connected to child porn. "I came here to find out who's behind the tapes and try to put a stop to it."

Gant blew air from between his lips. "That's what you say."

"That's the truth! Besides, it isn't child porn. Some of the actresses were dressed to look like young girls."

Again the air rushed out from between Gant's lips. "I'll repeat . . . that's what you say. Although I have to admit it's the type of sleazy thing you'd pull, Marlowe. Getting a piece of the child porn trade but covering your butt with girls barely of age. Not out of character for you."

I don't know if it was the heat—so bad I was surprised some of us weren't lying on the floor with the kid's corpse— the smell of shit and piss, or a delayed reaction to what I'd been just through, but I went for Gant. If it hadn't been for Steve Moore and my attorney I would have got him, too. They both grabbed me, held on tight.

Gant looked stunned, but only for a moment. "Let him go. Let's see what kind of a tough guy he is."

My heart was racing and I was fuming. I struggled against the grips of Steve and my attorney. It took a few seconds for my mind to come back from the brink and realize what an assault on Gant in front of all these witnesses would mean. Jail. For me. That's what it would mean.

"What about a gun?" Connolly asked, releasing my arm when he realized I'd relaxed. He raised his briefcase again in Gant's direction. "Did you find one?"

I already knew the answer—they hadn't. The look of disgust on Gant's face told my attorney the answer too. Connolly looked at me. "Have you given a statement?"

I nodded. "I also told them the kid mentioned an old man before he died."

Gant snickered. "That could be you, Marlowe."

"Or you, Gant," I said.

"Along with half the people on the seacoast," Connolly interjected.

Steve finally let go of my arm and stood there awkwardly. I guess he was caught between a rock and a hard place. He'd said next to nothing to me since he'd arrived. What could he say with all these others present? I'd find out later how he felt.

"I'm taking my client out of here, Lieutenant. He's suffered enough for today, walking in on a horrendous scene like this." My attorney ended his little speech with a loud sniffle.

I didn't know if Gant was scowling because of the sniffling or because he didn't have me roped and hogtied to a murder rap. Anyway, he waved the back of his hand at us, said, "Get your *client* out of here, Connolly. For now. Don't go far, Marlowe. I haven't finished with you."

That was all my attorney and I wanted to hear. Connolly took me by an arm like I was his date at the prom and we headed for the door. I glanced at Steve. His back was toward Gant and he rolled his eyes at me. I felt bad for Steve. I seemed to have a knack for placing him in uncomfortable situations.

It was good to get out of the apartment and almost as good to get out of the building. It was hot and humid outside and that's all the wind carried—heat and humidity. Still, it was a blessing to have some air that didn't carry the stench of death on it.

In the parking lot my attorney said, "You're in hot water, Dan. You going to tell me what the hell this is all about?"

"Yes, I am. At least what I know, which isn't much. But not right now. I've got something I've got to do."

That something had been bothering me the whole time I'd been in the slaughter house. What if somehow I had led the killer or killers to Early?

Maybe the killers had seen me talking to the delivery kid and had followed him back to Early's apartment. Or maybe they'd just tracked him down in the same manner I had.

It didn't matter right now. What was really gnawing at my brain was something tied to that, though. I was worried that there was a chance that whoever was responsible for the double killing upstairs might have also found out about Skye. I had to warn her. I didn't want anything like what had happened to Early and the kid happening to her. I had enough on my conscience.

"Where are you going?" My attorney wiped sweat from his forehead with the sleeve of his sport coat.

"I've got to warn someone that they might be in danger from whoever the hell killed those guys."

I started toward my car. "Have you got A/C in your car, Dan?" Connolly asked.

"Of course," I said, without stopping.

"Well, you might need some legal advice on a job like that." Connolly hurried to catch up to me. "I'm coming along."

I stopped. "Mr. Connolly, you charge by the hour. I can't afford it."

Connolly held his free hand up, made it shimmy. "Don't worry. You won't be on the clock for this trip. And I've told you before, it's James."

I looked at him skeptically.

He saw my look, said, "Well, to tell you the truth, I haven't got anything else to do today and my car's A/C is on the blink. I think I'd go mad if I have to drive another mile in it."

I believed that. I didn't see where his car was parked but every time I'd seen Connolly in the past, he'd been driving what could be generously called a heap. I shrugged. "Okay then."

We hopped in my car. "The A/C, man," Connolly said, pointing at the dash panel. "Put it on."

I did. It blew as hot as the wind. It would take a few minutes until it cooled. Connolly and I both rolled down our windows until it did.

"Where are we going?" Connolly asked, ending in a loud sniffle. I didn't like his sniffles but I was used to them by now.

"Salisbury, Mr. Connolly," I said, as I pulled the car out of the complex's parking lot.

"James, Dan. James."

I'd forgotten to call him by his first name. It's hard to override the good manners you're brought up with. And it does feel odd calling your attorney by his first name. At least it does for me. Besides, I wasn't really sure how chummy I wanted to get with James Connolly, Esquire. His sniffling had told me the first time I'd met him that it might be better to keep our relationship purely on a business basis. On the other hand, I was quite a bit older, so the *mister* bit was probably out of place.

"Okay, James."

"Where in Salisbury?"

"You'll see when we get there. I've got to pick someone up on the way."

Chapter 16

I WANTED TO pick up Shamrock before seeing Skye. Skye knew him better than she knew me and maybe she'd be more apt to take my warning seriously if Shamrock was there to back me up.

It was dark when Attorney Connolly and I pulled up in front of Shamrock's cottage on a side street off Ashworth Avenue. I didn't bother going in. I tooted the horn. Shamrock opened the front door, came to the driver's side window. All I had to tell him was that I needed him. He looked at my face and at who was sitting beside me, then went back to his cottage, locked the door.

As Shamrock was locking his door, Connolly got out of the front seat and hopped in back. "It'll be easier for you to talk to him."

"Hello, Solicitor," Shamrock said to Connolly once he was settled in the front seat.

"You remember Shamrock Kelly, right?" I said to Connolly.

"Of course I do," Connolly answered, sniffling a bit. "And you can call me James, too, Shamrock."

Shamrock gave me a discreet glance. I did nothing except turn the car around and get back on Ashworth. As I drove, I brought Shamrock up to speed on what had recently transpired.

When I was done, he said in a bit of a shaky voice, "Sweet Mother of Mary, you say they used an iron on his face?"

"It wasn't pretty," I said.

I could see Shamrock shudder out of the corner of my eye.

"And now you're afraid they might hurt Skye?"

We were in Salisbury now and not too far from our destination. Even though I had the A/C cranking, I was still sweating. "Maybe," I said, "I can't take the chance they won't."

Shamrock turned toward me. "But why would they go after her, Danny? Aft . . . after what they did to the Bartender, they must know what they wanted to know."

Shamrock was right. Why would they go after Skye if they already had the information they wanted? They wouldn't. *If* they'd found out what they wanted to know. Considering their interrogation methods, there was only a small possibility that they hadn't. But like I said, I couldn't take that chance. Not with the girl's life. Especially if the killers had followed me to the Delivery Kid and then followed the kid to Early. They also could've followed Shamrock and me to the Midnight Reader and found out we'd met with Skye. If anything happened to her, it would be my fault.

So I had to warn her. Having Early and the kid on my conscience was more than enough.

"You're probably right, Shamrock. Still, I have to give her a heads-up and make sure she'll be all right."

"Why didn't you tell the cops, Danny, and have them do it?"

I could tell by Shamrock's voice that he was keyed up and probably wished he'd doused his cottage lights when he'd heard my car horn.

"First of all, I'm not squealing on that woman. She's got enough problems without the police jerking her around about porn films. Second, Gant was there. You think he's going to be in a hurry to protect anybody I ask him to?"

Shamrock was shaking his head as I spoke.

"He'd drag his feet for days before he got around to seeing her. And when he did, it wouldn't be to issue a warning or to protect her, either. It'd be for rousting her, that's it." I took a deep breath. "I figure the animals who used Early for ironing practice won't be able to iron more than one victim a day. Even a psycho probably needs to get drunk after something like that. So I'm hoping they won't make their next move until tomorrow at least. Gant would definitely be too late, though. Hopefully, we won't be."

When we reached the Midnight Reader, I pulled the car as close to the front door as I could. It was night and that meant there were quite a few more customers compared to when Shamrock and I had been there in the daytime. The neon lights of the business were flashing brightly.

"You might as well wait here, James." I said, looking over my shoulder. "She doesn't know you. It might be better."

Connolly nodded and sniffled. "Leave the car and the A/C on."

Shamrock and I hurried into the store. The overhead lights were bright and the A/C was on. I spotted Skye immediately. She was dressed exactly as she had been the last time except her little thong bikini was pale blue not black. She was in the furthest aisle from the cash register, talking to a man. I gave Shamrock's arm a tug and headed that way.

When we reached them, Skye turned to us, a surprised look on her face. "Hi, guys. That was quick but I'm busy right now. You'll have to wait your turn."

The man she was talking to was quite distinguished looking. Taller than me, pure white hair, combed backwards just so. He had a pencil-thin mustache, and although his clothes were casual, they were expensive. I pegged him at about seventy and imagined that he had driven down from one of the oceanfront mansions in Rye. I could understand why Skye wanted us to wait. But we couldn't. This was life or death.

"We have to talk to you, Skye," I said. "Not business, personal. And *very* serious."

"It can't wait?" she asked in almost a begging tone.

"No." I answered.

She must have seen the seriousness in my face because she looked resigned, then turned to the distinguished gentleman and said in a cooing voice, "This'll only take a minute, honey. You wait right here."

She didn't look too hopeful that he would. And I could understand why—you couldn't tell how he felt about the interruption. This guy was the old Yankee type who could keep the same expression through a bitter divorce proceeding. Still, I guessed that no matter how he felt about waiting for her, Skye was more concerned about one of the other hostesses jumping this guy's bones the second we walked away with her. After all, from what I knew firsthand about establishments like this, they didn't often get someone who didn't have to check their wallet to see what they could afford before accepting a proposition. This fellow definitely had a good credit score but probably never had to take advantage of it.

The three of us left the gentleman behind and headed for the far front corner of the shop. Skye led the way. I watched her as she walked. She had spike heels that matched the color of her bikini. Her thonged tight ass swayed nicely as she walked. She had a tan with no tan lines. All set off by her short blonde hair and gold jewelry.

When we reached the corner and a semblance of privacy, Skye turned around. "All right. What the hell's so important that you have to take me away from a paying customer?"

Then she looked at me, lowered her voice. "I told you I'd call."

As I began to tell her why we were there, she stretched, trying to see around Shamrock and myself, to see if her customer had been stolen yet. She kept looking in that direction as I spoke. As my story continued, her gaze shifted to me and her eyes slowly widened.

When I finished talking, she spoke and her voice shook. "An iron? And you think they might be looking for me?"

I shrugged. "It's possible."

Shamrock had been quiet up until now. "We just want to make sure you don't get hurt, lassie."

"They can't hurt me here," she said. Her voice shook harder. "Not with Larry around."

I didn't have to ask who Larry was. I was sure she was referring to The Refrigerator. And she may or may not have been right. The Refrigerator was a big boy all right. But the animals who had taken care of the Bartender and Delivery Kid had used guns and an iron. For all I knew, The Refrigerator might become a whimpering punk with the business end of a gun jammed in his gut. Or at the sight of a hot iron close to his face.

"Maybe, maybe not," I said. "I'd advise you to get out of here now and go somewhere, anywhere except home. A girlfriend's place?"

"I can't leave here now. I'm working. Besides, one of the other hostesses gave me a ride."

"We can give you a ride wherever you want to go," I said.

"Aye, lass, we can," Shamrock confirmed.

"Jesus Christ," Skye said. She had her arms wrapped around her chest. Still I could see her arms shaking. "Larry won't like it. He won't let me leave."

"Forget Larry," I said. "This could be life or death. Yours."

She shuddered. "Please don't say that. All I can think of is that hot iron and . . ."

Just then I heard a familiar booming voice behind me.

"What's going on here? Is this work?"

Shamrock and I turned to face Larry, the human refrigerator. He wore a black short-sleeve T-shirt stretched tight across his massive chest and upper arms. The business name was stenciled across its front. The bright light made his shaved head shine and his gold earring glint. He didn't look happy. But I guess he probably never did.

Skye cleared her throat. Her voice was still none too steady. "Larry, I'm going to have to leave. Something's come up."

Larry looked like he'd just been insulted. "What something?"

"It's personal," Skye said.

"Ain't nothin' personal here," Larry said, raising his already loud voice. "Unless your house is on fire, you ain't going nowhere. Can't you see how busy we are?" He waved one arm at the shop.

He was right about that last part. There were quite a few patrons scattered around the place. I noticed one of the other hostesses leading the distinguished-looking gentleman to the back area. That hadn't taken long.

"Larry, pleeease," Skye said.

She was genuinely terrified and I thought she might actually break down and cry. Whether Larry picked up on her sincerity or not, I don't know. I did know that he didn't care either way.

"Nobody's going nowhere, girl, until their shift is over."

A few patrons glanced toward us, but quickly looked away when Larry half turned and swept his eyes across the premises.

"Now, Mister . . . ahh . . . ahh . . . Larry," Shamrock began, "this is a very serious situation. This lass is in danger. We're going to escort her to safety."

Larry looked at Shamrock like he was surprised my friend could talk. "Shut the fuck up, pinhead. No one's in any danger when I'm here." He tapped his big thumb against his huge chest. Then he looked at Shamrock's white restaurant outfit and smirked. "And what's with the clothes? You an ice cream man or something?" What passed for a smile crossed his face.

Shamrock didn't respond. I didn't blame him. I figured we were just about to get thrown out of the store when the front door flew open and in stormed my attorney.

His head swiveled from side to side like a duck in a shooting gallery. When he spotted us, he made a beeline in our direction.

"What's taking you guys so long?" he said when he reached us. His sniffling had increased two-fold.

Before we could answer Larry said, "They're coming right now as a matter of fact, buddy."

Connolly turned to Larry. He only came up to the bigger man's chest and I imagined The Refrigerator could use Connolly for a barbell if he wanted to get some exercise in. Still, Connolly's words came out as if Larry were no larger than a dwarf. "And who might I ask are you?"

Larry was taken aback for a moment. "Who am I? Who the hell are you?" he finally said.

I saw a sliver of hope and jumped in before Connolly could answer. "This is my attorney, James Connolly."

Larry looked like he wanted to pop someone's head off, but at the same time he seemed hesitant to speak. It was almost as if the president of the local chapter of the Hell's Angels was standing in front of him instead of a slightly built, sniffling lawyer.

I shouldn't have been surprised. I'd learned long ago that lawyers sometimes made certain businesspeople more nervous than an armed robber storming through their establishment's front door. Especially if said business was operating in a gray area to begin with. And maybe if said businessperson had had very unpleasant experiences with various lawyers in the past. Those were the only reasons I could think of to explain Larry's turnaround—from Godzilla to Bambi in no more than a long minute.

"Well, what do you need a lawyer here for?" Larry asked, in a much softer voice.

"We don't," I said. Then, trying to sound ominous, I added, "I hope."

"What's the problem?" Connolly said, looking sternly at Larry.

"No problem," Larry answered. The big man actually sounded timid and I almost felt sorry for him.

Still I took full advantage of the situation. "Well, Attorney Connolly, I've told this man," I said, nodding at Larry, "that there's been a serious personal problem for Skye and she must leave work now. For her safety."

"And?" Connolly didn't soften his look.

"He doesn't seem to want to let his worker leave during this emergency."

Larry held up both hands, palms out. "Now wait a minute. You didn't say it was an emergency. I just thought . . . well . . . maybe you wanted to take one of my girls off-premises for some action. Guys try that, you know."

"Well, that's not what's happening here," Connolly said. He was looking intently at Larry and the bigger man was actually averting his eyes.

"Okay, okay," Larry said. "I would never keep an employee from an emergency."

"I wouldn't advise it," Connolly said. "If she were harmed or suffered damages, there could be serious and costly legal ramifications for you and this business."

The big man looked like someone had held a gun to his head, pulled the trigger, and dry-fired it. He actually gulped. "Yeah, you can go," he said, looking at Skye. Then, I guess to save the last of his self-respect that my attorney hadn't already torn to shreds, he pitifully threw in, "But you make sure you're on time tomorrow for your shift."

Connolly glared at him.

Larry quickly added, "Well, you know, if your emergency is all straightened out."

What happened next kind of shocked me. Larry turned on his heels and fast-walked away from us as if he were fleeing a band of angry gorillas.

Why would I ever need a gun again? I'd just bring James Connolly and his law degree along with me whenever I feared I might end up in a tight spot because apparently he could intimidate cops, shady businessmen, and maybe even King Kong if it came to that. I shook my head. I was in the wrong racket.

"I have to change," Skye said. She hurried down an aisle to the back of the shop where I assumed a dressing room was located.

"What now?" Shamrock asked.

"We'll give her a ride to her friend's place," I said, "and that'll be it."

Chapter 17

SHAMROCK WAS RIDING shotgun in the car again. Connolly and Skye were in the backseat. Skye's small pink gym bag and purse on the seat between them. She'd changed into white cotton shorts and a light blue blouse. Neither were overly suggestive. If I hadn't known her profession, I would've thought she was a beach waitress with a night off. The only thing unusual was the blouse's long sleeves at this time of the year. And I knew what they hid.

I pulled my little green Chevette out of the strip mall. "Where do you want to go, Skye?" I asked.

She didn't answer.

I glanced quickly over my shoulder. "Skye?"

"I want to stop at the set."

The set? If she meant what I thought she meant, we were already on our way. "What set?" I asked.

"Where they make the adult films, where else?"

Shamrock was rustling around on his seat and Connolly was sniffling away behind me.

"All right," I said, "but why?"

"Because the guys who run it were good to me. I want to give them a heads-up. Those maniacs you told me about might go there if they know about it."

I nodded as I drove. This was good. The "Set," as Skye called it, was what I'd been hoping she'd turn me on to in the first place.

"Will they be working at this time of night?" I asked.

"Will they be working?" Skye repeated as if I'd asked a stupid question. "The director's always on some type of uppers. Coke, meth, something."

"Okay, where am I going?"

She gave me directions. When I reached our destination, which was on Route One in Seabrook, I saw the "Set" was no more than a Quonset hut. Much larger than the usual but still the same one-story, cheap metal, uniquely shaped building. It was set back quite a bit from the main road and stood by itself. No cars were in the small lot. The building was solid with no door. There were no signs as to what was inside. Everything around it was dark.

"It looks like they're closed," I said.

Skye reached over, touched my shoulder, then pointed toward the side of the building. "No. Out back. That's where the door is."

I maneuvered the car around the building to the back. Sure enough there were about a half-dozen cars scattered around the rear. Skye pointed again. There was one door on this side. I pulled the car up as close as I could to the door without blocking it.

Skye started to exit the car, her small purse hanging from her shoulder. "You guys can come too."

"Are you sure?" I asked.

"Absolutely. You're with me."

I hadn't noticed but Shamrock and Connolly had piled out of the car before I'd even asked my question. Probably couldn't wait to actually see a porn movie set. My desire to see anything new had been dampened by the vision I had in my mind of Thomas Early's steam-ironed face. It was just starting to hit me. Like PTSD. My hand dropped to the pocket of my shorts. I'd left the Xanax at home.

I followed Skye to the metal door. She knocked three times. I stood to one side of the door, Shamrock stood to the other. Connolly stood behind Skye. A small metal grate in the door about head high slid open. Light poured from it.

"Who's that with you?" a voice asked.

The voice sounded oddly familiar.

"Just good friends," Skye answered. "They're cool."

A lock was thrown on the other side, and the door slowly opened. Skye hadn't given us any explanation as to who the pornographers inside might be. Mafia? Outlaw Bikers? Heavies from Boston?

I let Connolly and Shamrock follow Skye in first. I felt very uncomfortable as I stepped through the door after them. The door closed behind me.

Skye held her finger to her lips. "Shhh."

I muscled my way between Connolly and Shamrock who were frozen to their spots. I froze beside them.

The warehouse-like room was ablaze with overhead fluorescent lights. Directly in front of us was the infamous "Set." There was a bed in the middle of the makeshift stage which was wood and raised off the floor by a few inches. Surrounding the stage were two or three large lights on stands pointed directly at the bed. On the bed were the *actors*. Two women, one man. They were all nude and at this distance the women looked fairly attractive; the man not so much. In front of them was the cameraman. He was operating some type of movie camera on a tripod. Beside him, seated in a canvas chair marked "Director," was a man with a black beret on his head.

Aside from these people, the only other person in the cavernous warehouse was a large man standing between us and the action, his back to us, the word "Security" in large letters on his T-shirt. I assumed he was the person who let us in. I had a sensation of deja vu.

I turned to look at Shamrock beside me. He was as motionless as if he'd just been frozen solid, his blue eyes big, glazed, and staring at the stage. Connolly was the same except his tongue danced around his lips and he kept loosening an already loose tie. Skye stood in front of us.

The director was giving the actors some instructions that I couldn't make out. When he was done, he lifted his hand and the cameraman shouted over his shoulder, "Quiet on the set."

I wondered why because I didn't see any microphones and the porn video Shamrock and I had seen was soundless.

A few seconds later, the director shouted, "Roll 'em. Action!"

That voice? I thought I'd heard that one before, too, but I didn't dwell on it. I was distracted by the *action*. The three actors were going at it all at once. It appeared in this scene that the two women were supposed to use their hands and mouths on every possible *inch* of the male actor and both at the same time. Judging by the wicked grin on his face he was enjoying it. I noticed that what he lacked in looks was made up by the size of his manhood. It was the size that makes most other men feel more than a bit inadequate. I watched. What else could I do?

There were groans, moans, and little whimpers. One of the sounds was coming from Shamrock. I gave him an elbow. Connolly was still loosening his tie. If he kept it up, the knot would soon be down to his bellybutton. Skye was looking around the warehouse and back at us as much as she was looking at the set. She didn't seem interested one way or the other in the sex action. I guess to her it was just three workers doing their jobs. To me, I hate to admit, it was a little more than that. The warehouse was growing warmer and stuffier by the minute. When we'd first come in, I'd been pleased to feel the rush of nice cool air. But now, even though I could hear the hum of large A/Cs, it seemed they just weren't working.

Finally, after what seemed an hour but was closer to fifteen minutes, the tension reached a peak. And in more than just the actors. Connolly was still fidgeting around with his tie and I was having to poke Shamrock occasionally. The scene came to what I knew was called the "Money Shot." There was no doubt that the male actor wasn't faking his passion, and as far as the females, well if they were pretending, then they ought to head for Hollywood. When everyone, at least on the stage, was drained dry, the director shouted, "Cut!"

I felt my blood pressure start a downward drift. Shamrock started to move again, from foot to foot. Connolly cleared his throat and stopped tugging at his tie. Skye approached the director, leaned over his shoulder, and spoke to him. He nodded vigorously, jumped up from his canvas chair, and turned to face us.

I almost had a heart attack right then and there.

"Jesus, Mary, and Joseph," Shamrock whispered.

There, standing in front of us, with one hand on the director's chair and the other tugging at the black beret on his head, was none other than Eddie Hoar!

Chapter 18

TO SAY IT was a surprise to find my old *friend* Eddie Hoar directing porn films was an understatement. For a long minute maybe, then all of a sudden it made perfect sense. Who else would be directing cheap porn films on the seacoast? If it hadn't been Eddie, it certainly would have been someone like him.

I wasn't the least bit surprised when the man with the security T-shirt turned around and headed toward us. Derwood Doller, Eddie's long-time partner-in-crime.

Eddie and Derwood were a pair of Hampton Beach hustlers. Small-time hustlers but they'd been around for many years. Eddie was the brains of the duo, which wasn't saying much. Derwood, who was lacking in the brains department, made up for it with his large size.

Shamrock and I had had the misfortune to have been involved with them in more than one unsavory situation on the beach in years past. Although Eddie and Derwood had never been known to be violent, their petty scams always seemed to attract a very violent reaction. If you happened to be close to them when the reaction happened—which Shamrock and I had—you'd get sucked right into it. That's why now, as Eddie headed in my direction with a big smile on his face and that stupid black beret on his head, I got an apprehensive feeling and a warning flutter in my stomach.

"Dan! Dan Marlowe!" Eddie said, coming up, grabbing my hand, and shaking it. His hand was clammy.

Eddie was about a head shorter than me and skinny. His semi-long, stringy salt-and-pepper hair hung below the beret. He had beady eyes that resembled a rodent's. For that matter, except for his pockmarks, his entire face resembled a rodent's.

"Eddie," was all I said.

Derwood Doller stepped up to his side. Derwood was about a head taller than me and a lot heavier. Some of his weight was muscle, I suppose, but you'd have to look under a lot of flab to find it. Still, he could handle himself; I'd seen him in action before. His hair was short, brown, and he grinned a lot.

"And Shamrock Kelly," Eddie said, glancing in my friend's direction. Shamrock grunted. Eddie continued. "And you all know one of my star actresses, Skye, I see."

Skye beamed.

"And who's this gentleman?" Eddie asked, nodding toward Connolly.

Before I could answer, Connolly whipped out a business card and thrust it into Eddie's hand. "James Connolly, Esquire. Attorney-at-Law," he said.

"This is Eddie Hoar and Derwood Doller," I said to Connolly.

Eddie studied the card. "A lawyer, huh? Maybe I can throw you some business one of these days, Councilor."

Eddie half turned, raised his arm, and indicated the stage behind him. "As you can see, I've got quite a successful business going here. And it won't be long before I might need a good mouthpiece to renegotiate my lease."

Connolly sniffled. "I specialize in criminal law, Mr. Hoar."

"Shiiit," Eddie said. "I won't need the services of a criminal lawyer. My business is protected by the United States Constitution." Eddie started to hand the card back.

Connolly didn't accept it. I thought he might correct Eddie's naivety about how much protection he could expect from the First Amendment when the local powers-that-be got their ire up about Eddie's activities. But he didn't; there was no need. He could see the future as good as Madame Stella. "Just keep the card, Mr. Hoar. You never know."

"I know," Eddie said. He shrugged. "But what the hell." He stuffed the card in the pocket of his lime-green polyester pants. The pants were held up by a wide white plastic belt. His shirt was the same material as the pants but yellow in color with green piping. The shirt was open to his chest showing scraggly black hair and a thick gold chain, which I assumed to be either fake or hot, hanging low from his skinny neck.

"What brings you gentlemen . . ." Eddie stopped in mid-sentence, snorted heavily, swallowed. Derwood frowned. Eddie continued, ". . . to my enterprise?"

"Look, Eddie," I said. "We've got something we want to talk to you about."

Eddie held up his hand, a sly grin on his face. "Don't say anything more."

He turned to the actors and cameraman who were lounging around the set. "All right, gang. Call it a night. I've got an important business meeting now."

The crew grumbled. One of the actresses said, "Are we gonna get paid for a full shift, Eddie?"

Eddie looked at the actress like she was a poor orphan. "Of course you are, darling. You never have to worry about that with me."

More grumbling from the crew, but they started to gather up their clothes. I didn't blame them. I knew from firsthand experience that collecting money from Eddie Hoar was like trying to retrieve money already invested in a get-rich-quick scheme.

"Right this way, gentlemen," Eddie said. "And lady," he added, grinning at Skye.

He led the way to a series of three doors at the far end of the building. On the door at one end was the word *Star* painted crudely in purple. The door on the other end, *Director*, in orange. The middle door had the word *HEAD* painted sloppily in black on it. The paint had run. Eddie, of course, opened the *Director* door and led the way in. He flicked on a light switch as he did.

Once we were all inside, Eddie took a seat behind a big expensive-looking polished wood desk. It, too, had to be stolen. Unless maybe it had come with the Quonset hut. Although I could easily picture Eddie and Derwood humping the desk out the back door of some business they'd burglarized in the dead of night.

Eddie motioned for us to sit. There were only two chairs—cheap metal folding ones with paint splotches on them. I indicated for Skye to take one. Connolly took the other. Shamrock and I stood. I don't think Shamrock would have sat if there'd been ten chairs. He hadn't looked happy since we'd found out this operation was an Eddie Hoar enterprise. Derwood was standing to one side of Eddie, behind the desk.

I glanced around at the walls decorated with Polaroid shots of what I assumed were Eddie's stable of actors and actresses. They weren't framed, just stuck haphazardly on the walls with pushpins.

I tried to get down to business. "Eddie, we've got a problem. There's—"

Eddie held up his hands, palms out, and smiled benevolently. "No need to explain, Dan. I know your problem. You'd like to make a little extra bread. Times are tough for you, I bet. Well, you've come to the right place. You've seen my operation—high class. I can give you the best adult film tapes between here and L.A. At a good price, too." He sat back in his swivel chair, a smug look on his pockmarked face. "You'll be dealing with the main man. Me!"

"Look, Eddie—" I started before being interrupted again.

Eddie leaned forward in the chair, speaking to me like I was a little kid. "And you want to make sure my product is so good that you don't get stuck with anything. Don't worry. Between the quality of my films and the people you know on the beach, the tapes'll fly out of the High Tide. You'll make a lot of money."

I was about to explode when Shamrock said in a loud growl, "Will you shut up, Eddie. Dan's trying to tell you that you've got big trouble."

Skye nodded rapidly. "He's right, Eddie. Someone's been murdered."

She had been looking more and more tense since we'd entered the warehouse. I wondered if it was time for a shot.

"Murdered?" Derwood Doller said, his eyes the size of poker chips.

Eddie's eyes suddenly rivaled Derwood's in size. He snorted loudly. "What are—" His voice cracked, he cleared it, continued. "What are you talking about?"

I told him the story, almost everything. The thugs who beat me, the ransacking of my house, the murder of Thomas Early and the delivery kid.

By the time I'd finished, Eddie looked like Dracula had just drained him. Derwood not much better.

"An *iron?*" Derwood said, his voice shaking. "On Tommy's face? I told you we might get in trouble for this, Eddie. I'm gettin' outta here."

Derwood made a move for the door. Shamrock and I jumped to block him at the same time, although I wasn't sure we could stop Derwood if he was determined to leave. He was stupid but plenty big. And tough.

Fortunately, Eddie spoke up quickly. "Hold it, Dumwood. Dan'll help us."

Eddie had always had a strong hold on Derwood and the big man stopped in his tracks. He looked sullenly at Eddie. "Don't call me that, Eddie. You know I don't like it."

"Yeah, yeah, whatever," Eddie said. Then to me he said, "What can we do, Dan?"

He looked so scared, I think I would've given him a Xanax if I'd brought them with me.

"First of all, I want to know why these thugs, and maybe whoever murdered your distributor Early and his driver, want these tapes and what tapes are they?"

"Well . . . I don't know—" Eddie began.

I banged my fist down on the desk. Eddie moved back with a start.

"Don't bullshit me, Eddie. You may want your ugly face steam cleaned, but I don't want mine tampered with!"

Derwood let out a little whimper. "Tell him, Eddie. Tell him or I will."

Eddie gave up. Between snorts he told us the entire story and because of Derwood's nods, I believed it was true.

It seems that Eddie and Derwood had broken into some storage units in North Hampton. In one of the units they'd found expensive movie equipment, which was now out in front of the stage, and a machine for making duplicate VHS tapes. They'd also lugged a safe from the same unit, and because they were lucky if they could open a can of beans, it took them a week working on the safe, day and night, to get it open.

"What was in it, Eddie?" I asked

"In what?" Eddie answered. I wasn't sure if he was being dumb or evasive. Knowing Eddie, it could be either.

"The safe," I said. "The damn safe."

"Nothing, Dan," Eddie said scowling. "After all that work. Ain't that right, Derwood?"

The big man nodded. "That's right, Eddie."

It didn't figure. The thugs who'd beat me on the beach wanted some tapes returned. And Early and his delivery boy had been involved with video tapes. So was Eddie. Just coincidence? I wasn't sure. But I still had to find out what video tapes the thugs were looking for and where they were if I didn't want to end up like Thomas Early.

"Are you sure there was nothing in that safe, Eddie?"

Skye excused herself to use the bathroom. She left the office, taking her small purse with her.

Eddie shrugged. "Just some porn tapes."

My ears perked up. "Porn tapes? Where are they?"

Eddie flicked his wrist. "I tossed 'em. They was junk. The rubbish guy took them the day after we got that goddamn safe open."

"What about . . ." Derwood began.

Eddie cut him off. "Shut up."

I banged on the table again. It seemed to have worked last time. Papers fluttered on the desk.

"*You* shut up," I shouted, leaning across the desk toward Eddie. He cowered back in his chair. Looking at Derwood, I said, "Go ahead, Derwood. What were you going to say?"

Derwood looked a bit embarrassed. "Sorry, Eddie. But we got to tell Dan everything. Those guys sound real mean and I don't want them catching up with us. Maybe Dan can help. He has before."

Eddie's little black eyes blazed as he glared at Derwood. "Can't you ever keep your mouth shut, Dumwood?"

Derwood stuck his lower jaw out and began breathing heavily through his mouth. "I told you not to call me that, Eddie." He took a lumbering step toward Eddie. Eddie jumped to his feet.

Shamrock hurried over and put his hands on Derwood's chest. "Easy big guy."

Seeing that Shamrock had Derwood under control, Eddie slid back into his chair. "Ahh, can't you take a joke?"

I reached across the desk, grabbed Eddie by his shirt with my left hand and held my right fist in a threatening manner. Eddie's prominent Adam's apple slid up and down.

"All right, all right," he said. "Take it easy. Christ."

I let go of his shirt, moved my hands to the desk. He removed a ring of keys from his pants pocket. Skye had returned from the bathroom. She looked refreshed and was more animated than before she'd left. Connolly had also taken his turn in the bathroom. He was just sitting back in his chair. Sniffling more than ever. I didn't need a weatherman to know which way the wind blew, but right now I didn't care. I had more important things on my mind than what my attorney and a sex worker were doing in the bathroom.

Eddie used one of the keys to open a bottom drawer in his desk. I took my hands off the desk, straightened up. Eddie came up with an unmarked VHS tape. He looked at it like it contained images of one of his children on their death bed. He stood, walked over to one of the filing cabinets in the room. A TV sat on top of it, with a VHS player on top of that. Eddie turned both on, slid the tape into the player.

I had no idea what we were going to see. I could only hope it would be something that would help me out of this jam and help clear my name as head pornographer of Hampton Beach. Maybe help save the lives of more than one person in this room, too, including me.

I kept my fingers crossed that it wouldn't be just another run-of-the-mill skin tape. Something inside told me it wasn't.

Chapter 19

EDDIE HIT THE lights. The little office was dark and silent except for the incessant sniffling from Eddie and my attorney. Then the tape started and it looked like nothing more than I'd been seeing a lot of lately—a cheap porn film. This one looked like it had been shot in a hotel room somewhere, but certainly not the Ritz Carlton. The place was your standard dump, one and a half stars at best. And the two participants were on a bed that probably would have squeaked if there'd been sound.

The female actress appeared all of sixteen. She wore pigtails and had a young girl's breasts. The man's face I couldn't see because the youngster was riding on top of him, facing the camera and he was on his back facing the other way. I could see long black hair streaked with gray spread out on the pillow underneath his head.

The only other thing of interest was a Winnacunnet High School jacket hanging on the bedpost. The girl's, obviously.

I was just about to call an end to watching this perversion, when Skye audibly sucked in her breath, then said, "Hey, that's Jillian! She used to work with me."

"Jillian?" I said, looking at Skye. My eyes had become adjusted to the darkness and I could see her fairly well. "Larry uses kids?" I added, disgusted.

"She isn't any kid," Skye said. "She's older than me. She just looks real young. And the way they got her hair and no makeup and the high school jacket—that makes her seem even younger. Larry used to let her play that part at work sometimes. The pervs liked it. They must've known she was of age but I guess they got off pretending that she was a young girl. Sick bastards!"

I agreed but now that I knew I wasn't watching child pornography, I turned my eyes back to the TV—just in time to see Jillian roll off the man under her. The camera zoomed in for a close-up of Jillian's face that gave nothing away about her age. If I hadn't been told she was over eighteen, I would've sworn she was at least a couple of years younger.

The man turned around clumsily on the bed and propped himself up on his elbows, facing the camera, which had pulled back from the previous shot. He was bombed, eyes at half mast. I wasn't sure he could even see, he looked so bad. But I was proven wrong quickly.

Jillian, the young-looking porn actress, was kneeling on the bed at his side. His head went toward her chest and those small, pert breasts. I had to admit, they looked perfect for the part she was playing. His mouth zeroed in on one of her brown nipples as if it were a magnet. The camera zoomed in on his face, as his mouth opened and sucked in almost her entire breast. I sucked in my breath, heard more than one other person in the room do the same. Not because of the erotic scene. Those of us who hadn't already seen the tape had recognized the male participant at the same moment.

"Jesus Christ," Skye said, "That's Lonnie Ellison."

Indeed it was. There was no doubt about it. It *was* Lonnie Ellison. How could we not recognize him? Ellison was a world-famous rock star and the seacoast's most famous resident. He'd been at his pinnacle in the big-haired 70s as lead singer for the group Sponge. Many platinum albums and years later, they were rock royalty, with Ellison being the most famous of the group. Now they kept their extravagant world tours down to one every five years or so to coincide with any new album that was being released.

I'd heard Ellison was worth a couple hundred million bucks. I knew where he lived, too. Everyone on the seacoast knew that. An oceanfront mansion in Rye, New Hampshire.

Connolly moved forward in his chair. "He looks trashed."

"Wait'll you see what comes next," Derwood said.

Just then Ellison pulled his mouth away from the girl's breast, turned, and reached over to a table beside the bed. It had a single lamp on low. He took a kitchen plate from the table, turned back to the girl. He almost lost the plate in the process. He picked up a cutoff straw from the plate, and without even making a line, stuck the straw in the middle of a large pile of powder and snorted away. Again he almost dumped the plate, barely saving it in time so he could repeat the process with his other nostril.

He handed the straw to the girl. She did the same with it, just not as greedily.

By the way they both instantly went at each other like wild animals, I was sure the powder was cocaine. I felt my bowels grumble. Judging by the look on Ellison's face, he probably had other substances in his system as well.

The debauchery continued and became more degraded. Finally, I said, "Okay, Eddie, we've seen enough. Turn it off."

"Shouldn't we watch the rest," Shamrock said, "just in case there's something else we ought to know?"

I looked at my friend, furrowed my brows. "We got the idea."

Eddie got up, turned off the VCR, and flicked on the lights. He sat back in his swivel chair.

"So what's this all mean, Dan?" Connolly asked.

"I don't know. Eddie, how many tapes like this were in the safe?"

Eddie shrugged. "I don't know. Dozen, maybe."

"A dozen?" I said. "Of Ellison?"

"Naw," Eddie said. "Other . . . ahh . . ." He hesitated.

"What?" I asked.

"Well, the chick was the same one. But the guys were all different, I think."

"Did you know any of the other men except him?"

Eddie shook his head. He didn't look like a very happy director. "Just him. I figured I'd keep it for posterity." Then added, "You know. That's a little piece of history."

"Eddie!" It was Derwood and he looked both angry and frightened. "Tell him the truth. These guys are gonna help us."

Eddie glared at Derwood. Then to me he said, "Well, I wasn't going to really do it. Just if things ever went sour in the movie business."

I was losing my patience. "Do what?" I said, banging my fist on the desk again. It worked.

Eddie spoke in a rush. "All right. All right. I mentioned to Dumwood here—"

"I don't like that, Eddie," Derwood said, his fists clenching and unclenching at his sides.

"Knock it off, both of you," I said. "We're not here to see you lamebrains go at it."

Derwood unclenched his hands and Eddie continued. "Like I said, we was just going to give it a shot if the film industry didn't treat us right."

Now it was my turn to ball my fists. "Give what a shot?"

Eddie saw the fists. "Okay, okay. We were thinking of selling the tape back to him. Ellison. You know—the young girl, the blow. He wouldn't want that to get out. I think he's still married, too. And a few bucks wouldn't hurt him. Hardworking men like Derwood and myself need a little extra sometimes."

"That's blackmail my friend," Connolly said.

Eddie licked his lips. "What'd you bring your lawyer with you for, Dan? To scare us? I said we was just thinkin'. No law against thinkin'. We woulda never done it. Would we, Derwood?"

Derwood shook his head. "I wouldn't have. I don't know about you, Eddie."

"Thanks for the support Dum . . . err . . . Derwood."

The two men glared at each other.

"Knock it off, you two. We haven't got time for this. For all we know we could have visitors any second."

Eddie leaned forward in his chair and peered nervously around me at the door.

Derwood said, "Maybe we should get out of here now."

It sounded funny hearing a voice shake on such a big man. But I couldn't blame him. What Eddie had told me had put an uncomfortable idea in my head.

"You didn't recognize anybody else on the other tapes, did you?" I asked.

Eddie shook his head.

"Did you know anything about Jillian being mixed up with Ellison?" I asked Skye.

She picked at her neck as she spoke. "No, nothing. And that's funny because if I was dating him, I'd sure be telling everyone."

Yes, she would. Anyone would, unless . . .

Eddie had given me an idea. "Give me that tape, Eddie."

The tape was on Eddie's desk, close to him. "Uhh, uhh. I think I'll keep that."

"Think again," I snapped. "I'm not asking. I'm telling. Maybe that tape is what the goons who beat me senseless want. And whoever murdered your distributor, too, if it wasn't them. That might be the only thing that can save our lives. Yours and Derwood's included."

"Give it to him, Eddie," Derwood said. "I don't want to meet these guys. No way."

I reached out for the tape. Eddie's eyes were glued to my hand all the way as I picked up the tape. He didn't try to stop me. It would have been ugly if he had and he must have known that.

"Now I think it's best if we all get out of here before we have visitors," I said.

Eddie shot up from his chair. We all made for the door.

On the way out of the office, Skye said, "I got to visit the ladies room."

That didn't make me happy. Time was of the essence. Connolly added, "Me too."

I almost blew my cork. "Why don't you two just go in together," I said in disgust.

To my surprise, they did just that. Skye went into the room marked HEAD with Connolly following. They closed the door behind them.

"I ain't waiting for them," Eddie said. "I'm getting outta here. Derwood, take the camera and stuff."

"I wouldn't bother with it, Eddie," I said "Your days as a movie mogul are over. That equipment belongs to cold-blooded killers that you ripped-off, and if you take it, it'll be one more reason for them to come after you and Derwood."

Derwood let out a little whimper. "He's right, Eddie. I'm not taking it."

"All right," Eddie said, in a tone that told me he hated leaving anything of value behind. But that was trumped by the fact that he didn't have a brave bone in his skinny little body. "Let's go."

Before they could take five steps, I said, "Where are you going to go?"

"Home, where else?" Eddie said over his shoulder.

"They might be there waiting for you," I said.

Eddie and Derwood froze in their tracks.

"He's right, Eddie," Derwood said. "They probably used that iron to make poor Tommy tell them where we live. But where else can we go?"

Just then the bathroom door opened and Skye emerged, followed by my attorney. They both looked a bit guilty but quite chipper.

"Are you two ready now?" If we didn't get out of here in time, I had more than one person I was going to blame and probably strangle.

The three of us, along with Shamrock, walked up to Eddie and Derwood. They were arguing about where they could safely go for the night. Apparently, they didn't have many options. Every time Eddie mentioned a possible person they might hide out with, Derwood would throw cold water on it by reminding Eddie that he, Eddie, either owed said person money or had ripped them off in one of his little scams.

It sounded like Eddie was on the wrong side of most everyone on the seacoast. Those he wasn't, probably wouldn't have wanted to associate with him anyway. Not after they got a good look at him. A person didn't have to be too perceptive to realize what Eddie was all about.

"What about your aunt's place, Eddie?" I asked. Eddie and Derwood had holed up there another time when Shamrock and I had unwittingly gotten caught up in one of their antics.

"My aunt's place?" Eddie said. "Yeah, sure. Why didn't I think of that? She's in Florida all the time now. She's gotta boyfriend down there. That'll work."

That settled, we all headed for the door. When we reached it, Eddie hesitated, grabbed Derwood by the arm. "We got to turn off all the lights and A/C."

I should have known Eddie was stalling but he had a doctorate in how to get out of tight jams, while I had only a high school diploma. Skye, Connolly, Shamrock, and I stepped out into the parking area in the rear of the building.

The lights of a car parked at the far end of the lot popped on. They were aimed at the door and the light hit us right in our faces. I turned. The door was open a crack but before I could grab it, someone inside—probably Eddie—closed it and I heard a deadbolt thrown.

The bastard had sent us through the door first to see if anyone was lurking outside. When he'd seen the headlights though the crack of the door he'd left open, he had his answer.

I almost started banging on the door, then realized that, if we did get in the building, we'd be trapped. I was unarmed. I assumed my companions were, too. I hated making a break for it, though. That would help Eddie. Whoever was in that car had no way of knowing there was anyone left in the warehouse. If they wanted blood, they would naturally come after us. And as we led them away, Eddie and Derwood would flee safely into the night.

I hated that part of it, but making a run for it at least gave us a chance. Trapped in a warehouse with two armed animals breaking the door down, we had next to no chance at all. I'd deal with Eddie later.

"Come on, slowly. Get in the car," I said. I was hoping the car with the bright headlights might turn out to be just some kids drinking beer.

That possibility was shot down the instant we scrambled into the car and I started the engine. The mystery car roared to life and jumped forward. I slammed the Chevette into reverse. The mystery car was trying to block us in. I spun the wheel and pulled around them, missing the other car by inches. I jammed the Chevette into drive and drove. The chase was on.

Chapter 20

IT WAS A weeknight and late enough for traffic to be light as I pulled out onto Route 1. Shamrock was beside me riding shotgun. Skye and Connolly were in the back seat again. The mystery car was right behind us. I'd shoved the tape under my seat.

"Who the hell is that?" Connolly asked. His voice was high and quivering. I supposed the drug he'd done in the bathroom back at the warehouse wasn't helping him with his nerves any.

"Could be the two looking for the tapes," I answered. I tried to keep the Chevette at a reasonable speed. Every time I accelerated, though, the car behind us followed suit.

"Well, stop and give them the damn thing," Connolly said.

"That might be a good idea, Danny," Shamrock said. He had his feet planted on the floor like he was using the gas pedal and brake.

"Don't shtop," Skye said. "They'll pobably hurts ush." Her words were slurred, but still, she made the most sense.

"They might," I said, swerving around two cars and running a red light. The mystery car followed. "This tape might not be what they want anyway. Even if it is, they might also want the ones Eddie threw away. The ones we haven't got."

"Well, we can stop. Find out." Connolly was looking over his shoulder at the car following us. I could see him clearly in the rearview mirror.

"You don't know these boys," I said. "I do. If it's who I think it is, I had the pleasure of meeting them on the beach. If I wasn't convinced then that I never wanted to see them again, what they probably did to Early and the kid has convinced me."

Connolly groaned.

Shamrock said, "Now we did it."

I looked at Skye in the rearview. The heroin, too strong to be overridden by any coke Connolly might have given her, had her on the nod now. Her chin was against her chest. She was the lucky one.

"Take me back to my car," Connolly said.

"I'm not worried about your damn car. I'm worried about us. This could be big trouble." I came to a traffic circle, followed it halfway around, and flew down a two-lane road. There was no traffic but there were houses on either side. The mystery car followed.

We hadn't gone more than a quarter mile when I heard a familiar sound.

Both Shamrock and Connolly turned and looked out the rear window.

"Sweet Jaysus, Danny, they're shooting at us."

I took another glance in the rearview mirror. Just then something flashed on the passenger side of the mystery car. I stomped on the gas and the little Chevette jumped.

"Want to stop now, *James*?" I yelled.

"My car," Connolly howled. "Get me to my car."

He disappeared from the rearview. Apparently he'd burrowed down onto the floor. I couldn't blame him. I would have done the same if I didn't have to drive the damn crate.

He'd made his seat change just in time. The rear window of the little Chevette exploded. My whole body jerked like I'd just sat on a tack. I glanced at Shamrock beside me. He was leaning over, his head below the dashboard. My stomach flipped.

"Shamrock!" I yelled, reaching out and shaking his shoulder.

He tilted his head, peeked up at me. "I'm all right, Danny," he said in a shaky voice. "Just getting out of the line of fire."

I wished I could've gotten out of the line of fire.

Where had the bullet gone? I looked in the rearview. Skye was still on the nod and in the same position as before. Her head down and in the clear from any shots.

"Look at this, Danny." Shamrock was sitting up a bit, pointing a thick finger at a hole in the front windshield between the two of us. It was spidering. Where the bullet had exited. I hadn't even noticed it. And it had been that close. I swallowed hard.

"Take me to my car. Please! My car," Connolly whined.

"Screw your . . ." I shouted, then it dawned on me where the attorney's car was—the Hampton Police Station. It was quite a distance and maybe the Seabrook Police Station was closer, but for the life of me, I couldn't remember where the hell the Seabrook station was. I drew a big blank—from fear maybe—though I should have remembered. I'd been in the place for at least one overnight visit back in the day.

The little Chevette was flying and we were coming up on an old train bridge. It was only wide enough for one car at a time to pass under and, as luck would have it, another car was coming in the opposite direction right toward us. It was going to be close. I had seconds to decide if I wanted to try it.

I was almost ready to slow down and risk the gunmen behind catching us, when I heard two shots slam into the rear body of my car. That caused my foot to almost drive the gas pedal through the floorboards.

I squeezed the steering wheel with both hands almost hard enough to crack it and shouted, "Hold on."

Shamrock grabbed the dashboard and braced himself in his seat, his head almost touching the roof. There was no reaction from Skye but Connolly yelled, "What the fuck?" from the floor.

Only yards from the bridge, I could see the approaching car begin to fishtail. The driver must have realized what was about to happen. I couldn't blame him if he had no interest in playing chicken with a maniac. Slamming on the brakes might not do him any good though. It was going to be close. Very close.

We flew through the underpass just as the other car reached it. My hands were bone white on the steering wheel. The sides of the two cars screeched as we scraped together, sparks flying in the dark.

I glanced in the rearview as we cleared the underpass but I didn't let up on the gas, not yet. The car we'd just struck had slowed and was still in the underpass. Someone's horn blew furiously. I could see the mystery car flash its headlights and slow.

By the time I was ready to make the next turn, I could see that the mystery car had untangled itself and was coming up fast.

Tires squealed as I spun the Chevette into a hard right turn. I floored the gas and headed for Route 286 which led to 1A and the beach. Within seconds I could see a green light ahead. I didn't let up on the gas.

In the rearview I spotted the headlights from the mystery car pulling onto the street behind us. If that green light could hold a few more seconds, it would give us more time. I shook the steering wheel with my hands, trying to get a little more speed out of my jalopy. It didn't help.

Shamrock shouted, "Slow down, Danny. You won't make the turn."

I did slow down but not much. I went into the turn on yellow, and if it's possible for a Chevy Chevette to take a turn on two wheels, mine probably did. At least that's what it felt like.

When I straightened the car out again, I saw we were lucky. Like I said, it was a late weeknight and traffic was light. Nonetheless, I had to zoom around a couple of cars on the two-lane road. Behind me I heard screeching car tires and blaring horns. The mystery car was still with us. They'd blown a red light and were driving other cars off the road as they came.

We flew down 286 and when we passed Brown's and Markey's, two seafood restaurants on opposite sides of the road, I said, hoping for some levity, "Where do you want to eat, Shamrock? Brown's or Markey's?"

He didn't smile but he still threw a joke back at me. "Markey's, of course. I need a beer and fast." Markey's sold beer; Brown's was BYOB.

Even though I'd started the exchange, I didn't have the inclination to laugh. We were coming up to a light at the corner of Route 1A. It was a red light and some cars were backed up at it. But I wasn't stopping for anything now. There were two car slots on our side of the road occupied by cars waiting for the light to change.

I wasn't waiting. I veered to the left—into the wrong lane—swerved around a couple of cars, shot onto Route 1A, and fishtailed into the lane that would take us to Hampton Beach. Horns sounded behind us.

Traffic was still sparse. Behind us another blast of horns. I didn't have to look in the rearview to know it was the mystery car driving other vehicles off the road as it tried to catch us. Shamrock was sitting bolt upright now, face white as a seagull, hands the same color, squeezing the dashboard. A little case of deja vu materialized in my mind as I flashed on another time we'd been in a car chase like this. I prayed this one ended up better than that one had.

Route 286 is a straight shot on its two-way, four-lane blacktop. Homes on the right, marsh and a couple of strip malls and small businesses on the left. As I was going through a green light at an intersection, I could see the Hampton Bridge ahead. Luck was with me again. Many times, especially in the summer, traffic is at a dead stop. It can often take an hour or more to get over the two-lane bridge. Because this was a late weeknight, with no traffic backup, it looked like we might get over the bridge without having to slow down. Unless, of course, that damn bridge light came on red and the bridge began to open. You see, the Hampton Bridge is a drawbridge that opens periodically for boats, often at very inconvenient times as far as vehicle traffic goes. Like right now. If the red light came on and the drawbridge opened, we could be in big trouble. On the other hand, if our luck was running hot, the bridge could open just as we got across, leaving the mystery car trapped on the other side.

I flew across the bridge, pleased that we'd gotten our first lucky break. Looking in the rearview, I realized that was all the luck we were going to have. The bridge didn't open behind us, and as I drove past the state park, I could see the mystery car pass a car on the bridge and get in behind us. The bastards wouldn't give up. What did they intend to do if they did stop us? There were still some people around. Would they dare use their guns in front of potential witnesses? I didn't want to find out.

There was sporadic traffic on Ocean Boulevard and I easily maneuvered around it. I had to slow down a bit though. At the corner of M Street, I swerved to miss someone who'd just stepped off the curb in front of Beverages Unlimited, a convenience store. The young guy jumped back onto the sidewalk, swore, and gave me the one-fingered salute as I passed.

After just missing a pedestrian, I didn't dare take my eyes off the road. "Are they still behind us?" I asked.

Shamrock turned in his seat. "They're still back there, Danny. What are we going to do now?"

"Hold on."

We'd just reached F Street, the street that ran along this side of the Casino. I took a left, weaved around one car in front of us, and headed toward Ashworth Avenue at the end of the short street.

"Here they come, Danny." Shamrock was still turned, looking out the rear window.

There was almost no traffic on Ashworth Avenue, the street that ran parallel to Ocean Boulevard. Its one-way traffic ran in the opposite direction. I ran the Chevette right up to the stop sign, slowed but didn't stop. Of course I bumped into the side of the only moving car within a hundred yards. A Ford Escort. I hadn't hit it hard enough to injure anyone. But from what I could see, the people inside—in addition to their shock at the impact—looked none too happy. At this point, I couldn't have cared less. I'd worry about the mishap later.

"They're behind us," Shamrock screamed. "He's getting out of the car."

In the rearview I could see a figure exiting the passenger side of the mystery car, but I couldn't make out a face. I backed the Chevette up, dropped the car into drive, and attempted to get around the Escort. The Escort's driver must have thought I was trying to pull a hit-and-run because he moved his car forward, trying to block me in. He beeped his horn and flashed his lights, both driver and backseat passenger shouting and gesturing angrily at us out their windows.

"Danny!" Shamrock yelled just as the man from the mystery car jogged up to Shamrock's door, reached to open it. "He's got a gun!"

I stomped on the gas, driving the Chevette hard against the Escort. The sound of steel grinding against steel could probably be heard up on Boar's Head. The Escort's driver blasted his horn. I pushed his car out of the way like I was driving a Cadillac boat and he was driving a . . . well . . . a Ford Escort.

Once the Escort was out of the way, I gunned the Chevette, careening into a parking lot on the other side of Ashworth—directly toward a cinder block building. Glancing in the rearview, I was surprised to see the man who'd been out of the mystery car hopping back in and the car zooming after us. Either they were crazy or they didn't realize where we were. I held down the horn, making as much noise as I could as I jammed on the brakes and brought the Chevette to a halt just inches before striking the building.

That's when the dunces behind us must have realized where we were. Their car made a complete one-eighty and zoomed back onto Ashworth Avenue. I could hear a couple of horns beeping and could picture the driver of the mystery car forcing other cars off the road in an effort to get away.

After all, the little one-story cinder block building I was kissing with my front bumper was the Hampton Police Station. And I was making enough noise to wake a twenty-year old after a beach drunk.

I let up on the horn and was out of the car exchanging papers and trying to placate the driver of the battered Escort by the time a cop showed up. It didn't look like the Escort had too much damage beyond what the car had already had. *And* no one had been injured.

I gave the Escort driver a hundred dollars that he stuffed into his pocket, and we agreed to keep this *accident* between us and forget insurance companies. He'd more than likely already collected money from his insurer on the already-damaged area of his car and wouldn't have any luck if he tried again.

It took me longer to persuade the cop that there was nothing going on except a run-of-the-mill fender bender. I even convinced him my window damage was from vandalism a day ago that I would have fixed right away. Why didn't I tell him the truth? A couple of reasons. Skye was, as unbelievable as it seems, still comatose in the backseat. I didn't want to see her get in trouble. Also I didn't want her to get me in trouble if she was holding.

And if I told this cop what was really going on, Gant would probably find out. If he did—for that matter, if anyone else but this summer cop found out—the tape I still had under the front seat might be confiscated. I didn't want that. That tape might be good insurance. People insurance. For myself, Dianne, Skye, and maybe even Shamrock and Connolly now that whoever was in the mystery car had seen them, too.

Also, I had a sense that it would be a good idea to follow up on the tape and the Lonnie Ellison angle. See where it led. I had to do that before the boys in the mystery car or the guys on the beach—if they weren't the same people—came back. I was sure they would. I was also sure that they'd be back way before the cops followed up any clues the tape might reveal.

So I had to follow up myself. And quickly.

If I wanted to live.

Chapter 21

IT WAS A hard sleep that night. What was left of it anyway. I'd left Connolly at the police station with his car, given Shamrock a ride to his cottage, and brought Skye home with me. First, after shaking her awake, we took a chance and made a pit stop at her place for clothes. We'd had no trouble. I know what you're thinking, but I had no ulterior motive. She was plenty shook up after I told her about the car chase she'd slept through. Suddenly, the girlfriend's house didn't seem so safe. I agreed. And besides, it was too late to go prowling around her friends' houses. So I took her to my place.

The next morning, I let her sleep. She'd used one of my children's bedrooms, so I'd quietly gotten ready for work. Before I left, I made a call and arranged for a mobile glass company to come by the Tide and replace my car windows. I left for work, taking the porn tape I'd gotten from Eddie along with me. I had a kernel of an idea. I arrived at the Tide and parked. I hid the tape in the car, walked across Ocean Boulevard, and went through the back door of the restaurant.

Dianne was in her office. I stepped in. "You busy?" I asked.

"Not really," she said unconvincingly. "What's up?"

I sat in a chair in front of her desk and told her almost everything that she didn't already know.

Her face turned pale. "For the love of god, Dan. *You* found those murdered bodies?"

I nodded.

"Your name wasn't on the news."

"Probably 'cause I wasn't charged with anything."

Dianne picked up a piece of paper; the paper shook. Just something to hold on to, I guessed. "So that's definitely why they broke in here and into my apartment? Looking for these tapes?"

"Probably," I said. "Dianne, I'm sorry." I started to get up from the chair.

"No!" Her green eyes narrowed. "One of those men was tortured. We could be too. Just give them the tape, Dan."

I didn't like saying it but I had to. "I can't, Dianne."

Her face flushed with anger. "What do you mean, you can't? Have you gone completely crazy?"

Maybe, but I had to answer her like I hadn't. "They most likely don't want just this one tape. They probably want the ones Eddie Hoar threw away, too."

She looked at the ceiling and rolled her eyes. "You don't know that until you give it to them. Give the damn tape back, Dan. Today!"

"I have to clear my name, Dianne."

"Clear your name of the kiddie porn rumors? If you're dead, it'll be too late for that. And what about Shamrock? Do you want to see him tortured and murdered?" She stopped, swallowed. "And what about—"

I interrupted her. I couldn't bear the idea of anything even remotely like what had happened to Early, happening to my beautiful Dianne. I couldn't even talk about it. "Nothing's going to happen to Shamrock or . . . anyone."

"How the hell do you know that?"

"I just know," I lied. I didn't really know shit, but I had to make sure nothing happened to either Shamrock or Dianne. And I would.

She hesitated, looked at me intently. "There's something else, isn't there?"

She knew me too well. I told her about Skye staying at my cottage.

Dianne pursed her lips. "How long is she going to be at your house?"

I had to tread carefully. "Not long. But she really is in danger. I couldn't let her just go home."

"Mmm."

Dianne looked down at the papers on the desk in front of her. I could tell she wasn't seeing them. I figured I had better get out of there before the conversation went any further down the Skye road.

I jumped up from the chair, headed for the door. "I'm late. I'd better get opened up."

"Yes," Dianne said, "you do that."

I scurried through the kitchen; waved a greeting to Guillermo, the Tide's head chef; and pushed through the swinging door into the dining room. A couple of the waitresses were finishing their setup duties in preparation for lunch. I'd just reached the end of the partition and was about to step into the bar area, when there was a loud banging on the front door. I glanced at the Budweiser clock over the back bar. 11:00. I hadn't realized it was that late.

I got the key from the register and walked to the door, accompanied by another series of knocks. Not too many, considering Eli was on the other side of the door. And he didn't like me being late. He had to get started on his daily beer ration after all.

I unlocked the big wooden door, swung it open. Eli had to step out of the way to let me get the door open.

"You're late again," he grumbled, squeezing by me into the bar. Paulie followed. He smiled and shook his head. His long hair swayed. I let the door close and trailed after the two of them.

When they both had taken their positions and I had beers in front of them, I puttered along, trying to get the bar in order.

There were the standard comments the three of us made every morning. Then Eli started in.

He had the pilsner glass against his lower lip, not sipping from it. Just holding it there and looking over it at me.

"What did ya think of them guys gettin' murdered, Dan?" he asked too nonchalantly.

I whacked at fruit on a cutting board and tried to keep my eyes on what I was doing while I talked. Eli was very perceptive. I knew he was watching for my reaction.

"Terrible." I held my breath, hoping that would be the end of it.

Of course it wasn't. Eli wasn't going to let it slide. Not Eli. This was an important piece of gossip in a very boring life. His.

"I guess you just *heard* about it, huh?" he asked.

I didn't answer. Obviously, Eli had gotten wind that I'd been at the death scene and maybe even that I'd found the bodies. I glanced at Paulie down at his end of the bar. He had a silly grin on his face. Every so often he'd puff on his cigarette butt, blowing huge, perfect smoke rings toward the ceiling.

When Eli realized I wasn't going to answer, he tried another angle, one where he didn't have to come right out and say he'd heard I'd been at the scene of the crime.

"One a the dead guys was a bartender on the beach back in the day," he said, again trying to act nonchalant. He'd finished his beer and held the glass up, jiggling it. I took the glass; gave him a refill.

"You musta known him, Dan. Both being bartenders and all."

"I didn't know him." That was mostly the truth.

"You know where he lives?" Eli asked, trying another tack.

I knew he was going to follow on this course until he had me so boxed in I'd have to confirm the rumors he had obviously heard about me finding the bodies. I didn't feel like getting into that with anyone. Especially Eli. Once I admitted I had found the bodies, he'd tell his version of the story, which would include me, to everyone who pulled up a stool for the next couple of hours and I'd be peppered with questions I didn't want to answer until my shift was over. And probably for days afterwards.

I grabbed a Lite for Paulie and rushed it to his end of the bar, hoping to derail Eli's questions. And besides, there was something I'd been planning on asking Paulie anyway. Discreetly.

"You know where Lonnie Ellison lives?" I asked in a low tone, as I delivered Paulie his beer.

I knew where the rock star lived—oceanfront in Rye—but I wasn't sure of the exact location. It had been pointed out to me in the past but I couldn't remember the specific mansion he lived in, just the general location.

Paulie let another smoke ring drift from his mouth. It rose toward the ceiling and mushroomed out when it hit. "Sure, I know where he lives." He gave me an address.

"Hey," Eli shouted. "Talk louder. I can't hear you."

That was the idea but it was hopeless. I leaned my butt against the backbar, so I could see them both.

"You ever deliver to him?" I asked in a more normal voice. Paulie had worked at more than one post office during his long career.

"No." Paulie said.

"I'm just wondering if you think I could get an autograph if I went up there?"

It sounded lame to me and apparently to Paulie, too, judging by the odd look he gave me.

Eli looked at me like I was suddenly a little light in my loafers. "An autograph? Ha! When'd you start collecting them things?"

I shook my head. "Not for me. One of my kids."

Both Paulie and Eli looked at me skeptically.

"Your kids are interested in an old rock dinosaur like him?" Paulie asked.

"Anyone who's famous, I guess."

Eli harrumphed.

Paulie spoke. "I know guys who deliver packages there all the time and you can't just go up to the front door. You can go up to the gate but it won't do you any good. They got cameras and intercoms and they won't answer for anyone who wants an autograph."

So I had to think of a way to get past the cameras and intercom and gate. And I did. The idea wasn't ingenious, but it was the only thing I could come up with. And if Lonnie Ellison's mind worked anything like mine, I thought it might work.

Right now though I had to get Eli and Paulie off the subject of my sham autograph hunt. They were going back and forth about how to land an autograph from Ellison, tossing around names of people I could approach, from the head of the Casino Ballroom to the owner of Joe's, a high-end meat market in North Hampton that they assumed Ellison patronized.

I tried a couple of times to get them talking about something else. I didn't have any luck. Eli kept jawing about Ellison and the autograph I was supposedly seeking. At least he was focused on that instead of the murdered men. It was better. Finally, their drinking shift was over. Eli and Paulie marched out the front door without Eli mentioning the dead men again.

I did my best to forget about Eli and autographs and dead men and spent the rest of my shift on autopilot, serving my customers. But in the back of my mind I was going over how I was going to get into that gated mansion and what I was going to say to Lonnie Ellison when I did.

Chapter 22

IT WAS ABOUT 5:30 when I reached Lonnie Ellison's ocean-front mansion in Rye. It sat back about a hundred feet from Ocean Boulevard which was all that was between the massive home and the Atlantic Ocean. An eight-foot high ornamental metal fence surrounded the property. You could see the home through the fencing which was constructed in such a way as to make it very difficult to climb over and get to the other side.

I pulled my car off the road and up to a small turnaround in front of the gate. I parked and got out and approached an intercom box attached to the gate. Two cameras peered down at me from the top of both sides of the gate. Just as Paulie had said. I pressed the button on the intercom. It made no noise and nothing happened. I tried again. Still nothing. I wasn't going to give up. I glanced at the camera above me and continued tickling the button.

Finally, the intercom squawked and a male voice said, "What do you want?"

"I'd like to talk to Lonnie Ellison for just a minute."

"Sorry," the voice from the box said. "He doesn't talk to anyone."

"Can you see this?" I asked, holding up the video tape I had in my other hand and facing it toward one of the cameras. "This is a movie starring you." I was taking a chance that it was Ellison speaking.

The camera whirred as if it were zooming in for a close-up.

For almost a full minute nothing happened. I was just about ready to start poking the button again when there was a loud metallic click from the gate and it swung open.

The voice in the box said, "Drive up to the front door." He didn't sound too happy. Whether it was Ellison or someone else, I couldn't be sure. I did as I was told though.

I left the car in the middle of a much larger turnaround up at the house. A house that reminded me of Southfork on the *Dallas* TV show. I got out and marched up to the front door. I had the tape in one hand.

Ellison stood in the doorway. I recognized him right away. He looked like the pictures I'd seen of him back in his heyday—with maybe fifteen or twenty years of substance abuse and debauchery added to the mix. In his mid-forties maybe but hard to tell. His hair was long and black with that weird red tint that told me it was a dye job. Probably done since the porn flick because he'd had some gray in that. He wore expensive jeans, a long-tongued Rolling Stone T-shirt, and was barefoot. He was short, maybe five-seven or eight, and couldn't have weighed more than a hundred and forty pounds. He motioned me inside. We walked down a long corridor and stepped into what I'd call a great room.

The room was huge with a vaulted ceiling and a gigantic chandelier. It was littered with expensive furniture and more expensive paintings hanging on the walls. I'm no antique or art expert, but I had no doubt they were all the real McCoy.

They *felt* expensive, if you know what I mean. The windows looked out on the rear of the property with a view of a large backyard about the size of a golf course and beyond it, a tree line. Ellison nodded for me to take a seat. I sat in one of those high-backed fragile-type chairs you're always afraid are going to collapse beneath you. Ellison stood looking down at me. I shifted in the chair, feeling very uncomfortable.

He looked both angry and a bit nervous at the same time. "Who are you and how'd you get that, if it's what I think it is?" He tipped his chin toward the tape in my lap, then sat in a luxurious antique love seat across from me.

I told him who I was and most of the story. Not all, but most. He didn't interrupt; just listened.

When I was done, he said, "How much do you want for that?" He looked toward the tape.

I shook my head. "I don't want anything. And even if I did, I wouldn't pay if I were you. You've already paid enough, I'd guess."

Ellison sighed. "You'd guess right, brother. Those fuckin' scumbags got me all fucked up over at a strip club. Probably tabbed my drink. Then the chick took me to some rundown motel and they made that movie. I'd never be with an under-age kid if they hadn't drugged me."

I smiled. "I've got news for you . . . you weren't."

Ellison leaned forward, put his hands on his knees. "Weren't what?" he asked warily.

"The girl in this video is over eighteen. Not by much but she's of age."

His eyes widened. "You're kidding me, right?"

"No. She's of age. Was when this was filmed." I held up the tape.

"Are you sure about this?"

"I'm sure. I've talked to people who know her."

He thumped his thigh with a fist. "Those assholes. I should've known. But she looked so young and I couldn't remember a damn thing."

"You could've checked it out more," I offered. "Hired a PI or something."

"Like you, Farlowe?"

"It's Marlowe and I'm not a PI. I'm a bartender down at the High Tide in Hampton. I told you that."

"Well, you missed your calling." Ellison shook his head in disgust. "They told me if I put anyone on their trail, copies of the tape would go to the police and my wife. I couldn't risk that."

I looked around. "Your wife here?"

He snorted. "No, she's in our place in New York. Too boring for her here."

I glanced around the room. "I like this kind of boring."

Ellison let out a half-hearted chuckle. "Yeah, me too."

I fidgeted around in my uncomfortable chair. "How much do you pay them?"

"Plenty," he spat out. "I leave an envelope out in my mailbox after nine at night the first of every month. It's just like a pension check for the jerks."

"I can't promise you'll get any of it back, but how would you like to help me shut these characters down?"

Ellison rubbed his chin, was silent for a minute. Then, "I'd like to help but I think I'd still prefer that the cops or my wife not see that tape. Even if the girl was old enough. My other half wouldn't be happy with me. Not that she is now. And the cops . . . well, they might make something out of the controlled substances. And there's the damn tabloids."

I nodded knowingly. "Still, these people will probably try to shake you down forever, and when you do stop paying they might send the videos out just for spite."

"Then you think they got copies of that?" Ellison nodded toward the tape in my lap.

"I don't know. It's possible."

Ellison looked distressed. "Jesus. Maybe I should keep payin' the bastards." He thought for a moment. "On the other hand, if you're right and she's over eighteen—"

I interrupted. "I'm right. She's over eighteen."

"Okay. Then no problem there. As far as the extramarital sex goes . . . like I said, my wife'll be pissed, but this won't be the first time and I've gotten through it before. So that'll blow over eventually. The coke, though—and there was smack, too, but I didn't know that at the time. At least I don't think I did. Can you be charged for snorting on camera? I've never heard of it. But if the *Enquirer* and those other rags pick it up . . . shit, on the other hand, that'd be a million dollars of free publicity. My agent'd be happy. He hasn't been happy for years."

"Well?" I asked, trying not to hold my breath.

"I don't know what the hell to do. Maybe I need some legal advice."

"A lawyer?"

"Yeah . . ." Ellison began but then stopped. A double worry line between his eyes deepened. "But what if I decide to just keep paying anyway? Then my lawyer will know about it all. I don't want that." He looked stumped.

I took out my wallet, removed a business card, and handed it over. Ellison starred at the card, then looked up at me. "This Connolly guy any good?"

"He's gotten me out of a couple of jams."

"I hope he's discreet and not too expensive."

"He's not expensive."

Ellison stood up. "All right then. I'll call him. See what he says. I don't want those damn tapes floating around out there. Especially if I'm not going to pay anymore. And now that I know the girl wasn't a minor, maybe I can take a chance and help you."

I started to speak but he hurried on. "I may still want my name kept out of this, though. I don't know yet."

"I'll do the best I can. But remember what you said."

He cocked his head, gave me a quizzical look. "What?"

"A million dollars of free publicity."

"I did say that, didn't I?"

I could almost smell his brain cells burning as he imagined being number one on the Billboard charts again.

Finally, "All right. I'll call this lawyer. Leave me a number where I can reach you."

I did and got up from the fragile chair. Ellison escorted me out to my car. I could see him in the rearview as I drove away. He was still standing there, watching me, when I exited the gate and pulled onto Route 1A south.

To my left was the Atlantic Ocean. The sun was shimmering off it. The tide was high and the waves were breaking on the rocks below. Out beyond the scattered power boats and sailboats was the Isles of Shoals, a group of small islands about six miles off the coast. The sky was so clear I could almost count the buildings on Star Island.

I rolled the window down and sucked in a huge lungful of clean salt air. If I'd been able to, I would've driven like that all the way back to Hampton Beach. Just savoring that salty air. Hot, humid air. After a minute, though, I almost couldn't breathe. Salty air or not. I closed the window, turned the A/C on high, and sweated while I waited for it to work.

Chapter 23

THE SUN WAS still bright by the time I got back to my cottage. Skye was puttering about. She looked very anxious, averting her eyes and licking her lips, her skin pale. She was a good-looking woman but she didn't look good now. Within minutes I knew why. There was the beep of a horn out on the street. Skye gave me a sheepish grin and walked out the front door. I didn't ask where she was going. I had a good idea and I wasn't happy about it.

She returned in about five minutes, something clenched in her hand. She hit me with the sheepish grin again and hurried to the bathroom. I heard her lock the door. I grabbed a beer. It was early but I'd need it tonight. And probably more.

When she came out of the bathroom, Skye joined me in the living room. I was in my easy chair. She sat across from me on the sofa. I had the television tuned to a newscast. She had on worn jeans and had pulled her legs up underneath her, Indian-style. The denim material pulled tight along her thighs. Her short blonde hair was unruly, almost wild, but attractive. She had on a man's long-sleeved shirt, no bra. Her nipples pushed at the tight material. The shirt was knotted under her breasts exposing a tanned firm midriff. I tried not to look. I wasn't too successful. The drug—heroin, I assumed, with maybe a little coke thrown in—had transformed her. Minutes ago, she had been a sniveling wreck, barely holding it together. To look at her now, you'd never have suspected she was a junkie.

Even so, I was pissed and I told her so. "I don't want anyone delivering any dope here. I have enough problems with the Hampton cops without them thinking I'm doing heroin, or whatever it is, down here."

She pursed her lips. "I'm sorry, Dan. I didn't want to. I had to. I won't do it again. I promise."

I knew that was an impossible promise to keep. Still, I said, "Well don't, please."

What else could I say? I'd known what she was before I'd brought her here. And I'd left her alone. What else could I have expected? Unless she was carrying a hidden pharmacy around with her. And that could've been worse. Of course, she'd have to make arrangements to cop the drug. I must've known that. I wasn't naive. So I was as guilty as she was.

We sat in silence for a while. I drank beers. She sipped one. Finally, I stopped stewing over what had happened and told her about the Lonnie Ellison blackmail plot.

She grimaced.

"Do you think you can get in touch with the girl who was in the film with him?"

She shrugged. "Jillian? Maybe. I know where she works now. Ogle's." She was referring to a well-known strip club over in Seabrook.

"Do you know when she works?" I took a swig of beer. I was drinking faster and earlier than usual tonight.

She smiled. I noticed for the first time that she had beautiful teeth. I knew that wouldn't last long. But that knowledge wasn't helping me right now. I was turned on. I couldn't deny it. I fought the feelings.

"That's no problem. You just call over there, ask when she's dancing. Guys are always calling the clubs. Finding out when their favorite girls are dancing."

I hadn't known that, but it made perfect sense. I got a phonebook from the cabinet under the TV, found the number and called it. A gruff-sounding male answered. There was rock music and voices in the background.

"Can you tell me when Jillian is working next?" I asked.

"Jillian? Yeah, she's workin' . . ." The important part was drowned out by the background noise.

"When's that?" I said.

"Clean out your ears. I said she's working tomorrow at eleven and all afternoon."

"Thanks." I hung up the phone and said to Skye. "She's working tomorrow afternoon."

Skye leaned back on the sofa. The material of her shirt stretched tighter against her breasts. I wondered if she had implants. Implants or not, they were nice.

"Not a busy shift," she said. "But not as many girls working, either." She was silent a few seconds, then said, "What good do you think it's going to do going over there? She's not going to tell you anything."

She was probably right, of course. Why would Jillian give anyone up to me? But I had an idea. "Maybe she'd give the information to someone else."

Skye cocked an eyebrow, stared at me. "Like who?"

"Lonnie Ellison, maybe?"

She did a double-take. "Are you crazy? Why would she tell him anything? Especially if she was involved in black-mailing him. Forget it."

I couldn't. It was the only idea I had. "What if we convinced her that Ellison was genuinely interested in her? That he hadn't been able to get her out of his mind since the time they'd been together?"

Skye shook her head slowly. "Uhh. I dunno."

I leaned forward in my chair. "He's worth a couple a hundred million dollars. *And* he's not getting along with his wife. *And* we all know how famous he is."

She sighed. "Jesus. I don't know about her, but I'm interested."

I held my hands out, palms up. "Come on, what do you think?"

She opened her blue eyes wider. They sparkled. I wondered again if she'd taken some coke in her jolt. The thought made me nervous and my bowels churned.

"Well, she'll be leery. Tempted though. She might give it a shot. It's a once-in-a-lifetime chance, hooking up with someone like that." Her eyes got a little dreamy. "Never having to work—let alone strip—again." She looked up at the wall behind me. "You probably could get some info out of her. People have taken a chance for a lot less."

That was for sure. A lot less. So we'd have to convince this Jillian woman that she had a chance to hook up permanently with Ellison. A wealthy rock star but also a person she'd been involved in blackmailing. Of course, she'd probably been no more involved than a mannequin would've been. Others had to be behind this. We could use that fact to our benefit. She was just an ancillary player in the scheme and we'd make it appear that's how Ellison looked at it. If her greed trumped her suspicions and we could get her to believe that, then we'd also have to convince her of some fairly benign reason we wanted to know who was running the extortion plot. Something that wouldn't spook her or cause the culprits to chop her head off if they heard about our inquiries. I didn't want any more dead bodies on my conscience.

"Please keep my name out of it though, Dan. You said they might be after me already, but if they aren't, I don't want them to be."

"Of course."

Skye stretched luxuriously, her shirt doing the breasts-accentuating routine again. "I'm going to bed," she said. She kept her eyes on my face as she stood up, took a couple of steps, and put one knee on the arm of my chair. Her jeans were very tight. Her crotch was at my eye level.

I grabbed the beer off the end table. Tried to take a casual sip. It felt as casual as the first drink of water after a three-day trek in the desert.

Her eyes were mapping my face. "I want to thank you for letting me stay here. You've probably saved my life."

"That's . . . hmm . . . okay," I said.

She pushed my hair back with a soft hand. "Want me to thank you, Dan?"

I stuttered again. "You . . . ahh . . . just did."

She moved her hand so her fingers were light on my cheek. They felt warm. She looked into my eyes, a slight grin on her face. I couldn't look at her for more than a few seconds. I'd never made it with a porn actress before. At least I didn't think I had. Not one this good-looking, anyway.

If she knew about the inner tug-of-war going on in my beer-soaked brain, she didn't show it. Just kept looking at me and touching me like she was wondering how much longer I'd hold out. Then she must have figured she'd given me enough time.

"You're a funny guy, Dan. Sleep tight." She bent, gave me a peck on the forehead, and headed for the kitchen and the back bedroom.

I started to say goodnight after her, but it came out like I was just learning a new language. Completely unintelligible.

I sat there for a few minutes, in a mental battle with myself. One army's general said, "Stay put." The opposing one said, "Go to her bedroom." Images of Skye behind the little window in the booth at Midnight Reader flooded my head. When I couldn't take it anymore and thought the good guys might lose, I jumped up, went to my bedroom and retrieved the Xanax, popping one under my tongue. I could taste the dissolving chemical as I went to the fridge and returned to my seat with two cold beers.

It took another thirty minutes before I was conscious of what I was watching on TV. It was a long night to say the least. The night I almost went to bed with a porn actress.

Chapter 24

THE NEXT DAY I had off from work. That was good because the gruff voice on the phone at the strip club had told me that Jillian was working the afternoon shift, starting at 11:00. Who would be interested in going to a strip club that early—except me, of course—I had no idea. Skye prepared a nice little breakfast of fruit, bagels, and juice. About all I had in the house. She looked good and seemed in fine spirits. I knew what that meant.

As soon as I finished eating, I made a call to Lonnie Ellison. I explained the situation. I had a bad feeling that being as well known as he was—and married—the last place he'd want to go would be to a strip club. Especially after what had happened to him. I was wrong.

"You bet your sweet ass I'll go," he said over the phone.

I explained what he'd have to do to make this little excursion productive.

Again, I thought there might be some hesitation. Again, I was wrong.

"No problem. I always wanted to get into acting." He chuckled, then hesitated. "I'm going to bring my attorney along though."

"Your attorney?" I asked.

"Yeah, James Connolly. The guy you hooked me up with. I called him last night."

"Oh? How do you know he'll want to come?"

He made a snickering noise over the phone like I had no idea how the world operated. "Don't worry, he'll come"

It took less than a few seconds for even a dumbbell like me to realize he was probably right. Not only was Attorney Connolly in dire need of clients, but Ellison was a potential gravy train of legal work. I'd read quite a few articles back in the day about his adventures with the law.

"Just want to make sure I don't get in over my head," he said. "I tend to do that sometimes. At least I used to."

"Do you want me to come up there and get you?"

"No. The lawyer and I'll pick you up in a couple of hours."

Boy, the guy was sure of himself. He had Connelly's schedule committed without even confirming it with him yet. But I guess anyone would've been a little cocky if they'd lived his kind of life. I gave him the directions to my cottage.

"All right. *Ciao*," he said before hanging up.

I had one more call to make, to Shamrock of course. If I didn't cut him in on this little jaunt, I'd never hear the end of it. As I expected, he was raring to go. I didn't mention Ellison though. Still, Shamrock said he'd be out on his front porch in five minutes, waiting for me.

I knew he was joking about the five-minute part and that was good because Ellison showed up three hours later at around 1 p.m. I thought it best for Skye not to come with us. It might make Jillian suspicious that Skye had put the finger on her. Or maybe she'd wonder why Skye hadn't tried to rope Ellison for herself. And besides, Skye wanted to keep her name out it. So I asked her to stay put and not answer the phone or the door while I was gone. Not just because the bad guys might be looking for her, but it had also dawned on me that they might come here looking for me and stumble on her. Too bad I hadn't been smart enough to think of that earlier. She said she wouldn't let anyone in. I also reminded her what I'd said about no dealers showing up. She assured me she wouldn't call anyone. She looked pretty together, so I was hopeful that she wouldn't break her promise.

A new pearl-gray Mercedes sedan sat in my driveway, driven by Lonnie Ellison. In the passenger seat, with a big grin on his face, was my attorney—James Connolly, Esquire.

I hopped in the back and directed them to Shamrock's cottage off Ashworth Avenue. He was standing on his porch, in dungarees and a T-shirt with a map of Ireland on it. He hurried down the steps and got in the backseat beside me.

Ellison had barely turned the car around and headed back onto Ashworth before Shamrock was leaning over the front seat between the two men. "Hey, I know you. You're . . . you're . . . you're . . ."

"Lonnie Ellison," Ellison said.

Shamrock bobbed his head up and down. "Yeah, that's right. You're Lonnie Ellison, aren't you?"

I could almost sense Ellison frowning. "Last time I checked that's who I was." I realized he'd probably had this same exchange hundreds . . . no, maybe thousands . . . of times before.

"I just saw you—" Shamrock began before I jabbed him in the kidney. "Ouch" he said, looking at me sheepishly. "Ahh . . . oh, yeah."

I gently grabbed Shamrock's arm and urged him to sit back.

"Are we going to Ogle's now?" Shamrock said, trying to change the subject.

"Yes," I answered.

The ride was uneventful and it was close to 1:30 when we pulled into the parking area for the Ogle strip club. There were only a few cars in the large lot. We walked in the front door. A mountain of a doorman gave us all the fisheye as we came in. He did a double take when he saw Ellison. He jumped to open an inner door and held it for us like he was a royal footman. There was no cover charge at this early hour.

It took a minute to get accustomed to the dim lights. I'd never been in this club before but there wasn't much original to see. There was a fairly large stage toward the back, centered and surrounded by captain's chairs that ran all the way around three sides of the stage. The rest of the area was furnished with a few dozen two- and four-person tables, all with chairs. On the stage was a semi-nude redheaded dancer swinging around a pole. Her hair was thick and long and she was well illuminated. The throbbing beat of some new popular rock song came from speakers around the large room. I'd heard the song recently but had no idea what the hell it was. I listened mostly to classic rock.

Surrounding the stage, on the chairs, were maybe a half-dozen men scattered about, nursing drinks and staring dumbly at the dancer. Only a few of the tables were occupied. I wasn't surprised because of the hour. I assumed this type of business picked up as soon as the five o'clock work whistle blew.

I was surprised when the doorman who'd let us in dashed up beside us and, coming as close to a bow as is humanly possible without actually doing it, said, "Right this way, Mr. Ellison."

The doorman's huge arm arced out, directing us to follow him. We did, Ellison leading the way. We were taken to a table for four, as close to the stage as possible without actually being on it. The doorman pulled a chair out for the rock star; the rest of us pulled our own chairs out.

"Your server will be right over," the doorman said. He had a smile on that almost split his face. I doubted he looked like that at any other time. "If there's anything I can do, just ask."

"Yeah, sure," Ellison said, holding up one hand and shimmering it like he was a king dismissing a subject. And maybe he was. The doorman lumbered toward the bar, grabbing a cocktail waitress along the way. He had a few words with her and the bartender. Then he barked the word "Go" to the server and she headed our way, bumping into chairs as she came.

She was a wisp of woman. Thirties somewhere, maybe, but tough to guess with her hard face. I wondered for a moment if she'd been a dancer at one time. Was this where many of the dancers ended up after they were too old to gyrate on stage?

"What can I get for you gentlemen?" she singsonged in a tone I was sure she rarely used with other patrons. Not with a face like that.

We all placed our orders but you wouldn't know any of us were alive except Ellison to judge by our server. Her eyes never left Ellison. There was no reaction from him. He was probably used to all this fawning. When she had all our drink orders, she excused herself and made a beeline for the bar, only banging into one chair as she went.

"Well, do you see her?" Connolly asked.

"I sure do, laddie," Shamrock said. He was turned in his seat, staring at the redheaded dancer who was now wearing only a G-string. She was doing a series of splits and slides. She was a very agile woman and I hoped she didn't get a splinter

"Not her," Connolly said. "I mean the one we came here for. The one in the movie."

We all looked around. Except for the redhead on the stage and the bar waitress, there were no other women visible. Apparently, like most strip joints, the dancers rotated every thirty minutes or so. Unlike Boston and larger cities, the girls here weren't mingling with the customers. Maybe they weren't allowed to. Or maybe the pickings weren't worth it until the after-work rush.

Just then I noticed that a corner of a floor-length drape off to one side of the stage had been peeled back and at least three or four female heads were bouncing around, jockeying for position, all looking in our direction. I was sure they weren't looking at me.

"Look over there," I said, nodding in the direction of the ogling women.

"I think I see her," Ellison said.

The waitress returned with our drinks. She was visibly nervous. I was amazed that a guy like Ellison could have such an effect on people. And I fantasized for a moment what it would be like to be him. That's when I remembered an old quote by some writer with three names: "Fame is very agreeable, but the bad thing is that it goes on twenty-four hours a day." Twenty-four hours a day? I wouldn't like that. Another saying came to mind: "Watch out what you wish for. You might get it." So I dropped the dream.

When the waitress was done delivering our drinks and staring at Ellison, she excused herself. Before she could turn, our rock star said, "Tell Jillian to come over for a drink." He said it like a command and I felt a bit embarrassed.

But I got over that quick when the waitress replied with something I surely wouldn't have gotten. "Yes, sir. Right away." Like she was a Marine grunt and Ellison was her drill instructor.

I shook my head and watched as she scurried toward the bar, frantically signaling the doorman along the way. The big man had been looming in the background, keeping an eye on us all this time. He pushed off like a cruise ship and met her at the bar. They had words and then both hurried over to where the other dancers still had their faces peeking out from behind the black drapes. They saw him coming and the big drape dropped shut. When the big man reached it, he fumbled around for a moment, trying to find his way in, and finally did.

"What now?" Connolly asked.

"She'll be right over," Ellison said, as if there was absolutely no chance that she wouldn't be. From what I'd seen so far, I figured he was right.

Shamrock was back to watching the red-headed stripper whose act had just finished. She was snatching up a small scattering of bills that had been thrown on stage by the half-dozen men on the stools. Ellison was sipping cognac from a very small glass. Connolly had a vodka-and-tonic. Shamrock and I both had our Heinekens, no glasses. We knew where we were.

There was some loud talking from behind the curtain. The music had stopped between acts but I still couldn't make out what they were saying. I was sure the doorman was giving Jillian her marching orders as far as coming to our table. *If* that was even necessary. A few seconds later, I was proven right. The same corner of the drapes, where the dancers had recently been checking out Ellison, suddenly opened a bit and *that* girl, Jillian, stepped from behind it. Well, not really stepped, more like rolled from behind it. She was on roller skates and she used them expertly to maneuver around obstacles to reach our table.

The first thing I noticed when she rolled up and came to a stop was the uncomfortable look on her face. She must have been thinking of her dalliance with Ellison and wondering if his visit was going to have unpleasant consequences. The second thing I noticed was a large pair of artificial breasts and that she was dressed appropriately for her job. Tight baby-blue satin bikini outfit with lots of thin gold chains wrapped around different parts of her body. These girls must like gold chains, or maybe it was what the guys liked.

"How are you doing?" Ellison said, as if greeting a long lost friend. He twisted around, pulled a chair from a table behind him, and positioned it at our table beside him. She looked hesitant. Then I noticed her glance toward the bar. The doorman was standing there watching, his big arms folded across a massive chest. Jillian quickly sat in the chair. She looked like someone who thought she might be on her way to jail.

Connolly and Shamrock gaped at our new companion. I guess I did, too. Her getup encouraged that. She was attractive. Short brown hair and huge beautiful eyes. And yes, as the video had shown, very young looking.

"Would you like something to drink?" I asked.

"No."

I was surprised. I'd been sure that she would have ordered a $20.00 glass of ginger ale. But I should have known this woman wasn't in work mode. She was in frightened mode, very frightened mode. Whether it was Ellison or the doorman who scared her more, I didn't know. Maybe both. She clenched her hands together on the table. I realized I'd probably have the same trepidation in her position. For all she knew, the police were outside, waiting for a signal from Ellison to come in and arrest her for blackmail or whatever the hell they might decide to charge her with.

Rock music began to blare from the sound system again and a new dancer took the stage. Shamrock and Connolly turned to watch the performance. I kept my eyes on our guest, waiting for Ellison to get the ball rolling. I didn't have to wait long.

"I've been thinking about you a lot since that night," he said to her.

She glanced at him suspiciously. She didn't say a word. Ellison continued. "I don't think I've ever enjoyed myself that much and I've been trying to find you. I finally have."

I could see in her eyes that she didn't believe a word he said. But he continued with a long spiel of smarmy talk. Within ten minutes he'd just about told this strip club dancer, who'd been part of an extortion plot against him, that he was in love with her and wanted to marry her.

And I could tell she still didn't believe a word he said. But I could see the wheels spinning behind her big brown eyes. Listening as Ellison talked about giving her a ride in his Mercedes to his oceanfront mansion in Rye, so she could take a tour of it. And more. I almost felt sorry for her. She didn't have a choice. If there was one chance in a million he was serious, it could be her only hope to get out of this hole she worked in and out of this life, a life the older girls had probably told her wouldn't last long. If there was even a prayer that Ellison had really become hooked on her, she couldn't risk blowing it. It was a long shot, but I was sure she'd heard stories of wealthy men falling hard for strippers and taking them for wives. It had happened. Not often, but it had. And she knew she was never going to meet another multimillionaire rock star in this dump or any dump for that matter. That was for sure.

Ellison cuddled in close to Jillian, whispered in her ear. I turned to join Connolly and Shamrock in ogling the dancer on the stage. I couldn't have been watching more than five minutes when Ellison suddenly stood up and said, "Let's go."

We all got up from the table. Jillian rolled back toward the curtain she'd come from. The three of us followed Ellison across the room and out the door into the lobby.

"Where are we going?" Shamrock asked, beating me to it.

"I'm giving you guys a ride home, then I'm coming back here," Ellison said.

We walked out the main door into the bright sunshine. Connolly and Shamrock looked dejected. Back in the Mercedes, I said, "Did you find out anything, Lonnie?"

"Of course I did," Ellison answered. I was in the back-seat on the passenger side. He had a smug expression on his face. "The place they filmed me at is called the Weeping Willow Motel. I didn't even know the name of the place."

I glanced at Shamrock. Naturally he said, "I know where that is."

"Did she tell you who was behind it?" I asked, as we drove along Route 1A in the direction of Hampton.

"Nah, Dan," Ellison said. "She doesn't know who put it together. Some lowlife offered her the job. She never met anyone else. The guy running the camera in a rigged closet didn't even talk to her and she claims she didn't get a look at him. She says she thought the whole thing was a birthday present from some of my friends."

Glancing at me over his shoulder for a moment, he added, "You ought to be able to handle it from here. I can't do everything for you."

I let that comment slide. From the little time I'd been with this guy, I'd come to realize I couldn't blame him for being deluded into thinking there was something special about him. He'd probably been treated the same way he'd just been treated in the strip club for decades now. And most likely everywhere he went. So instead of taking offense, I asked, "Why are you going back?"

A sly grin came across his face. "We're gonna party. She can get some good coke and hot girls."

"Oh," Shamrock said. Now he sounded dejected.

"Any of you guys want to come?" Ellison asked. "My treat."

My stomach churned. I thought about it for a long minute. It was lucky I only had one beer in my belly or I would've disappeared on the seacoast for who knew how long. Connolly had already jumped on the opportunity when I finally said, "No, thanks."

"What about your friend?" Ellison asked, jerking his head toward Shamrock seated behind him.

Shamrock looked at me. I looked at him. "It's up to you," I said.

He looked as sad as a man who'd just lost his long-time girlfriend. "I have to work tonight," was all he said.

I felt for him. It would have been too late for him to call Dianne and get out of a shift that started in a couple of hours. And maybe it was for the best. He probably wouldn't have been in any condition for his early morning duties the next day, anyway.

"Maybe next time," Ellison said.

Ellison and Connolly were going back and forth jovi- ally while Shamrock and I sat silently in the back seat as the luxury car glided over the Hampton Bridge. Ellison dropped us off in front of my cottage. Shamrock and I watched as the big car turned around and headed back for the strip club.

"You want to come in?" I asked.

"No," Shamrock answered, sounding as low as an Irishman can sound. "I'll just go home and get ready for work."

There couldn't be much to that—except throwing on his whites. "You want to come to the Weeping Willow with me when I go?" I'd already decided the motel should be checked out.

"I dunno."

"I might need backup."

That cheered him up just a bit, maybe one notch. "Sure, I'll come, Danny. Just let me know when."

I watched Shamrock as he walked away in the direction of his cottage. He seemed to be dragging his feet. I couldn't blame him. I didn't feel great either. What kind of a show and how much cocaine Jillian and her friends were going to have for Ellison and Connolly, I couldn't imagine. Or maybe I could. Shamrock, too. That was the problem.

And with Ellison footing the bill, money was no object.

My stomach started to grumble. Inside my cottage, I popped a Xanax and visited the bathroom. Finally, forty-five minutes later, my stomach got the message that I really wasn't going to indulge and it quieted down. My mind took a lot longer.

Chapter 25

THE NEXT DAY at work was just another day in paradise unless you want to take into consideration Dianne's coldness towards me. She wasn't too thrilled with Skye staying at my cottage and I couldn't blame her. Still, I couldn't ask Skye to leave yet. Her life might be in danger and I felt responsible.

Nothing out of the ordinary happened until I got a shout from one of the waitresses that there was a call for me. I took it on the bar phone.

"Hello?"

"Marlowe?" I recognized the voice as one of the thugs I'd met on the beach. Big Man.

"Yeah?"

"We want those tapes and we want them yesterday."

"I don't have them."

"Those clowns you know do."

Apparently, he knew about Eddie and Derwood and hadn't been able to find them, or he wouldn't have called.

"They threw them all away." It sounded lame and I felt my voice shake a bit as I said it.

"Bullshit! You either get those tapes, Marlowe, or we'll cut off your cock and shove it in your mouth. *And* we'll do worse to your girl and your Mick friend."

This time my stomach fell to the basement. I had to stall. "You'll have to give me a little more time."

"We already gave you time, asshole. Get 'em now or we'll get you. *And* the others. I'll call you soon. And you better have 'em." He slammed the phone down.

I hung up the phone gently, walked around the bar, and out into the kitchen. I caught Shamrock just as he was about to punch out.

"We got trouble," I whispered.

His light complexion suddenly became paler. "More than we already got?"

"Can you hang around a while until I get off?" I asked.

He nodded gravely; didn't say another word.

About an hour later we pulled up in my car at the end of a cul-de-sac. On the drive I'd told Shamrock about the unpleasant phone call. I pulled into the tiny driveway of a well-kept mobile home that was one of many in the mobile home park. Shamrock and I were about the only ones who knew about Eddie's aunt's Seabrook home. She spent most of her time in Florida. Eddie and Derwood had used her place in the past when they'd been hiding out from blowback from one of their crazy schemes.

It was still light out. I noticed the curtains were all drawn and closed but I didn't miss the movement when someone inside pulled the shade back an inch and peeked out for a long second. We got out of the car, went up to the door. I opened the storm door and knocked on the inner one. There was no response.

"The screwballs," Shamrock said. "Let me try." He reached over my shoulder and banged forcefully on the door numerous times. "Open up, Eddie. We know you're in there. We aren't leaving."

It took another minute of Shamrock banging on the door before it finally opened. A man wearing a black floppy hat, sunglasses, and a few days' old beard stood there. Eddie. Shamrock and I brushed past him into the main room of the neat mobile home. Well, the outside was neat anyway and the inside probably had been, too, at least before these two buffoons had decided to use it as a hideout. Now the place was littered with empty beer cans and pizza boxes. The place stunk of stale beer and old butts. *And* the smell that people using meth sometimes gave off. Between the ridiculous disguise Eddie was wearing and him rushing to the window, pulling back the corner of the shade again, and peeking out, I didn't have any doubt who was indulging in that foul drug.

"Jesus Christ, what the hell are you two doing?" I asked.

"I ain't doing anything, Dan. It's him." Derwood sat in a barrel chair on the other side of the room. He scowled and nodded in Eddie's direction. Derwood was dressed normally for him—old jeans and a baggy navy-blue T-shirt.

Eddie dropped the corner of the shade, turned to face us. "Did anyone follow you?" he said, speaking faster than I thought anyone capable of.

"Eddie, shut up and sit down," I said. "And take off those stupid sunglasses and hat."

He sat on the couch and began fidgeting.

"The glasses and hat," I said, making a circular motion near my eyes with one finger.

Eddie removed them. If his eyes had any pupils, I couldn't see them.

Shamrock and I remained standing. There was nowhere to sit anyway. All available seats were littered with debris.

I got right down to business. "I need those tapes, Eddie. All of them."

Eddie whined. "I told you we got rid of them."

I turned toward Derwood. "Is that true?"

"We tossed most of 'em in a dumpster, Dan. They're long gone."

"And you only kept the one?" I asked.

Eddie's foot was jiggling like someone with a late-stage neurological disease. "Yeah, yeah, yeah, we—"

Derwood interrupted. "Tell him the truth, Eddie. We're in a bad jam. Dan and Shamrock are tryin' to get us out of it. They done it before."

Eddie spoke through clenched teeth. "Shut up, Dumwood."

Derwood started to get up from his seat. "I told you not to call me that, Eddie. It makes me mad."

I stepped over to Derwood, put my hand on his shoulder, and motioned for him to remain seated. He sat.

"As for you," I said, looking at Eddie. "Let me see the tapes."

Eddie hesitated.

Shamrock rushed toward him, his face flushed and his large hand balled. Eddie cringed.

"All right, all right," he whimpered.

Shamrock stopped. Eddie slowly adjusted himself, but his dignity was long gone.

"Get them, Eddie," I said. "Now!"

"There's only one left," Eddie said. He tried to stop jerking around. He wasn't having any success. The drug coursing through his brain was too strong for any human being to overcome until it dissipated on its own.

"Is that true?" I asked Derwood.

"It is, Dan. We tossed the rest."

"Get it," I said, looking at Eddie. "And put it in." I pointed at a television on a table in the corner with a VCR player below it.

Eddie got up, reached under the couch cushion he'd been seated on, and came out with a VCR tape. He held it in his hand, stared at it. His hand shook.

I was losing my patience. "Put it in, you stupid fuck."

Eddie wasn't used to hearing me swear. He almost catapulted out of his seat and over to the VCR. He fumbled with the tape, finally sliding it into the player. He pressed some buttons and hurried back to his seat. Shamrock and I continued standing as the tape activated and some figures appeared.

It was another porn film. Looked like the same location and bed as on the Lonnie Ellison tape. An actress I didn't recognize was earning her money. And she was dolled up to look like a kid. The male co-star was fat and bald. He wore only black calf-length socks. He would have been perfectly cast if this was a 1950s skin flick.

I watched the sexual shenanigans for a few minutes. Except for an old man having sex with a pretend under-age girl, I didn't see anything else of note. That is until the camera zoomed in on the bald man's face. I didn't need to see the results of a blood test on the bald man to know he was looped. He was conscious but barely. His eyes weren't focusing on anything. And if the actress wasn't struggling to support him occasionally, I think he would have done a header over the side of the bed.

And there was something else. I stared at the man's fat white face. And then it struck me. "Turn it off, Eddie," I said.

Eddie jumped up, turned off the VCR, and returned to his seat. He looked at me as he licked his dry lips. "See, Dan, nothing. Just another skin flick." His voice shook.

"Bullshit!" I said. "That's that state rep. What the hell's his name, Shamrock?"

Shamrock arched his red eyebrows. "State rep. It is? I dunno what his name is."

I turned back to Eddie. "You do. What is it?"

"Huh?" Eddie answered, looking like a drunk trying to bluff in a poker game.

"I'll beat your arse," Shamrock bellowed. He took a step toward Eddie again.

Eddie threw his hands up, cringed again. "Okay, man. It's Walter Fishbain. I only knew it was him 'cause I happened to see his picture in the paper that day."

I shook my head. "So you held that one back, too. Along with Ellison's. Why?" Before Eddie could answer, I said, "And he's also a rich real estate developer. You must've figured you could shake him down if you got the chance."

"Nah, nah." Eddie said, his eyes darting from me to Shamrock and back again.

"Tell the truth, Eddie," Derwood said. "I told him I wasn't interested in any of it, Dan. That's blackmail. That's way too heavy for me."

I looked from Derwood back to Eddie. It was way too heavy for Eddie, too. I'd known him for a long time and he'd never been more than a relatively harmless small-time beach hustler. And most of his bumbling escapades had backfired. This probably would have backfired, too, so badly he would've gotten his head blown off.

"You're lucky we're stopping you before you could get involved in this, Eddie. You would have ended up in Concord State Prison until you were old enough to apply for Social Security. And that's if you were lucky. The two of you could just as easily have ended up in a barrel at the bottom of the Hampton River."

I could hear Derwood gulp even though it was Eddie's Adam's apple that was sliding up and down.

"Now get that tape," I said. "And give it to me."

Eddie didn't hesitate. He got up again, popped the tape, and handed it to me.

"Now you're both coming with us."

"Where to?" Eddie asked. His voice was still quivering.

"You'll find out when we get there," I answered. "You got us all into this. The least you can do is help get us all out."

Eddie adjusted the belt around his skinny waist. "I dunno if that's such a good idea."

Shamrock was on him in a flash. He grabbed Eddie's polyester shirt with one hand and shook his balled fist in Eddie's face. Eddie's eyes were huge; his pupils, pinholes.

"Help me, Derwood," Eddie squealed.

Derwood didn't move from his seat, just slowly shook his head. "I ain't helping you, Eddie. We gotta go with them. I don't want to end up in no barrel."

Eddie held his hands up, palms out. "Okay, okay."

"You bet your arse okay," Shamrock said, loosening his hold on Eddie's wrinkled shirt. Not that it hadn't needed an ironing even before Shamrock had scrunched it.

It took a few minutes to get them out the door. Eddie had to hit the bathroom first. He came out sniffling like a sick dog and doing a quick marionette-like step across the room.

We finally got them out of the mobile home and into the backseat of my green Chevette. I drove carefully through the well-kept mobile home park and out onto the main drag. We were on our way to the Weeping Willow Motel. I wasn't sure why we were headed there, just that I had to keep trying different options, and hope that, like a broken clock, even an amateur detective was right twice a day.

Chapter 26

IT WAS AROUND 7:00 but hot as hell for this time of day on the seacoast. The heat wave marched on. My car's A/C wasn't working properly, as it often wasn't. Eddie had bitched about the heat the entire drive. A lot of his discomfort was more likely due to the sky-high level of his meth-induced blood pressure. I'd had to keep a rein on Shamrock to keep him from going over the seat after Eddie a couple of times.

When we finally pulled into the Weeping Willow Motel's parking lot, on the border between Salisbury and Newburyport, I'd just about had it with Eddie's incessant complaining. "Get out," I said. "We're all going in."

"I think I'll wait here," Eddie said. He had his shades on, his floppy hat pulled low, and was staring through the window at the building. Apparently, he didn't like the look of the place. I didn't either.

The Weeping Willow Motel was a one-story wooden L-shaped building. A large square sign on a post out front displayed its name. One letter had been worn off—the *g* in Weeping. Probably all the letters had been a bright white at one time. Now they were tinted a swamp green that had probably dripped from the circle of trees that overhung the entire property. The roof of the motel had the same unattractive stains. Along the length of the building was a blackish-green discoloration that hinted loudly at a severe mold problem. There were maybe fifteen units which were most likely one-room jobs. The door closest to us was marked *Office*.

I turned to face Eddie. "You're going in," I said.

"I ain't been feeling too good today, Dan," he said, tongue flicking across his lips. "Have I, Derwood?"

Derwood scowled at Eddie. "Knock it off, Eddie. You felt good enough to get wired, that's for sure."

Eddie glared in Derwood's direction. "Thanks for the help, Dumwood."

"How many times I gotta tell you not to call me that," the big man shouted. "You know I don't like it."

He reached over, pulled Eddie's floppy hat down over his eyes, and then used his left arm to put Eddie in a head lock. With his other hand he ground his knuckle into Eddie's head. A nice old-fashioned noogie. Eddie howled.

I didn't mind seeing Eddie being abused, but I'd had enough. Matter of fact, I'd seen the whole act with these two many times before and I was sick of it, sick of them. I grabbed Derwood's arm and tried to pull it away from Eddie's head. Derwood was big and strong and it took me a full minute, reminding him why we were there, before he let me pull his arm free.

Eddie pulled off his crumpled hat and rubbed his head where Derwood had given him the knuckle massage. He put the battered hat on the seat beside him. I almost wished he'd kept it on. His hair was stringy and not too clean. Apparently, he didn't own stock in any shampoo companies.

We all got out of the car and trudged up to the office door. I led the way inside with Shamrock bringing up the rear so Eddie couldn't make a break for it. I wasn't sure now if it had been a good idea to bring them along. I had no hint at what to expect here and I guess I'd thought that an intimidating hulk like Derwood would be an asset if things got out of hand. Now I didn't know if an intimidating hulk outweighed the aggravation of having Eddie along or not. Still, Eddie was the cause of all this, and whatever happened from here on out, he was going to take the ride.

The office was small—a couple of cheap wooden fold-out chairs, a rack with local tourist attraction pamphlets, and a faded, chipped gray metal counter. On the counter was what looked like a guest register book, a black telephone, and a bell. I poked the bell twice.

A curtain behind the desk opened and out stepped a man who was the spitting image of Stromboli in the *Pinocchio* movie. Black full beard, bald on top with long black unkempt hair hanging down the sides of his head. He had beady black eyes and a Hawaiian shirt that barely contained a monstrous beer belly. He was about as tall as me. Maybe even the same age. Although he could have been anywhere from forty to sixty-five. One of those types.

He sized the four of us up with his sly little eyes. When he gave up trying to figure out what kind of accommodations four guys like us would want, he said, "Yeah?"

Just another cordial local businessman. I reminded myself to check in here sometime soon. When the Bates Motel had their *No Vacancy* sign on.

I didn't have much time to beat around the bush with this character.

"I'd like to ask you a couple of questions," I said.

Stromboli's eyes narrowed until they were almost invisible. "Yeah?" He was a man of few words.

"Back on March 10 who rented room 116?" I asked. Ellison had given me the date and the room. He'd remembered that much somehow.

"Why?" Stromboli rested hands with hairy knuckles on the counter.

I didn't have a good answer ready for that. Instead I took my wallet from the rear pocket of my shorts and removed a twenty-dollar bill. I dropped it on the counter beside Stromboli's hairy hands.

He glanced at the bill. "Hah!" was all he said.

Some people might have just retrieved their money but not me; I was too cynical. Especially concerning this guy. I repeated the process and let another twenty float down to the counter.

Stromboli snatched both bills up and made them disappear behind the counter. He slid the registration book over in front of him, opened it, and began flipping through the pages. Finally, his fat finger stopped on a notation. "John Smith." He had a big ugly grin on his bearded face.

I grabbed the book, spun it around toward me. I'd paid forty dollars after all and I wanted to make sure I was getting the correct information. I looked down at the book. Shamrock and Derwood were looking over my shoulders. I ran my finger down the listings, saw the date and room number. And yes, the registrant's name was none other than the infamous *John Smith*.

"Who's John Smith?" Derwood asked.

"Never mind," I answered. I spun the book back around to face Stromboli.

"Anything else I can help you gentlemen with?" he asked, a smug look on his ugly face.

I knew it was useless but still I said, "You remember anything about this John Smith?"

Stromboli guffawed. "I'm lucky I can remember anything about who checked in yesterday."

I believed that at least. "Thanks," I said. I wasn't happy but there was nothing else to do. This was a dead end. At least for now. When I turned to leave, I noticed Eddie wasn't in the office. "Where's Eddie?" I said.

Both Shamrock and Derwood shrugged.

As we left the office I spotted Eddie slinking out of the front door of a motel room a few doors away from us. He hurried toward our car, hopped in the back seat. I don't think he realized he'd been seen.

When we were all back in the car, I turned on Eddie. "What the hell were you doing in that room? Or should I say rooms?"

He was as nervous as a tax dodger during an IRS audit. "I just had to take a piss, Dan." His eyes darted around as he spoke.

"Bullshit! You could have done that in the office."

"Yeah, but I didn't want to interrupt your investigation," Eddie said.

I had to give him credit; he was trying the best he knew how.

"Aww, Eddie, tell Dan the truth," Derwood said. "He's trying to save our lives." Derwood looked at me. "He was probably rippin' off the room. Maybe more than one. Eddie can move fast. Right, Eddie?"

"Shut up, Dumwood."

"Don't call me that, Eddie." Derwood's face darkened and he leaned toward Eddie.

"Forget that," I said to Derwood. "We haven't got time for another round of this comedy sketch." Derwood's face lightened a bit and he sat back.

"How'd you get in?" I said, looking at Eddie who was looking everywhere but at me.

Derwood answered for him. "Oh, Eddie's good at that too. He can get into most of these old motels with nothing but a driver's license. Although sometimes he uses a little pry bar if the license don't work. Right, Eddie?"

"Mmm," Eddie said.

"What did you get, Eddie?" I demanded. "Give."

"I didn't get—" he started. Shamrock turned and slapped Eddie hard on the top of his bare head.

"Ahh," Eddie squealed, throwing his hands up to protect himself from more possible blows. He peeked out from between his fingers and when he realized Shamrock wasn't going to slap him again—at least not yet—he put his hands into the pockets of his polyester pants. Both hands came out clutching bills.

I grabbed them. It was nothing but a bunch of ones and fives. Couldn't have been more than fifty bucks there. "You jackass," I said. "We could all get in trouble for this."

"Eddie don't care about that when he's wired up, right, Eddie?" Derwood said.

"Shut up, Dum—" Eddie began before stopping. Lucky he did. This time I would have let Derwood have his way with him.

I tossed the situation around mentally for less than a minute, wondering whether I should return the stolen dough to Stromboli. But I figured that could easily start trouble, especially if Stromboli didn't believe restitution was enough punishment and called the cops on us. That would be bad.

Finally, I said, "I'm going to mail this money back here anonymously. And Eddie," I looked at him with the hardest look I could muster, "don't ever pull anything like this again when you're with me."

"And that goes double for me, arsehole," Shamrock said.

Eddie sulked as I pulled the car out of the lot and headed back.

I was still as clueless as ever as to who was behind all this. And worse, how it would end up.

Chapter 27

BY THE TIME I dumped Eddie and Derwood at the mobile home and dropped Shamrock off at his house, it was almost dark. I was looking forward to a beer and just unwinding for a few minutes if that was possible. The second I opened the door of my cottage and stepped inside, that possibility faded.

Dianne sat in my easy chair. Skye sat across from her on the couch. They both looked at me. My stomach soured.

"Hey," I said, looking at Dianne. She appeared as if she'd come from work except she had a fancy flowered blouse on. There was a glass of water beside her on the table. "What are you doing here . . . honey?"

"Oh, I just thought I'd drop by and say hi to you and meet Skye."

I cleared my throat.

"Hi, Dan," Skye said. She had her legs under her, Indian-style again. She must have had a shot recently. And not too much—she looked okay. That was about the only thing positive in this situation. The rest of it, not so much.

I headed for the kitchen. "Anybody want anything to drink?" I asked on the way.

Dianne said, "No." Skye just shook her head.

I grabbed a Heineken, opened it, and, not bothering with a glass, returned to the living room. I hadn't heard the ladies say a word to each other yet. On the other hand, I supposed I was lucky I hadn't stepped in on a bloody cat fight. I wondered what they'd discussed before I arrived.

I could have sat on the couch beside Skye, instead I sat in the only other chair in the room, one I rarely sit in. The table with Dianne's water glass separated my chair from Dianne's. I took a good gulp of beer.

"Where have you been?" Dianne asked. I noticed a slight frosty tone to her voice.

"Shamrock and I went up to the Shillelagh for a beer," I lied. It wasn't that I didn't want to tell Dianne where I'd been, it was that something told me it might not be a good idea to get into this conversation with both of them here.

Dianne took a small sip of water. Her lips looked uncommonly thin. "Skye's been telling me some of what's been going on."

"Oh," I said warily.

Dianne leaned toward me a bit. "You didn't tell me that—"

I interrupted. "I hadn't had a chance to tell you yet." I knew Dianne wasn't too happy about Skye staying here with me, so I certainly didn't want to antagonize her more by her thinking I was telling things to Skye that I was keeping secret from her.

Skye hadn't said anything since she'd first greeted me. Even with the dope in her she looked a bit uncomfortable now. I didn't blame her. Though nothing had happened between us, I was uncomfortable, too. And for some reason, I felt a bit guilty.

"Skye and I have come to a decision," Dianne said. She looked at Skye and then back at me. "She's going to come stay with me."

I didn't take my eyes off Dianne until she looked at her water glass and took another sip. That's when I glanced at Skye. She shrugged, gave me a *what are you going to do* look.

I knew I had to tread gently with this one. I took another swig of beer. It didn't taste good. "Are you sure that's a good idea? This could be dangerous."

"No more dangerous than it is here," Dianne said. Her irritation—or was it anger?—was showing now. "No one will know Skye is staying with me. And *I've* got a gun."

She was talking about her pink-handled peashooter. But, gun or not, I really did believe Skye moving in with Dianne could be dangerous and I didn't like the idea. Dianne did though, and a quick glance at Skye told me the reason why. Skye was a stripper and a very good-looking one at that. I hadn't said anything about her looks when I'd told Dianne she was staying with me. I'd had a feeling that would have caused some problems, especially since Dianne knew how I was, or more accurately, how I'd been in the past. Now that feeling had been proven right. And Dianne looked adamant. Still, I had to try one more time to stop the proposed change in living arrangements.

"Can I talk to you in the kitchen for a minute?" I said to Dianne.

She didn't answer, just got up and walked from the room. I followed. Skye gave me a shrug as I walked by. In the kitchen Dianne started to speak. I held my finger to my lips. Skye could easily hear us from where she sat. I grabbed Dianne's hand, led her into the small bedroom that was the furthest away from the living room, and quietly closed the door.

"I don't think this is a good idea, Dianne." We were facing each other, standing only a foot apart. The two shades were up. Except for some light from neighboring cottages, the room was dark.

She raised her voice. "I don't care what you think. That woman's staying with me." She had her arms folded tight across her chest.

I knew Dianne well enough to know she meant business. I wasn't going to sweet talk her out of this. She picked her battles and I could clearly see she'd picked this one. I gave it one more shot.

"You know she's a junkie?"

"I *know* that. And she's a *pretty* junkie, too. I don't want her *or* her dope here with you." Then as if she'd realized she'd come off a little too distrustful, she added, "She'd be safer at my place anyway. No one will know she's there. And this cottage . . ." she looked around, "isn't the safest spot on the beach in the best of times."

"Yeah, but—" I began.

"But nothing, Dan. That's it. *She's* coming home with me."

And that was that. "All right. But you've got to be careful. Don't let anyone know she's with you. And if you see anyone or anything suspicious, you've got to promise you'll tell me right away."

"Who else would I tell? Now come on."

We paraded back to the living room. Skye apparently hadn't moved.

"It's all set," Dianne said to Skye. "Let's go."

"She's got to pack her bag," I said.

"She already did," Dianne said.

Skye uncurled those long legs from under her, stood up and walked to the middle bedroom, returning with her small suitcase.

"Do you need a ride?" I asked.

"No," Dianne answered. "My car's out front."

I hadn't noticed it.

"Thanks for everything, Dan," Skye said.

I hoped Dianne didn't take that wrong. Skye leaned into me and I gave her a peck on the cheek. Funny, I felt like I'd miss her. Underneath everything, she was a good person. I could tell. Skye opened the door, stepped out onto the porch. I tried to kiss Dianne as she passed me; she turned away.

When they were gone I had another beer, this one with an iced mug, and pondered what had just happened, along with everything that had come before it. As usual I was confused. Maybe it was for the best that Skye stayed with Dianne. My cottage was dangerous. Besides, Dianne knew me very well. Skye was super hot and I'd somehow resisted her come-on once. Would I have been able to resist twice? Maybe I'd been kidding myself that nothing was going to happen between Skye and myself. And the more I thought about it, the more I realized that it was even odds I had been. Kidding myself, that is.

Now I would never know. But that was a good thing. Wasn't it?

Chapter 28

THE NEXT MORNING at work things were just as I'd thought they would be. Dianne was as frosty as a January day on the beach, although I could tell that she was glad to have Skye out of my house if nothing else. We exchanged pleasantries. She'd defrost—eventually.

Eli and Paulie were their regular selves. Paulie entertaining; Eli irritating. I went through the motions for the entire shift. I couldn't get the threats from that phone call out of my mind. I wouldn't have given up all the tapes even if I'd had them. Which meant I had to decide what I was going to do if the thugs tried to follow through on their threats.

I'd been wracking my brain, trying to come up with some way to extricate myself and my friends from this predicament and coming up with nothing. Near the end of my shift I received another one of the rare calls I got at the Tide.

"Mr. Marlowe," the voice on the line said. "This is Walter Fishbain." The state rep who'd been filmed with his pants down.

"Yes?" I said, puzzled.

"I'm wondering if you could drop by. I'd like to talk to you for a minute."

I hesitated. I wondered if he somehow knew that I had the incriminating tape he'd "starred" in. I couldn't think of any other reason for the call. And I also couldn't come up with a single reason why there would be any danger in visiting him. He was a prominent businessman and politician, after all. Also, I had nowhere else to turn in my inquiries and he was as good as anyone to pump for information. Probably better. Besides, it would keep me moving. If I kept moving, even an amateur like me might stumble into a way out of this nightmare.

"Okay," I said. "I get out of work at five and then I'll have to take a short walk to get my car."

"Do you have a gun, Mr. Marlowe?"

"Yes. Why?"

He didn't answer that. Just spoke quickly, giving me an address over in town, and I told him I'd be there as soon as possible.

After my shift ended, I retrieved my car at the cottage. I also grabbed my .38. Why Walter Fishbain had asked if I had a gun, I had no idea. But now that he'd mentioned it, it seemed wise to bring that gun along. I headed to Fishbain's home. There was still a lot of daylight left, a beautiful daylight with clear skies but hot as hell. My clothes stuck to my body. I would have chopped off my right arm for better A/C in my car. But that would have to wait. Dough was short.

Walter Fishbain lived in a new development over in town. Very exclusive. In fact, one of the most expensive streets in Hampton for sure. The cul-de-sac was lined on both sides with McMansions, a little more than a half dozen, most with *For Sale* signs out front. All of them had similar facades, though none were totally alike. The lots were huge. The area was new enough that most of the trees were in the growing stage. I pulled into the driveway of Fishbain's abode and stopped before a three-car garage. On my right was a silver Jaguar sedan.

Before I got out of the car, I stuffed the gun in my rear waistband and pulled out my shirt to conceal it. I got out, walked up to the door. I gave the button a tickle. I could hear chimes play inside. I got no response, so I tried again. The Jag I'd parked beside told me someone was home.

Then a voice from inside said, "Come in."

I turned the doorknob. The door was unlocked. I pushed it open slowly, stepped inside. The shades were down. I stood there, trying to get accustomed to the lack of light, when someone to my side, near the door, said, "Marlowe."

I turned just in time to have a bright flash go off in my face. Between the dark, the flash, and the camera held in front of the photographer's face, I couldn't see who it was. And I didn't have time to try.

I heard a *whissh* behind me, and at the same instant, a thud like someone snapped a wet towel against a concrete block. Unfortunately, it wasn't a concrete block—it was the back of my head. And if it had been a wet towel that hit me, it must have been wrapped around a lead pipe.

Pain seared through my head, back to front, like I'd been shot with a small caliber gun and the slug was still bouncing around in my skull. A bright red curtain fell over my eyes and my legs buckled. I don't remember hitting the floor because by that time another curtain had fallen and this one was as black as the Devil's heart.

~ * ~

I HAVE NO idea how much time passed before I opened my eyes. I was in semi-darkness, sprawled out on the floor on my stomach. I moved nothing but my eyes. I hurt and

I was afraid I'd hurt more if I moved. I tried to remember what had happened. The picture flash, then someone had slugged me.

I couldn't stay on the floor forever, so I struggled to my feet. Believe me, it was harder to rise from that floor than to rise from the worst hangover I'd ever had. And that's saying something. I supported myself by grabbing the back of a chair in front of a roll-top desk.

I was in a study. In addition to the roll-top desk, there were expensive leather chairs that looked like you could easily fall asleep on them. There was a similar sofa. Probably worth more than my car. Again not saying much. The room itself was the size of my entire cottage.

I felt nauseous, as if I had food poisoning. I rubbed the back of my head and found an egg the size of . . . an egg. That's when I saw it—one foot, with a black sock and no shoe, sticking out from behind the sofa.

I forgot my head and stepped over so I could see behind the piece of furniture. It was a man's body. Brown slacks and a white short-sleeved dress shirt open at the throat. He was fat and on his back but I couldn't see his face. It was covered by a pillow. There was a large hole through the pillow with stuffing scattered about. Blood pooled around the pillow.

My heart beat like a trip hammer as I tried to put it all together. It didn't take me long and I didn't have to be a real detective to get the drift. The body was Walter Fishbain's. Just to make sure, I lifted the pillow, saw that it was indeed Fishbain, complete with an ugly bullet hole in his skull.

My stomach lurched. I didn't see the need to examine him further so I replaced the pillow. He was kaput. There was nothing I could do for him.

That's when I saw something else. Partially under the sofa. I leaned over, looked. It was a handgun. A .38. My hand went instinctively to my back waistband. My revolver wasn't there. I leaned closer to the gun on the floor. All the moisture was sucked right out of my mouth. There was a long deep gouge on the gun's handle—just like mine. I didn't think, I just picked up the gun. My hands shook as I examined it. One bullet was missing from the chamber. I could make a good guess where it was.

Whoever had done this was a mystery to me. But right about now that was the least of my worries.

It seemed I was the patsy for Fishbain's murder. That was a lot more important.

I could've stayed, should've stayed, but this frame was wrapped pretty tight. My gun near Walter Fishbain's body and my bullet in his head. And no one else here but me. Sure a bump on my head but the cops would peg that as a result of a struggle with Fishbain. And this *was* Hampton—Lieutenant Gant's stomping ground. I wouldn't stand a chance.

I needed time to clear my head. Think. So I did what they say you're never supposed to do in these situations—I left. Of course, the people who advise you to stick around never had anything like this happen to them. Believe me, it doesn't take much to convince yourself that you've got nothing to lose by beating feet. The worst that could happen was I'd be charged with murder, which I definitely would be if I hung around.

Just then I heard sirens. I had no doubt where they were headed. The final piece of the frame. I left quickly.

I was lucky leaving. Most, if not all, of the houses were still vacant. I didn't think anyone saw me coming or going. If they did, I didn't see them.

I'd barely driven out of Fishbain's street when two cruisers with sirens on and lights flashing passed me, going in the opposite direction. To Fishbain's, I was sure. I was shaking so badly I had to pull over for a couple of minutes on the way back to my place. I needed a Xanax, no two, and they were at my cottage. I drove with every muscle in my body held stiff and my hands white from squeezing the steering wheel.

Once inside the cottage, I washed two pills down with Heineken and debated what to do. It wasn't much of a debate. My thoughts were crazy and wild and I couldn't hang onto them for more than a few seconds at a time. Finally, the pills kicked in and my brain downshifted. I could examine a single thought now. And maybe follow any trail it offered. Where it would lead and how the hell I was going to get out of this lion's cage, I had no idea. But I had to keep trying.

Chapter 29

"DID YOU TAKE the gun, Danny?" Shamrock asked.

It was the next morning. Shamrock, Dianne, and I were seated in her office. Dianne was seated behind her desk. Shamrock and I perched on metal folding chairs. The door was shut tight. I'd just finished telling them about Walter Fishbain's murder and my gun at the scene.

"I did."

"Cut that out," Dianne said. She was looking at my leg. It was jiggling like crazy. I forced my leg to stop. "That was pretty stupid to leave," she continued. "Now they're going to think you did it for sure." Her green eyes were wide and she looked like she was a kid in a haunted house.

"Did you get rid of the gun?" Shamrock asked with a crack in his voice.

Dianne was all over him. "Shamrock! What are you saying? He's already incriminated himself enough by leaving the scene."

Shamrock wiggled around, blushed. "Sorry, Dianne. I just want to make sure he doesn't get pinched."

"Stop it!" Dianne shouted, then catching herself, she lowered her voice. "Dan hasn't done anything."

They were talking about me as if I weren't there. I suddenly felt very uncomfortable in the metal chair I was seated on. It might as well have been an electric chair the way I felt. I sighed. "He's right though, Dianne. I thought of getting rid of it. Maybe I still should."

Dianne almost came across her desk toward me. "Don't you dare! We'll go to Steve Moore. Tell him the story. You've done nothing wrong. You've got nothing to worry about." That's what she said, but she looked far from convinced. She slowly sat back in her swivel chair.

Shamrock and I glanced at each other. Dianne was a very positive, and, believe it or not, an old-fashioned type person in many ways. She believed in truth, justice, and the American Way. Shamrock and I—not so much. We'd been around more, seen more, and I was a very cynical person to begin with. I could already imagine the foreman of the jury standing before the court and pronouncing me guilty at my trial.

"I could toss it off the bridge," I said halfheartedly. "No one would know."

"If you do, I'll never speak to you again," Dianne said. Her eyes narrowed. Still I could see they were on fire.

Shamrock sputtered. "With your luck a fish'd swallow it and somebody fishin' off the bridge would catch it and he'd find the gun when he gutted it. Turn it in to the cops."

"Not funny, Shamrock," I said. I was frowning so hard I could feel the corners of my mouth drooping.

A light tapping sounded on the office door. "Come in," Dianne said.

The door opened. Ruthie stuck her red curly-haired head in. "Phone's for Dan," she said. She looked around, apparently felt the room's temperature, and retreated, closing the door.

I reached over, lifted the receiver of the phone plunked on Dianne's desk. "Hello," I said.

It was the *voice* again. My friend from the beach. I recognized it instantly. "You found our little surprise okay, *Mr. Marlowe?*"

"Yes." The trip hammer in my chest started up.

"Here's what you do. You got twenty-four hours to hand over the tapes. *All of 'em.* And you back off nosing around and forget every fuckin' thing you might have picked up on."

"I don't have any—" I started.

The voice interrupted me. "Clean out your ears, jackass. You got twenty-four hours. That's it. We've given you too many chances. If it weren't for the Old . . . we'd . . . well, never mind. Give us the tapes or we turn you in for the murder." He hesitated a few seconds. "On the other hand, maybe you won't have to worry about ending up in Concord. You and yours might be *dead.*"

He slammed the phone down on the other end. I returned the phone to the cradle.

Dianne stared at me with horror on her face. Maybe the person on the other end had been talking so loudly she'd heard him.

"Another threat," I said. "If threats were worth a buck, I'd be a rich man."

No one smiled, let alone laughed.

"I've got twenty-four hours to come up with the tapes or I'm going to have a murder rap hung on me," I said. Where were my Xanax when I needed them? Home of course. I chose not to tell the others what else the caller had threatened, hoping they hadn't heard it. At least not Dianne. I wasn't blind. I could see by her face she was plenty worried already.

"Maybe he's bluffing," Shamrock said. "They've threatened you before."

"That's for sure," I said, "but everything's escalating. And I think this guy's at the end of his rope. I don't think it's a bluff." I remembered the caller's unintentional reference to what I knew by now was the Old Man. That nickname again. It had to mean something.

"Mmm," Shamrock said. And maybe trying to cut the tension, he added, "No offense, Danny, but you've never been the best of poker players."

"You're right. But this isn't poker."

"What are *we* going to do then?" Shamrock asked.

I caught his emphasis on the word *we*. I wouldn't have expected anything else from my best friend. I decided in an instant to suck it up. I had to. I was more worried for Dianne and Shamrock than for myself. "We're going to have to find out who's behind this and quick."

"Oh, great," Dianne said, and I could detect a little catch between words.

I reached over, put my hand on the back of hers. "We don't have any choice, honey," I said.

"What about the police? Steve? Lieutenant Gant even?" she asked. But she said it without conviction. Even Dianne, who had a lot more faith in the system than I'd ever had, knew the cops couldn't take a crap in less than twenty-four hours, let alone begin and wrap up an investigation that, in this case, was on that short a time schedule.

"We can do it, Danny," Shamrock said, putting on a determined face. "I know we can."

"We don't have any choice," I said. "We have to."

Dianne looked at us like she was looking at two corpses in caskets. "Oh, Jesus," she said. "Here we go again."

Chapter 30

TOO BAD I'D already had my Cocaine Honeymoon. I had to move fast and I sure could have used the extra energy and insight the drug provided during that period in a user's journey. But I'd abused that option right off the table a long time ago. So I'd have to do it on caffeine alone. Beer and Xanax wouldn't help much, except maybe to knock me out at night for a few hours of sleep. And my schedule was so tight, a few hours of sleep was all I could hope for before the clock ran out.

I only had one lead as to who was behind this whole affair. And that was the two thugs. Big Man and Little Guy. Everything and everyone else I thought of were dead ends. So I decided to let the twenty-four-hour ultimatum expire. Sure, I was taking a big risk. Not just for me. For Dianne and Shamrock, too. But what other choice did I have?

The Old Man—if there really was such a person—had given me a timetable as to when I could expect some blow-back if I didn't act. And I couldn't act. It wasn't only that I didn't have the tapes they wanted. Not following their in-structions was the only way I might be able to flush them out on my terms and get to the bottom of this. Then I'd have a chance to clear my name, not only of involvement in the porn racket, but of murder too.

Which was why, close to forty hours after I'd received the threatening call at the Tide, I had myself stuffed into the closet in my bedroom. It was dark, after midnight. There was no door on the closet but it was on the far side, away from the doorway and the head of my bed. At this angle, anyone who came in the bedroom wouldn't be able to see me, especially if they had their eyes zeroed in on the bed. Also the door to the room opened inward, so if and when it was opened, it would offer me even more concealment.

My idea was that, when the thugs came—if they did— I'd be able to get the drop on them when they were turned, looking down at my bed. I'd covered some pillows on the bed to make it look like I was asleep under the blankets. The bedroom door was closed and the room was dark, but I'd left a table lamp on very low in the living room so when the bedroom door was opened there'd be just enough light shining to illuminate my visitors. After I stripped them of their weapons, I hoped to find out who they were taking orders from. I knew they wouldn't believe that I'd shoot them if they didn't talk, but they might believe I'd turn them into the cops if they didn't give me a name.

My .38 was at my side in my right hand. I'd considered using Betsy, my double-barreled shotgun, but considering the tiny size of the room, and how close I'd be to them, I was afraid they'd be tempted to make a grab for the gun's barrel. So I left Betsy in her usual lair under the bed—with both barrels loaded.

I could feel my palms sweating. I had drunk nothing. I had taken one Xanax pill around midnight just before I'd stepped into the closet. I was sure the thugs would wait until they thought I was asleep to make a move. At least that's what I hoped. So far I was right. But if they didn't come soon, it would all be for nothing.

Just then I heard it—a very light scrapping sound. So light I wouldn't have heard it, except my ears were like two raw nerve endings from straining to hear anything out of the ordinary. I couldn't make out what it was, or if it even was anything. I'd figured they'd probably come in the back door and I'd locked it along with the front. If I hadn't, they would have been suspicious. But the back door, unlike the dead-bolted front, only had a button lock on the doorknob, and the back was much more secluded than the front.

I tightened my grip on the revolver. The steel was clammy with my sweat. My ears felt like they were vibrating as I listened for any other sounds. I heard none. At least none that weren't the usual late night sounds of the summer beach—a motorcycle's roar somewhere up on the boulevard, the shouts and laughter of drunken kids a few streets over, the swoosh and muffled explosion of a bottle rocket being fired off somewhere down near the dunes.

A minute later, thinking the noise I'd heard was nothing, my slamming heart began to slow. That's when I heard the catch on the bedroom door snick. Whoever it was had turned the knob so quietly I hadn't picked up on it. My heart started its banging again as I brought the .38 up close to my stomach, pointing the gun in the door's direction. I would have given my left nut for the medicinal taste of another Xanax dissolving under my tongue. I fought to keep myself together until whoever it was had made it completely into the room.

A sliver of light from the living room became visible as the door crept open. The shaft of light widened across the bed as the door opened more. My breathing seemed to deepen. And it sounded loud to me. I hoped no one else could hear it. I could see more and more of the pillow dummy I'd formed under the blankets as the door slowly swung open. It stopped when it was a little more than halfway open.

That's when they stepped into view. They had their backs to me but I didn't need to see their faces to know who it was—Little Guy and Big Man. The tall one had come in first, his shorter partner beside and behind him just a bit. Big Man had what looked like an automatic pointed at the dummy on the bed. I couldn't see if his friend was armed.

"Marlowe. Marlowe!" Big Man shouted. "Get the fuck up."

The dummy didn't move. And I didn't give them any time to wonder why.

"Don't move," I growled. I was surprised at how steady my voice was. "Toss the guns on the bed."

It might've worked just like in the movies if there'd been only one person. But the short punk took a step sideways, then bolted into the living room. Probably heading for the back door.

"Shoot him!" Little Guy screamed as he ran.

If it hadn't been for Little Guy, I truly believe Big Man would have tossed his gun on the bed—unless he was suicidal, which I doubted he was. But with his friend making a screaming dash for it, he went on automatic pilot.

He spun in the semi-darkness and shot in my direction. I'd already crouched low, so the slugs from Big Man's gun slammed into the back of the closet behind me. I didn't give him time to get a bead on me now that he was facing my way. I let off one shot.

Big Man screamed as the slug tore into his upper torso and knocked him back a step. He stumbled from the room and headed for the back door after his partner.

I didn't chase them. I'd been caught off guard by the outcome of my trap and had made no plans to deal with a result like this. My hope of getting them to talk was kaput now. No sense chasing an armed man—possibly two armed men—between cottages in the dead of night, not if I didn't want to get shot too.

I spent more than a few minutes trying to pull myself together. By the time I saw the gumball lights of the first police cruiser splash across my blinds, my nerves had quieted down from a ten to maybe an eight or nine. I hadn't even had a chance to call the cops yet. My neighbors, who apparently heard the shots, had taken care of that. They were good that way.

Chapter 31

"MAYBE I OUGHT to rent one of your bedrooms, Marlowe. I'm down here often enough."

It was Lieutenant Gant of the Hampton Police talking. He stood in the middle of my living room looking down at me sitting in my easy chair, his iron grey hair combed straight back. On this visit he wore a navy sport coat with light blue shirt and no tie. A couple of uniformed cops mingled about. A plainclothes cop was in my bedroom closet digging the bullets out of the wall. Almost every light in the cottage was turned on.

"Now tell me again what happened?" Gant asked. He smirked as he added, "At least what *you* say happened."

The smirk and his sarcasm didn't bother me. I was still too shocked from the close quarters shootout for him to rile me much. Still, I wished Steve Moore would show up. I knew he'd keep things from getting too confrontational between Gant and myself.

Gant must have had mind reading abilities because he smiled slyly and said, "And your buddy isn't going to show up. I made sure of that. Now answer my question."

I swallowed, then said, "I already told you, Gant. I was sleeping and woke up when I heard someone coming in the back door. I grabbed my gun and jumped in the closet. They came in the bedroom. I saw a gun. I told him to drop it. He turned and fired. I shot him and they both ran out."

Gant rolled his eyes. "I don't believe you, Marlowe. And it's *Lieutenant* Gant."

"Why? Because it's me?"

"That's only part of it." Gant took a step forward and to the side. He glanced in the bedroom. "You must sleep with your bed all made up."

It wasn't a question. I didn't like Gant but I had to admit he knew his stuff. I'd been smart enough to remove the pillow dummy from my bed but also stupid enough to make the bed again. I almost told him how I'd arranged to get the drop on the two goons when they showed up. Instead I decided to remain with my previous decision to keep quiet about that part. I may have violated some laws by that action and also Gant would probably use the information to undermine my story even more than he was already trying to do.

"I threw myself down on the bed when I got home. I was exhausted." It sounded thin but it was all I had.

Gant let out a puff of air. "Drunk or drugged-up is probably more like it. *If* it's even true."

Now I was getting pissed. I was conscious of my teeth grinding. I wanted to tear him another asshole but what good would it have done? He already was a pretty big asshole, and besides, it would just get me in this jam deeper. If that was possible. So I held my tongue.

"And your two visitors," Gant said, again sarcastically, "were the same two men who gave you a beating on the beach? Or so you claim."

"It isn't a claim, *Gant*. It was them."

Gant's eyes narrowed as he looked down at me. He was just about to explode when a uniformed cop came in from the kitchen.

"Lieutenant?"

Gant slowly turned his head to look at his subordinate. "Whattaya want?" he said. At least I wasn't the only one on the beach he was short with.

The cop cleared his throat. He was young but not a summer cop. Not *that* young. "I followed the blood trail like you asked." The cop hesitated, looked from Gant to me and back again.

"Forget him," Gant said. "*And?*"

"The trail led between some cottages and up to River Ave. That was the end of it. Maybe they had a car stashed there."

"Good work," Gant said, without any sincerity in his voice. "Now see if you can help him." He nodded in the direction of my bedroom and the plainclothes cop who was still rummaging around in there.

Gant turned back to me. "Why would anyone want to come in here to kill you, Marlowe?" Before I could answer he held up his hand, palm out. "Hold it. Maybe I ought to get my notebook out. On the other hand, there probably aren't enough pages in it to list all the lowlifes and the reasons why they'd want to kill you."

I ignored the snide comments but I didn't ignore the question. "Because I'm close to finding out who's responsible for not only the porn on the beach but also the murders of Tom Early and his employee."

Gant lowered his voice. "I think *I* already know. I just have to prove it."

I could feel the perspiration under my arms and on my palms. "I didn't have anything to do with any of that. I can't believe even you would think I was involved in porn and murder!"

"We'll see, Marlowe, we'll see." Gant actually had a little smile on his face.

I would have paid plenty to be able to wipe that smile off his face and get away with it. Just as I was getting nicely into a little daydream where I was slapping Gant silly, the cop who'd followed the blood trail came back into the living room from the bedroom.

"Here you go, Lieutenant," he said. He was holding a plastic evidence bag in Gant's direction. Inside the bag was my .38 revolver. Gant took the bag.

I was in a bind. I knew the police had found Walter Fishbain's body. With the bullet from my gun lodged in his head. Gant would check out the ballistics on my gun against every shooting committed within fifty miles of Hampton Beach within the past few years. He was dying to nail me. And that gun might put me in prison for life as soon as the tests came back.

Gant would be ecstatic.

I, on other hand, wouldn't be.

I wasn't sure what to do. I could keep my mouth shut and hope for the best. Hope for some crazy foul-up in the ballistic tests or some other type of lucky lightning strike. But I wouldn't hold my breath. Or I could take a chance and tell

Gant about being at Fishbain's home, getting slugged, and waking up with a dead Fishbain. And hope he'd believe me. But there was as much chance he'd believe me as there was someone would give me the deed to the Casino as a birthday present.

I was already a suspect in a porn racket and two murders. In Gant's eyes, I was already guilty of all that. For a moment, I wondered if I really had anything to lose by telling Gant the truth?

My slamming heart reminded me that I did. Especially after the murderer of Early and his driver was exposed, which I was sure he would be eventually. And that *anything* was a lot to lose. It was my life.

Chapter 32

I WAS JUST about to speak when there was a clomping of feet on my porch steps and some angry voices outside the cottage door. It was only a few seconds before the door opened and a uniformed cop stuck his head in.

"It's his lawyer, Lieutenant," the cop said. "Okay to let him in?"

I'd almost forgotten that I'd called my attorney's beeper and received a call back before the first cruiser had arrived.

Gant made a noise deep in his throat. "No, it's not okay." Then he sighed. "But let him in anyway."

The cop had barely gotten out of the way before James Connolly, Esquire, barreled through the door. Stumbling in right behind him was Lonnie Ellison, rock star. They were both loaded—eyes wild, feverish looking, and wearing the same clothes I'd last seen them in. Behind them came a woman, maybe in her early twenties, who surprisingly looked as sober as the speaker at an AA meeting. Not that that was the first thing I noticed about her. The first thing was the set of boobs leading the way—they were big, firm, with the upper halves showing over the top of a sheer white tank top. She didn't wear a bra and she didn't need one. The breasts were enlargements and someone had done fine surgery. Oh, did I mention she was good-looking to boot? I pegged her as a dancer at Ogle, although I didn't remember seeing her there.

"Stop right there," Gant bellowed. "I said the lawyer. You two can step out." He glanced at Ellison and the girl. I noticed his eyes lingered on her. It was one thing I couldn't blame Gant for.

"Hold on, Lieutenant," Connolly said, his eyes blinking rapidly. "They're with me."

"All the more reason to throw them out," Gant said.

Ellison took a step and stood beside Connolly. Neither of them looked good.

"Do you know who I am?" Ellison said to Gant.

Gant smirked. "Yeah, someone I might run in for public intoxication. Is it drugs or booze, smart guy?"

Ellison actually raised his height an inch or so in a drunken way. "I'm Lonnie Ellison," he said.

I wouldn't have believed it if I hadn't see Gant's reaction with my own eyes. There was none. Or at least none that I'd expected. He stared at Ellison and actually swallowed. At the same time the detective who'd been digging slugs out of my closet wall showed up at the bedroom door. The two uniforms in the kitchen walked to the archway between the two rooms and peered in.

I'd already seen the awe Ellison had been treated with at the strip club, so I shouldn't have been surprised at this scene. But I was. Especially in regards to Gant. I'd always pegged him as the type of hard-ass cop who'd give the pope a tough grilling if it was ever necessary. On the other hand, Ellison had been a world-famous celebrity for a couple of decades now, not to mention he was the seacoast's most famous resident and maybe the wealthiest. Still, lots of people on the seacoast had only seen old newspaper pictures of him from fifteen or twenty years ago. I'd heard Ellison didn't like having his picture taken much anymore. And I could see why. He'd aged hard.

It took Gant a full minute to get being starstruck under control. I wouldn't have been surprised if Gant offered Ellison a seat and fluffed the cushions for him before he sat.

Instead, Gant jabbed a finger in the girl's direction. "Well, she's gotta go," he said firmly.

My heart sank. She was the only thing that had perked my mood up a bit.

The girl looked at Ellison.

He removed a set of keys from the pocket of his designer jeans and handed them to her. "It's okay, babe. We'll be right out."

She shook her long black hair, turned, and sashayed out the door. Everyone in the room, except Ellison, watched her go. Her ass was nice. I wondered if it had been rebuilt, too.

When she was gone, Connolly spoke up. "What's going on here with my client, Lieutenant?" His voice was off and his jaw muscles were twitching a mile a minute.

The detective and the two uniformed cops had returned to whatever they'd been doing before they came to see the rock star exhibit. Ellison's life must have been like being a statue at Madame Tussaud's Wax Museum. You know, that joint in London where they have all those wax mannequins of famous people. But I guess it was part of his job—putting up with the stares and the irritation. After all, he'd been paid well for it. That was for sure. And I'd seen many of the side benefits his fame gifted him. Still, I remembered that quote from George Harrison: "If you ever have a choice between fame and money, always take the money. Fame isn't what it's cracked up to be." I had a feeling George knew what he was talking about.

Gant had been smiling, looking in Ellison's direction, when Connolly had spoken to him. As Gant turned his gaze on Connolly, the lieutenant's smile flipped to a scowl. "We're conducting an investigation here, *counselor*." He spat out the last word. "There's been a shooting."

"Yeah, yeah," Connolly said, sniffling. "I already got all that from my client. Are you arresting him?"

"No," Gant said. Then he added ominously, "Not yet."

"And what do you mean by that?" Connolly asked, his jaw muscles still working overtime.

Gant held up the evidence bag in his hand, shook it a bit. My .38 was inside. "For one thing. I'm going to be looking into this more closely."

Connolly stopped the jaw isometrics and said, "What for? My client's the victim here, not the perpetrator."

"There's been other gun crimes on the seacoast I'd like to check this against."

"Such as?"

"Well . . ." Gant began, "there was a murder over in town the other day." Gant gave me a withering stare. "*Your* client was seen driving not too far away."

Connolly jumped on that. "My client *lives* in Hampton. Probably ten percent of the residents of Hampton could be accused of driving in that area at any given time. And what caliber was the gun?"

Gant scowled and didn't speak.

"Was it a .38, Lieutenant?" Connolly asked, sniffling and wiping his nose with the back of his forearm.

Gant continued to scowl and said nothing.

"No, I take it?" Connolly said.

Gant was fuming. He sputtered, "Like I said, there's . . . ahh . . . ahh . . . other crimes on the seacoast I'd like to have this gun checked against. See if it's been used in one of those."

"There'll be no fishing expeditions with my client," Connolly said.

I stopped listening. I was trying to understand what had just been revealed about the caliber of the gun that had killed Walter Fishbain. And the more I understood it, the better I felt. Like one of the boulders down at the jetty had just been lifted off my back. It had to mean I was off the hook. At least as far as that crime went. Apparently, my gun hadn't been used to kill Fishbain after all. That meant he'd probably been killed before I even got there, sometime after he was forced to make that call telling me to come up. Someone knew simply asking if I had a gun would plant the seed and tickle my paranoia just enough for me to bring my .38 along. Someone knew me well.

And what a setup it was. A setup that relied on me believing that my gun had been used in the murder. And I'd fallen for it—hook, line, and sinker. Maybe if I'd known more about firearms, I would've recognized that the head shot came from a different caliber gun. But I hadn't. *And* I hadn't been too anxious to inspect the wound closely. Not that it would have done any good. Sure, I could probably tell the difference between a .22 caliber wound and a wound from a Dirty Harry magnum but that was about it. Nevertheless, it was enough to know I was in the clear on this crime. At least as far as owning the murder weapon went.

Gant tried to drag even that out a bit more.

"What other guns do you own, Marlowe?" he said in his tough guy voice.

My attorney jumped in. "Don't answer that, Dan," he said.

I held my hand up to Connolly. "Don't worry, no problem."

And it wasn't. The only other gun I owned was Betsy, my double-barreled shotgun. And I did know that if Fishbain had been killed with a shotgun, he wouldn't have had much of a head left. Even though the wound I saw was ugly, most of his skull had been intact.

"Just my shotgun," I said. "Under the bed. Nothing else. And be careful. It's loaded."

Gant looked at me hard. "I'm not interested in shotguns."

"Come on," Lonnie Ellison said. "This is a real drag." He'd been standing off to the side, listening.

"Are you done here now, Lieutenant?" Connolly asked.

Gant called out to the two cops in the kitchen. "All set?" he asked when they stepped into the room.

The older cop spoke, "Done, Lieutenant. We—"

Gant interrupted. "Hold it for later."

The detective who'd been tossing my bedroom came in and joined us. He looked at Gant and shook his head. Gant dropped my .38, bag and all, on the chair beside me.

"All right, let's go," Gant said.

The three other cops trooped out the door. Gant started to follow them, then stopped, turned. "Are you driving, Connolly?"

My attorney smiled a strange crooked coke-smile. I didn't like it. "I've got my chauffeur waiting for me and she's as sober as a judge."

"Too bad," Gant said, putting on a wicked grin just before he turned and walked out of the cottage, slamming the door as he did.

"I wouldn't drive if I were you," I said. "He'll probably be waiting down at the corner."

"I've been around a little too long to expose myself to someone like Gant," Connolly said.

That was good thinking. But when he sniffled for the umpteenth time since he'd arrived, I wondered why he didn't apply that good judgment to all his questionable activities.

"Let's go," Ellison said. He was losing his patience with a side trip that had interrupted whatever the hell it had interrupted. "They're waiting for us."

"They?" I asked.

"Our chauffeur," Connolly said. "You saw her. And two other young ladies. And she's the plainest of the bunch. Want to join us?"

I didn't answer right away. I weighed the pluses and minuses in my head first. After all, this wasn't an invitation to go out for a beer. This was another invitation to a who-knew-how-many-days-long debauchery of cocaine, booze, and beautiful women who were probably all strippers and more. In the company of a famous wealthy rock star—who I'd heard say earlier the cost was all on him—and my attorney. And I *was* single, wasn't I? Well, technically, anyway. I wasn't married anymore. So those were all the pluses. At least that's how you could look at them, if you were so inclined.

On the negative side, there was only one thing. But it was a BIG thing. I'd be off the cocaine wagon before the chauffeur had driven the car down to Ocean Boulevard. And

I knew how that could end up. It always did. Except for the very beginning. My cocaine honeymoon. But like I've said, that was long past. Now, whether it was one day or a week, the experience wouldn't end pretty. And I could literally lose everything. I couldn't lie to myself about that. I shuddered, my body actually shaking.

"No, thanks," I said finally.

"Beep me if you need me again," Connolly said.

The two of them made a beeline for the door. As I was closing it behind them, I heard Ellison say, "Turn off your damn beeper." I couldn't blame him.

I took up residence in my easy chair. I felt good about refusing the wild ride with my attorney and the rock star. In a way. Still, what-might-have-beens occupied my thoughts for the next couple of hours. Even more than the gunfight. Even more than me almost being killed. Even more than me shooting a man who could be dead right now for all I knew. That's how strong a hold that stuff can have on you. A hold that lasts a long time. How long? I didn't know. I hadn't gotten there yet.

Chapter 33

I DRAGGED MYSELF to work the next morning, feeling little better than someone checking into rehab, and this after I'd refused the BIG temptation. Still, I was pleased that I had passed on the excursion with my attorney and the rock star. I wondered where they were right now. That was a thought that got my heart beating raggedly. I hoped they were all right and then pushed the rest of the unpleasant thoughts from my mind.

The first person I saw after entering the Tide was Dianne. She was at the speed table preparing baked haddock casseroles, one of our big lunch offerings. The smell of fish, butter, and cheese was strong and pleasant. Dianne glanced up at me.

"Can you meet me in my office?" I said, referring to a booth on the bar side of the restaurant.

She nodded, held up on one finger.

I walked out to the dining room, said hi to the two waitresses doing their lunch setups. At the bar, Shamrock was on a stool, reading the Boston Herald. I didn't let him get a word out, just said, "Can you join me in my office?"

He slid off his stool and I followed him to the back booth near the coffee station. He slid into the booth. I stopped to get a cup of coffee, glanced at him. He shook his head no. I sat on the bench across from him in the booth. He couldn't contain himself. He'd taken one look at me and knew I hadn't asked him for this powwow to discuss the tide tables.

"Jaysus, Danny. You don't look so hot." He had a butt going and was puffing nervously as he talked. "What happened?"

I let out a deep sigh. "Let's wait for Dianne."

Neither of us spoke. What would we have talked about? The weather? Shamrock smoked his cigarette and I sipped my coffee. We didn't have to wait more than a couple of minutes for Dianne to join us. She grabbed a coffee first, then slid in beside Shamrock. She looked good but tired. There were light shadows under her green eyes. Unusual for Dianne. But then I remembered she was hosting Skye at her condo and realized she looked pretty good, considering that and everything else that was going on.

Dianne looked from me to Shamrock and back again. "What now? Or should I ask?"

Shamrock licked his lower lip. "Danny's got something to tell us, Dianne."

Dianne rolled her eyes. "Oh great. Do I need a stiff drink for this first?"

I forced a smile. "You wouldn't take one even if I said yes."

Before I started my tale, I asked Dianne, "How's everything going with your houseguest?"

Dianne nodded slowly, arched her eyebrows. "Okay, but . . . ahh . . ."

"Ahh, what?" I asked.

"Well, she has gone out a couple of times."

"Nothing you can do about that."

"I know that, Dan, and I know where she goes when she goes out. She's a lot easier to live with when she comes back than before she leaves. Matter of fact, we're getting along pretty well and I kind of like her."

Dianne was right. I'd found that out myself. Skye was a lot more pleasant to be around after she'd had a taste. And her going out to cop whatever dope she was doing was a lot better than her supplier coming to Dianne's condo, even if Dianne wasn't there. Who knew what type of lowlife the dealer might be.

I told Dianne and Shamrock everything new and brought them both up to speed.

"For the love a god, Danny, you could've been killed!" Shamrock had a new butt in his mouth and was puffing like a locomotive.

"Yes, he could've," Dianne said. Her lips tightened until they almost disappeared. Her eyes narrowed to match.

They were both right, of course, and knowing that didn't help the anxiety coursing through my body.

"You have to bring this thing to an end, Danny," Shamrock said. "It's getting way too dangerous." He ground out his cigarette in an ashtray like he was quitting smoking forever. "'Course, I'll be glad to help you no matter what you have to do."

"Enabler," Dianne said, shooting knives at Shamrock with her eyes.

Shamrock shrugged. "If he's going to do it anyway, he needs me to watch his back."

Dianne turned her angry gaze on me. "I've been to this movie before, *Dan*. And you've been lucky so far. You can't be lucky forever. Remember, *you* have to be lucky every single time. These beach nothings you're involved with only have to be lucky once!"

She was right there, too. What could I say? "Dianne, this is blackmail and murder. And some of it's happening on Hampton Beach. Our beach. If I don't protect it, who will?"

"Dammit! Haven't you ever heard of the police? It's their goddamn job, not yours." She grabbed her cup, put it up to her lips too hard, and some dribbled down her chin. She wiped at her chin with her bare arm and slid from the booth.

"You're impossible," she said, storming away towards the kitchen.

Shamrock looked at me, shrugged. "She's just worried about you, Danny. And you know, you could have the police handle it."

"I'd either be dead or in prison by the time Gant cleaned it up. If he ever did." I picked up my coffee cup, finished the contents in one sloppy gulp.

Shamrock frowned. "Maybe you're wrong about that."

"Bullshit!" I almost shouted.

Shamrock's red eyebrows shot up. I could see in his face that he'd only been trying to ease my mind. It hadn't worked. I was on too tight a string. This whole situation was getting to me. Why shouldn't it? Murder, blackmail, fake kiddie porn. And there was one more thing—my kids, Jess and Davey. They were supposed to come and stay with me here at the beach for a week. That time was coming up soon and it was very important to me. I didn't see my kids much anymore. Not that I didn't want to; I wasn't allowed to. If this situation wasn't cleaned up by then, I certainly couldn't let them come to the cottage, putting them in danger. Who knew when I would be allowed to have them stay over again? I didn't want to have to find out.

I'd really ended up right in the middle of another sea-coast jam again, that was for sure. Not to mention a close call with a coke binge with my attorney and the rock star. Believe it or not, for someone like me, that was as disturbing as the capital crimes I was mixed up in. You see, my inner demons could defeat me as easily as a bullet if I wasn't careful. That was one of the few things I knew for a fact in this crazy life. And I had to remember it. Always.

"Sorry," I said.

Shamrock smiled. "No problem, Danny."

I was silent a minute before I spoke again. "I'm going to work."

I started to slide from the booth.

Shamrock's hand shot out and he touched the back of my hand. I glanced at his hand and then up to his face. He caught himself, pulled his hand from mine. He turned crimson, cleared his throat. Guys are funny that way. "You know you can count on me, Danny. I'm here for you."

"I know that, Shamrock."

And I really did. Shamrock's friendship was one of the few things in this life I could take to the bank. I smiled, slid from the booth, and headed for the bar, wondering what my next move would be.

Chapter 34

ELI HAD SOMEHOW already heard about the shooting down on the Island, as they called the area of the beach where I lived. He didn't know for sure it was me involved, but I could sense that he had his suspicions. I played dumb.

"And I heard the homeowner plugged one of 'em as they was gettin' away," Eli said. "Shot him good." He jiggled his Camel cigarette between nicotine-stained fingers as he spoke. Every so often he took a break from his spiel and took a few rapid puffs. Other regulars at the bar listened closely as did Paulie down near the picture window. Eli would glance at me occasionally with a grizzled, knowing look.

I tried to ignore him, tried to zone him out. The weather was good and still very hot, so there was a lot of both vehicle and pedestrian traffic outside on Ocean Boulevard to distract me from Eli. It worked a little, but not much.

Thankfully, Paulie and Eli finally finished their beer ration and punch-out time arrived. I was glad to see them go. Well, at least Eli. The rest of the day was uneventful. So far.

I left by the back door after my shift had mercifully ended, walked up to the corner of Ocean Boulevard, and banged a right in the direction of home. A large crowd, along with emergency vehicles, gathered farther down the strip in front of a competing watering hole.

For some reason my heart sped up. Why, I don't know. No way whatever was happening had anything to do with me. Or did it? I walked that way quickly, barely noticing the oppressive heat.

When I reached the opposite corner of the street that the side of the restaurant faced, I could see that the action wasn't in the restaurant but somewhere behind it. Police were trying to keep the crowd moving, trying to keep the congestion from building too much. There was a fire engine, ambulance, rescue truck, a couple of cruisers, and an unmarked car positioned in front of the restaurant and down along the side street toward the back of the building. Two officers were attempting to herd people onto Ocean Boulevard, bypassing the sidewalk in front of the building.

I bulled my way through the crowd and down the side street, hugging the building opposite the action. That's when I saw Steve Moore and he saw me. Our eyes caught each other's at the same time. He was across the street, near the rear corner of the restaurant. I took a few more steps to get a look around that corner and finally saw the big attraction—a green metal trash dumpster, just like the one we had behind the Tide. A few public safety people were standing around, most just talking.

Steve was standing beside another cop in plainclothes I didn't recognize. That man wore a short-sleeved shirt, tie, and had a gun on his right hip. Steve was decked out the same, minus the tie. Neither wore a sport coat. Who could blame them in this heat. Steve said something to the other cop. That cop glanced in my direction, nodded. Steve headed my way.

"What are you doing here, Dan?" he asked when he reached me.

"Coming from work. What's going on?"

Steve ran his hand across his forehead, made the beads of sweat that had been there disappear. "I heard about the trouble you had last night."

I didn't say anything. What was there to say? Steve probably already knew the whole story, or at least most of it. Gant's version anyway. And there wasn't much sense trying to set him straight in this crowd with whatever was going on.

Steve gave me a moment to say something. When I didn't, he said, "Take a walk over here with me, will you?" It wasn't really a question. He turned, squeezed between a couple of people, and headed back across the street the way he'd come. I followed.

When we'd both reached the cop I'd seen Steve standing with previously, Steve introduced us. "Dan, this is Sergeant Bill Walkowski." We shook hands.

"Dan Marlowe," I said.

Steve added, "Sergeant Walkowski's with Major Crimes. State Police."

Walkowski was probably in his mid-thirties with jet black hair in a Marine-type cut. Matter of fact, I would've bet he was an ex-Marine. He stood ramrod straight. I straightened up a bit myself. There was sweat rolling down my back. I wasn't sure if it was because of the humid weather or something else, even though I'd seen many sweat-stained shirts sticking to men's backs in the short time since I'd left the Tide.

"Inspector Moore told me about the incident at your home last night," Walkowski began. "Did you get a look at the two men involved?"

A sense of dread washed over me like a rising tide. "I know who they are." Then I quickly corrected myself. "Well, not *who* they are, but I've seen them before."

Walkowski put his hands on his hips. "That's good enough. Are you willing to take a peek for a possible ID?"

I felt like letting out a very big sigh. I didn't. Instead I just said, "Yes."

Walkowski looked at me like the Marine drill sergeant he might have been at one time. "It's not pretty. Steel yourself."

How the hell you *steel* yourself for what might be coming, I had no idea. Judging by my body's reactions, I certainly wasn't doing it instinctively. I swallowed hard and followed the state cop the few steps over to the dumpster. Steve walked beside me.

When I got close to it, I could see inside. Walkowski hadn't been exaggerating when he'd said it wasn't pretty. The dumpster was two-thirds full of green trash bags, each probably stuffed with restaurant refuse. On top of the trash bags were my friends—the two thugs, Big Man and Little Guy— both face-up. Whoever had dumped them had been considerate enough to put the smaller of the two on top. Still, I could see both of their faces clearly. Flies buzzed around both heads, seeming most interested in what looked like a small caliber gunshot wound in the side of Little Guy's head. One fly almost walked into the hole, then retreated. The buzzing of the flies grew louder as I looked. It seemed even hotter suddenly. I fought to keep my lunch down.

"Well?" Walkowski asked.

I nodded. "It's them," I answered, my voice cracking.

"That might be yours," Walkowski said. He reached over and pointed at a blood stain on the shirt in the left shoulder area of Big Man.

I said the first thing that came to mind. "Did I kill him?"

"Probably not," Walkowski said. "He's got a twin of *that* in the back of his head." He moved his hand to point at the fly attraction on the side of Little Guy's head. "Probably .22s. No exit wound. Bounced around in their skulls."

I caught a whiff of rotting garbage and something else. My stomach suddenly rolled like the sea and the taste of bile filled my mouth. I swallowed hard.

Walkowski continued. "The big one might have lost enough blood from your bullet to be out cold when he got the kiss-off though. If he was lucky. Anyway, the medical people'll tell us that when they're done."

I didn't want to be the first one to pull away from the scene but I was. And I didn't feel too bad about it. Walkowski and Steve were professionals; I wasn't. This little visual was going to stay with me a long time as it was. I didn't want to lengthen the coming unpleasantness. I moved back the few steps to where we'd been. Where I couldn't see or smell the dumpster's nauseating contents. After a few seconds, Steve and Walkowski joined me.

"Thanks," Walkowski said. "Shouldn't be hard to find out who they are. When did this incident at the cottage happen again?" Walkowski asked both of us.

I told him.

"At least now we have a good idea when they were dumped," he said. Then, as an afterthought, added, "I might like to talk to you myself, Mr. Marlowe. If you don't mind. Later."

I nodded. "Sure." I didn't feel like talking now anyway. My stomach was very queasy, like the time I ate bad mayonnaise.

"I'll see you later, Dan," Steve said.

"All right," I said, turning to go. I couldn't have picked a better time, unless maybe I'd left one minute sooner.

A black unmarked car with a flashing dashboard light came around the corner and drove slowly through a group of gawkers. It was Gant. He stopped his car just short of the dumpster and stepped out just as I walked by. He glared at me as I passed.

We both took a couple of steps in opposite directions and I could hear him saying, probably to Steve Moore, "What the hell is he . . ." before his voice disappeared because of distance and the crowd chatter.

Didn't matter though. I could imagine what Gant was saying to Steve *and* the state cop. Maybe Steve would set Walkowski straight when he got the chance. Then again, maybe not. Steve was walking a tightrope, having me for a good friend and being a Hampton cop. I couldn't expect him to speak up every time Gant or some beach busybody had something bad to say about me. He probably ran into that most every day. And besides, it was my own fault that there were all these negative rumors on the beach about me.

Right now though I was more concerned with keeping the contents of my stomach in place than what lies Gant might be telling. After what I'd just seen, keeping my stomach where it belonged wasn't easy. Still, I was oddly hungry. I hadn't had supper before I left the Tide. I'd had too much on my mind. Now I was glad I hadn't. It might have been a waste of good food. I wondered if I'd be able to hold down a few beers. If I couldn't, I'd have to figure a way out of this stone-cold sober. And maybe that wasn't such a bad thing. I couldn't have anything fogging my mind. And I couldn't waste time.

Because now I was certain the Old Man was real. And whoever the hell he was, he was tying up loose ends.

Chapter 35

I WAS BACK at my cottage, sitting in my easy chair, ruminating. The Old Man was real. I knew it now. But who was he? I still had no idea but even an amateur detective like myself could see that, whoever he was, he was smart and vicious. He was taking care of business—eliminating anyone who could put the finger on him in regards to the blackmail racket. First to go was Thomas Early, the porn distributor on the seacoast. I was sure now it wasn't his involvement in porn that had gotten him killed, but more likely that he was somehow privy to the identity of the Old Man and knew about his control of the shakedown scam. I wasn't sure though if he'd been killed because he had crossed the Old Man in some way, or if someone, like me maybe, was about to pick his brain and find out the identity of the Old Man. It didn't really matter. And Early's delivery boy? It was unlikely someone at that low level would have known the name of the Old Man. More than likely, the kid had just been in the wrong place at the wrong time.

Walter Fishbain? Maybe he'd been killed just to set me up but that was unlikely. More likely he had run afoul of the Old

Man in some way. Maybe stopped paying extortion money or maybe the Old Man knew that I'd found out about Fishbain and was worried that Fishbain might talk. I hoped that wasn't the reason. It would only be more baggage for my already overloaded conscience to deal with.

Next in the Old Man's hit parade were the two thugs, Big Man and Little Guy, both tossed dead in a dumpster like the trash they'd been. Probably right after the shootout at my cottage. Whoever had been waiting down on River Avenue for them, in what they'd probably thought was a getaway car, had most likely been instructed to take care of the two of them if their mission failed. The Old Man wouldn't have wanted a gunshot victim like the Big Man taken to a hospital where he might've been persuaded by detectives to talk. And whoever had actually shot the two on the Old Man's orders hadn't even taken the time to drive more than a few blocks up the strip before he'd killed them and dumped the carcasses. Fast and efficient. A pro for sure.

But I wasn't interested in the pro, other than maybe leading me to the Old Man. There were plenty of pros in the hit man business. Whether the hit man was connected to Whitey Bulger's Winter Hill Gang, the Italian Boston North End Mob, or one of the many qualified independents around the New England area, he could be easily replaced. It was the Old Man I wanted to unmask. Before he checked off another name on his list.

These were the thoughts that were running through my mind when the telephone rang. It was Skye.

"Dan, can you come up here?" Her voice seemed a little anxious, but that didn't overly concern me.

"Everything okay?" I asked.

"Yes, everything's okay."

I felt a bit wary but I said, "I'll be right over."

She jumped on that. "Not now. In an hour."

It would take her that long to go out, cop, get back, and take care of business. I felt less hesitant; all was normal. "I'll see you at Dianne's in an hour."

We both signed off. I puttered around the cottage doing much of nothing. The hands of the ship clock on the wall seemed slow, like the power company might have cut the amount of juice sent to the beach, as they did occasionally during heat waves like we were experiencing now. Finally, the clock got within range of the time I was waiting for.

I left, drove up my street and onto Ocean Boulevard. I squeezed my green Chevette into bumper-to-bumper traffic. The cars inched along so slowly a beach crab could've beaten me to Dianne's. The sidewalks were packed. It was well after supper time, still light out, and still hot as hell. I had the Chevette's A/C on full blast. It barely made the car bearable. How much of my distress was caused by the brutal weather and how much by my anxiety, which was gearing up again, I didn't know. I was sure both played a part.

I inched past Buc, the thirty-foot pirate who guarded the miniature golf course, but didn't get much farther. Ocean Boulevard was down to one lane and I instantly realized why. The authorities were still cleaning up the mess at the dumpster. I'd almost forgotten about it. I had plenty of time to remember as I inched along. It looked like the police were directing traffic to the far lane away from the front of the restaurant and the official vehicles parked there. I kept my gaze mostly to my right, towards the Ocean. I didn't want to get another glimpse of the crime scene. I'd seen enough.

Finally, after what seemed like an all-nighter, I was waved through the one-lane bottleneck in front of the restaurant by a rookie cop. I suddenly broke free from the traffic. Well, for twenty feet anyway, then got stalled again in standard Ocean Boulevard double-lane traffic. I was stuck in the jam right up to the Casino. Such was summer traffic on Hampton Beach. I finally broke free again after I passed the two-block long Casino building. From there I made the rest of the trip to Dianne's condo in jig time.

I got lucky, at least as far as parking was concerned. Someone was just pulling out of a metered spot. I grabbed it, fed the meter, jumped the knee-high guardrail, and dashed across the street.

A resident was just entering the building and I went in with him. I made my way to the second floor and knocked on Dianne's door. When there was no response, I tried beating the door a little harder. Still nothing. I tried the knob. Locked. I removed a ring of almost twenty keys from my pocket. I couldn't remember what half the keys unlocked but I was still hesitant to throw them out. I used the appropriate key and let myself in.

I caught a very light whiff of an unpleasant odor the minute I stepped in and closed the door behind me. "Skye?" I called.

No answer. I was in the living room, near the door. I was leery about moving through the various rooms. Glancing to my right, I saw that an armchair had been turned around so it faced toward the sliding glass doors of the balcony and the ocean beyond. The drapes were open wide and I could see the back of Skye's head. She was seated in the chair and if I hadn't suddenly had three or four symptoms of a pending anxiety attack and a queasy stomach, I would've assumed that Skye was enjoying the nice view in the pleasantly air conditioned condo. But my subconscious knew better.

I stepped over to the chair and as I walked around to the front of it, I said, softly, "Skye?"

When I saw the color of her face, I realized Skye was never going to answer anyone again. She was dead.

I took it all in at once. She was barefoot, dressed in cut-off jeans and a loose-fitting red blouse, her head tilted to one side. The spike was still in her arm. A short tan piece of rubber tubing was trapped between that arm, her side, and the arm of the chair. I didn't buy the "accidental" overdose for even a second. Skye's jean shorts were unbuttoned and the pockets look disturbed. But not so disturbed, I realized, that the police wouldn't rule the cause of death as "accidental." Still, with what I saw and with what I knew was going on with the Old Man, I doubted this death was self-induced.

Skye had been given a hot-shot. No doubt in my mind. Her pockets had been searched and probably the spare bedroom she was using, too. I went to check the bedroom out. A couple of things I picked up on looked out of place, like a couple of empty drawers left open, ones that Sky obviously hadn't been using. Dianne never would have left empty drawers open. Of course none of it would be enough to convince a cop this wasn't a death by misadventure. But like I said, it was plenty enough for me.

I was sure that Skye had called me here to give me some information about the identity of the Old Man. That seemed to be why everybody on the beach was dying. She might have even found out who he was, although that was unlikely. More likely she was either going to direct me toward someone who might know the name of the Old Man or give me a tip that would at least head me in that direction. Unfortunately, someone had found out about her meeting with me and had struck before I arrived. On the other hand, maybe said person hadn't known about our meeting. Maybe Skye was just another loose end the Old Man was tying up. The timing of the crime might have been luck on the killer's part, nothing more than coincidence.

Whatever, it was apparent the Old Man or one of his underlings had killed again. Another name had been checked off his list. What by now had to be a very short list, and growing shorter by the day.

I took a last look at Skye's face. I'd grown to like her. Underneath the stripper/junkie facade I'd seen a good person. Maybe because, through my own experiences, I knew the drug problem Skye had could happen to anyone. I also knew that the only difference between Skye and folks who were clean was that they hadn't tried the one substance, whatever it might be, that had their name on it. Most of them never would. Skye had.

I blinked hard, went to the phone. I couldn't just walk away from this death like I had with Walter Fishbain's. This was Dianne's place after all. I'd have to stay and face any unpleasantness that came from the cops, namely Lieutenant Gant. I called Dianne at the High Tide. The police would be next.

When Dianne finally came on the line, I said, "It's me. You'll have to come home."

She started to say something about the restaurant being busy. I interrupted her. "You'll have to come anyway. It's bad. Very bad." She didn't question me; I think she knew. She said she was on her way and hung up.

I called the police, gave the dispatcher the basics. Then sat in a chair out in the kitchen nook, far from the corpse. I didn't look at Skye again. I couldn't. I'd seen enough dead bodies recently to last me a lifetime. I hoped I wouldn't see any more. But I knew there was no guarantee. Not where the Old Man was concerned.

Chapter 36

ACCIDENTAL OVERDOSE. THAT'S what they chalked Skye's death up to. Just one more dead junkie on Hampton Beach.

I tried to convince the cops otherwise, but they didn't buy it. What did I really have as proof? A couple of pockets on Skye's jean shorts that looked like they could have been searched. The cops thought she could have done that herself. And the couple of things out of place in her bedroom, like the open empty drawers? The cops saw it as nothing more than my wild imagination. Even Dianne couldn't swear that Skye's room had been tossed.

So there we were: Dianne; Shamrock, who had driven up with her after she got my call at the Tide; and me. We were seated in Dianne's living room. Dianne and I were on the couch. Shamrock was across from us in a beige barrel chair. The chair Skye had died on was where it had been, facing the sliding glass doors with its back to us. The police had just left.

"She was such a nice lass," Shamrock said. "And such a terrible way to go . . . the dope. And by her own hand."

My eyes zeroed in on Shamrock. "You heard what I told the cops. She didn't kill herself."

"Aye, Danny, I heard you. But you can't be sure, she—"

I cut him off. "Was a junkie—but I'm still sure!"

Dianne ran her hand roughly across the top of her head. "Oh stop it! Both of you. The poor girl's dead. Does it really matter how she died?"

I should have let it lie there. But how the hell could I when I *knew* what had happened? "Yes, it does," I said. "Because I'm sure the Old Man was behind it and he's probably going to kill again to cover his tracks. We have to find out who he is and stop him. Fast."

"The Old Man, the Old Man, the Old Man." The words came from Dianne's mouth wrapped in sarcasm. "Do you know how ridiculous you sound? And that's to me. To the police it makes you sound like some kind of conspiracy nut."

Yes, I'd told the police all about my suspicions about a criminal known as the Old Man. A couple of them had looked at me like I was under the influence of a full moon. Gant had snickered. I sat up, put my hands on my knees, and looked at Dianne. "It's true though. And you know it."

Dianne's green eyes flashed. "I don't know it, Dan. I was agreeing with you before because I trust your judgment. Well, I did until . . ." Her voice trailed off.

I could feel the corners of my mouth drooping. I turned to Shamrock. "You believe me, right?"

"Well, Danny, I—"

Dianne cut him off. "For god's sake, Dan, don't put him on the spot again. He'd go along with you if you said the sand on the beach was on fire."

I didn't know what to say. No one else did either. If Dianne and Shamrock had doubts about my theory as to what was going on, I was in big trouble. I'd never have any luck convincing the police who was behind all this if I couldn't get my best friend and my girlfriend to agree with me.

And now a little doubt started to trickle into my own mind. What if I was wrong about everything?

What if Skye's death *had* been just an accidental overdose? It *was* possible. It *could* have been coincidence that she'd called me prior to getting off. Maybe so she'd feel straight talking to me?

And Thomas Early, the porn distributor, and his delivery boy? Well, maybe that was someone trying to move in on Early's action. Or maybe one of the Boston gangs wanted tribute and he didn't pay up. That *was* possible too, wasn't it? I read the papers. Things like that happened all the time.

And what about Walter Fishbain, the illustrious state rep? Christ, a guy who'd been in politics and business as long as he'd been could have had plenty of enemies. The person who set me up as his murderer could have been someone local who knew my reputation from years back and decided to take advantage of it by pinning the murder on me. So it didn't necessarily have to be some omnipotent blackmailer and master criminal known as The Old Man who was responsible for Fishbain's death either.

But why make me believe I'd murdered Fishbain when whoever was behind the murder must have known I'd find out sooner or later it hadn't been my gun that killed him?

To get me to stop my pursuit of the Old Man—for a while anyway? Maybe, maybe not.

And the two thugs, Big Man and Little Guy, who'd ended up in the dumpster with slugs in their respective heads? They could've easily been muscle for one of the Beantown criminal organizations I'd thought about earlier. Maybe they used the term "Old Man" just to throw me off the track. If they had, it had certainly worked. I was down a rabbit hole looking for a ghost. And apparently I was the only person on Hampton Beach who believed in ghosts.

And what about the blackmail of Lonnie Ellison, Walter Fishbain, and probably others on the seacoast? Anybody could be involved in something sleazy like that. It didn't take a Mr. Big in the background to pull the strings to make something like that work. I could do it, if I was so inclined.

I wasn't, of course, just as I wasn't inclined to give up my pursuit of this so-called Old Man. The person everyone said was just a figment of my imagination. I wasn't going to drop my inquiries because I *knew* he existed. I don't know how I knew he was real. I just knew. And if I had to go it alone, I would.

"I believe you, Danny," Shamrock said. "And I'll have your back well guarded. You can count on that." He nodded hard once.

"Ohhh," Dianne said, exhaling in a long sigh. Rubbing her hands together, she said, "I wish you'd just drop the whole thing."

"I can't," was all I said.

"That doesn't surprise me." She slowly shook her head. "I guess I'll have to be here to pick up the pieces then. Again."

I smiled.

Dianne jumped on my smile. "That doesn't mean I believe in this bogeyman you're chasing. I don't. You've been watching too many of those old noir movies. They put dumb ideas in your head." She hesitated. "But you are mixed up with some very bad people, and I don't want anything to happen to you . . . so I'll help if I can."

I hoped that wouldn't be necessary. Still, it meant everything to me that Dianne supported me. My confidence had been badly shaken. With the stress of dealing with one or more killers on the beach, my usual anxiety level had increased enough that Dianne's not believing in me might send me over the edge.

Over the edge meant crawling away to that little drug den off Ashworth Avenue. The one I used to almost live in not that very long ago.

Dianne and Shamrock were my handles. What I held onto to keep from falling apart. Not just in situations like I found myself in now, but in my life in general.

"Thanks," I said to both of them and I meant it. I stood. "I've got to get going."

Shamrock jumped up. "Drop me at my place, Danny?"

"Sure," I said. "Dianne, what are you going to do?"

"I'm going to go down to the Tide in a bit and close."

I heard a catch in her voice and noticed her eyes were filling up. I should have gone to her; for some reason I didn't.

Shamrock and I headed for the door. Dianne stopped us cold. "Wait a second," she said. "Can you two take that chair?"

She was pointing at the chair Skye had died in. I couldn't blame her for wanting to dump it. Before I could move, Shamrock was on it. It didn't weigh that much and he lugged it out without help. I held the doors. We had a hell of a time getting it in my small car but we finally did.

"I'll take it to my house, Danny. Bring it to the dump later."

On the drive, Shamrock chattered away about Skye's death. At least that's what I guess he was talking about. I wasn't listening. I was thinking. First about Skye. I had warm feelings about her that I hadn't realized I'd had. I pushed them from my mind and started thinking about the Old Man. I was going to pursue him further. But would it end up being worth it? I had no way to know.

Chapter 37

THE NEXT MORNING the phone woke me up. I stumbled out to the living room, answered it. The voice on the other end mumbled something.

"What? Who is this?" I asked.

"James. James Connolly." This time I got it. He didn't sound good.

"What's up?" I said warily.

"I got myself into a little jackpot, Dan. I need someone to bail me out."

That woke me right up. "Where are you?"

"The Hampton Police station." His speech was very thick. "They won't let us bail ourselves out."

"I'll be right there."

Before I could hang up the phone, Connolly said, "Bring enough money for my friend too."

I knew who he meant. "All right," I said.

I hung up, dashed back to the bedroom, threw on some clothes. Then I looked at the cash in my wallet. Not much. I had a credit card. I wondered if they accepted Visa for bail.

I ran to the bathroom, did some business, and made myself look human. Before I left, I grabbed a blank check.

On the short drive to the cop station, I thought about what kind of a jam my attorney could have gotten himself into. Christ, it could be anything! He'd been on a week-long toot, after all. With Lonnie Ellison, rock star. That meant an endless supply of money, coke, and women and probably no more than a couple of hours sleep here and there, if that. I knew the drill well. My heart sped up. Christ, I'd almost gone with them! Twice. I couldn't kid myself that I hadn't been badly tempted.

Then I had another unpleasant thought—what if I got them out of jail and they weren't done with their depraved run? What if they asked me again to come along? With all the added stress since their first two invitations, I wasn't sure I could refuse another time. The closer I got to my destination, the more I doubted I'd say no. But I had to. I just had to. If I didn't, everything would fall apart. If that happened, exposing some Old Man who ran the rackets on the seacoast would be the least of my worries.

The rest of the drive to the station house was like a vicious fistfight between my dueling personality traits. On one hand, my good side was trying to knock out its competition, battering away at it by telling me I might lose everything if I gave into temptation. On the other side, hammering away just as hard, was my bad side—or to put it more kindly to me, my animal instincts—jabbering away about the delights a once-in-a-lifetime escapade with a rock star and his coked-up female entourage could bring. If it had just been the women, my good side would have won hands down. But it wasn't. Cocaine was in the mix. And that was Big. Real Big.

Anyone who doesn't believe cocaine could be harder to refuse than beautiful women, hasn't experienced what I've been through.

By the time I reached the police station, my inner battle had reached a boiling point and the arguments were about as logical as a political debate in a lunatic asylum. Mercifully, just as I passed the front door into the station, someone called my name.

It was Steve Moore. He was a little way down the hall, standing in the door of his office.

I went up to him. My heart was pounding in my chest.

He nodded to the interior of his office. "Can I talk to you for a minute?"

"I've . . . got to bail someone out." My breathing was labored. It felt like I was almost panting. I hoped Steve didn't notice.

"I know. But they're already gone."

"Gone?" I said, as if Steve had just told me the sand on the beach was missing.

"That's right," he said, nodding.

My breathing moderated and my heart rate stabilized. It happened that fast. Because the possibility of joining my attorney and the rock star in their debauchery had ceased to exist, so did the inner battle in my brain. I felt a little disappointed but relieved and definitely drained as I followed Steve into the office. He closed the door and took a seat behind the beat-up desk. I sat in one of the two chairs facing him.

Steve leaned back in his swivel chair, studied me. "Yeah, the chief decided to let them go on personal recognizance. He didn't want all the out-of-town press showing up and disrupting the place. Besides it wasn't too serious a charge anyway."

I had to know. "What did they do?"

"They were caught inside the Crooked Shillelagh around 4:00 a.m."

"What the hell were they doing in there? The Shillelagh closes at one o'clock."

"What weren't they doing is more like it. The report says Ellison and Connolly were holding court in the place when the first cruiser arrived. There were a dozen people in the joint. Except for them, it was all women. A couple of the women had the kitchen going full bore and were preparing what looked like an early breakfast buffet."

I must have smiled because Steve scowled at me. "It's not funny, Dan."

Oh yes, it was. As a matter of fact, it was so humorous the smile on my face grew until it stretched my skin and started to hurt. Better still, I felt good. My inner struggle, the battle I'd experienced just minutes earlier, was a thing of the past.

I forced the corners of my lips down as Steve continued. "Most of the women were strippers. And two of them were playing bartender behind the bar, serving drinks. They even offered the first cops on the scene free drinks. And they were topless!"

The smile was back on my face, bigger than ever. I couldn't help myself. "Who were, the cops?"

Steve frowned. Still, I could see a little sparkle in his eyes. "You know who, smart ass. Anyway, the place was like Uncle Billy's Smokehouse and we're not talking cigarette smoke either. And there was coke too."

"So you got Connolly and Ellison on drug charges?" I asked.

Steve shook his head. "Nah. Neither of them had anything on them. It was all on the girls, and even though I'm sure it was Ellison's stuff, none of the girls wanted to talk. Especially after Ellison said he'd bail them all out, pay for their lawyers and any fines *and* they could continue with the party." Steve hesitated, then said lamely, "So your two friends only got a Disturbing the Peace charge."

"No Breaking and Entering?"

"No. Apparently, Ellison dazzled the owner earlier in the night and had his permission to be there. When the owner locked the front door and left, probably with a baggie of Ellison's blow, only Ellison and the lawyer were there. The owner claims he didn't know Ellison was going to invite his entourage over as soon as he left. I believe that. He's in a little trouble with the town himself now."

Suddenly there was the sound of numerous feet and laughter outside the door in the hallway. "What's that?" I said. "Reporters?"

Steve put his hands behind his head, leaned back in the chair, chuckled. "Nope. Too late for them with the rock star gone. But the girls aren't gone yet. It's probably some of the patrol guys making a pit stop. People been tramping past here for the past couple of hours. It isn't often we get almost a dozen strippers in our cells."

"A dozen?" I said.

"Want to take a look?" Steve said, smirking.

"No, I think I'll pass." Maybe cops could justify gawking at people in cages. I couldn't. Although under these circumstances, at least with the younger cops, I could understand it.

For all I knew, there could be a few dates made in those cells and love might bloom.

Damn, I felt good for a change. A lot better than when I'd walked through the front door. At first, I wasn't sure why that was so. Then it dawned on me that this little sideshow had gotten my mind off what was probably the most troubling situation I'd ever been in. And right behind that realization was another: this little escape wouldn't last more than a few more minutes. Then I would be back traveling a road lined with crime and murder and danger. A road only I had a chance to maneuver along safely, hopefully getting us all to the end in one piece. And I had to do it—now.

Chapter 38

AFTER I LEFT the station I had a shift to do at the High Tide. I made a stop back at the cottage first, collected a few things I'd missed in my haste to bail out my attorney and the rock star. When I did get to the Tide, all was as it should have been. I set up the bar, then did a lot of nothing, worrying about how I was going to wrap up the dangerous predicament that I was now deeply involved in.

I was actually happy when eleven o'clock rolled around and I opened the door. In trooped Eli and Paulie. At least I'd have a distraction from the problem running around in my mind, a problem that was driving me crazy because it was more frustrating than a defective Rubik's Cube.

Eli didn't disappoint me. He'd barely swallowed his first sip of draft beer and wiped his lips with the sleeve of his dirty white painter's shirt when he said, "I ain't sure I'll be comin' up here anymore."

Believe it or not, that was a pretty shocking statement. Eli, who'd been coming to the Tide almost every day since the business had opened—at the same time, to the same stool, drinking the same beer—was as unlikely to not show up as precipitation during a nor'easter. The bar was a big part of his life. Maybe the only real part. He had no family and his only friends were here. I knew that, even with his sour attitude toward life, the people here at the Tide were that life, his only life. Kind of sad, but better than no life at all. I knew other people like Eli without a place to go where they felt comfortable. They usually stayed in their dingy quarters, wherever that happened to be, and drank themselves to death. I didn't want to see that happen to Eli. I considered him a friend and almost like family, too. Even family could be annoying.

Eli stared down at his beer as I took a quick glance in Paulie's direction. Paulie shook his head, long hair waving, and frowned, a look that told me not to take Eli's statement seriously. Apparently, whatever was bothering Eli, he and Paulie had already discussed it. I watched Paulie for a few more seconds. A grin came across his face before he took another puff of his cigarette and let out a quick column of perfect smoke rings in the direction of the ceiling.

I said, turning back to Eli, "What's the matter?"

"You wanna know what's the matter?" He adjusted his stained painter's cap. "I come up here to relax, goddammit. And I can't no more." He screwed up his gray-stubbled face, arched those wild gray eyebrows, and gave me a hard stare.

I had a good idea what was coming. I could've reassured him right then that he was safe at the Tide, but instead I decided to let him run with it and get it off his chest.

When Eli realized I wasn't going to say anything, he continued. "Dead bodies in the freakin' dumpster." He pointed backward over his shoulder toward the dining area. "Only a couple a streets down. *And* shot in the head to boot."

I wasn't sure what to say. It was bizarre for Hampton Beach, that was for sure. I gave it a bit, trying to dream up a cockeyed theory on why Eli shouldn't worry about a couple of bodies being found in a dumpster a stone's throw from where he was trying to have a relaxing morning beer.

I opened my mouth but Eli raised his hand, waving it furiously. That shut me up and made Paulie down at the end of the bar snicker.

"I know what you're gonna say," Eli sputtered, "and I don't blame ya. Ya work here on the beach and don't want the customers scared away, do ya?"

I jumped in. "There's nothing to be worried about, Eli. They say that was just some mob hit or something that just happened to take place on the beach."

I should have known Eli would be all over that. If Shamrock was the number one man as far as knowing what was going on in Hampton Beach—and he was—Eli ran a close second. He knew how many times everyone flushed their toilet on the beach.

Eli looked at me through watery eyes and nodded. "And you'd know about that, too, wouldn't ya?"

Paulie cleared his throat. I could've asked Eli what he meant by that comment but I already knew. He'd picked up on some scuttlebutt about my involvement with the two dead thugs. How much, I didn't know, and I really didn't want to find out. Besides I had to tread carefully if I didn't want my name bandied about this bar and outside on the streets any more than it apparently had already been. So I didn't answer.

When he saw I wasn't going to respond again, Eli said, "Well, I just don't feel safe coming here no more. I ain't heard about nothin' like that happenin' since they found those guys on the chaise lounges. Remember that?"

I did. A few summers back two young men had been seen lying on chaise lounges out in front of an Ashworth Avenue motel on a sunny morning, apparently either watching the heavy traffic pass by or taking a snooze. Hours later, after hundreds of cars had driven by only feet away, someone on foot checked on them and found both young men dead. They had died sometime during the night before from drug overdoses. Not something you'd put in a tourist brochure, of course. But on the other hand, not on the same level as two bodies tossed in a dumpster with their heads ventilated, either.

"That was just an OD," Paulie said.

"That's right," Eli said firmly. "Nothin' compared to this." He held up his empty pilsner glass, wiggled it. I got a fresh glass from the ice in the sink and poured him another with a beautiful small foamy head.

Eli was taking his first sip of the new beer and I was wondering how I was going to extricate myself from this potentially incriminating conversation, when a waitress stuck her head around the partition that divided the bar area from the dining room.

"Dan, telephone," she said.

I hadn't heard it ring. At least not consciously. The phone rang off and on all day. The only time it registered with my brain was after the fourth or fifth ring, when it appeared everyone in the kitchen and dining room was too busy to answer it. Then I'd pick up the bar phone.

Whoever it might be, it would be enough of an interruption to derail Eli's conversation for another minute or two.

And that would be a good thing. Still, considering the type of phone calls I'd been getting lately, I was leery. I walked to the back end of the bar, reached under it, and grabbed the phone.

"Hello?" I said.

"Mr. Marlowe?"

Don't ask me how I knew, but somehow those two spoken words were all it took for me to know who was on the other end of the phone. The Old Man. I knew it as well as I knew I was Dan Marlowe.

"Yes," I said.

"Mr. Marlowe," the Old Man said, "it's nice to hear your voice. I've heard a lot about you."

It was a very smooth, educated voice and it didn't sound *old*; on the other hand, I couldn't really put an age to it.

I didn't know what to say and I didn't want to say the wrong thing. What if he hung up and I never heard from him again? What then? I didn't want to chance it. My mind was drawing a blank, so I said nothing.

The Old Man waited a few long seconds and when I didn't speak, he said, "I see you're not a man that goes in for idle chitchat." He chuckled. "I could've guessed that. So let's get right down to business. I want you to drop these foolish inquiries you've been making."

I got one word out, "I—" before the Old Man cut me off.

"I wasn't through, Mr. Marlowe," he said in a harsher tone. Then, returning to his more syrupy speech, he went on. "You're quite an impatient fellow, aren't you? Of course, I should be well aware of that. But put that aside. I'm willing to offer you something in return for your stepping back from your latest quest. Certain movie tapes being sold in your area have caused you problems. I can make that all go away. Those tapes won't be available on your precious Hampton Beach anymore. *And* I'll make certain that the proper authorities are informed that you had nothing to do with the business. How does that sound, Mr. Marlowe?"

It sounded good. At least the half about the porn being off the beach and my name being expunged from being involved. The other half, me giving up my search to find out who the Old Man was, not so much. I was involved too deeply and too many people—people who mattered to me—believed I was crazy, chasing a ghost. I wanted to redeem myself in their eyes by showing one and all that the Old Man really existed. Once again I chose not to answer his question for fear of saying the wrong thing.

He gave me that same long few seconds, and when I didn't respond, sighed. "I knew you were going to be difficult, Mr. Marlowe, so I've already put into motion a scenario that will put a very black storm cloud over the head of someone you care for. Matter of fact, I was so sure you would respond this way that you should be aware of the inclement weather very shortly." He hesitated, then added, "And believe me, this time it is for real," apparently referring to the phony Walter Fishbain frame that had derailed.

Now I spoke. Loudly. I didn't care if Big Ears Eli heard me or not. What the Old Man had just said had my anxiety symptoms suddenly in overdrive. I knew what this man was capable of. "What are you going to do?"

"Shut your mouth and listen," he said, dropping his civilized facade. Then, lowering his angry tone a bit, he continued. "I'm a reasonable man, so I'll agree to make the problem this person will find themselves in disappear *and* I'll still have the movies withdrawn from the beach and your name whitewashed as far as involvement with them goes. But only *if* you discontinue your pursuit."

I had to fight to keep my voice from shaking, "What person are you talking about? What have you done?"

"I've said enough already, especially on the telephone," he said smoothly. "I'll be in touch with you as soon as you know the answer to your two questions. And that should be very soon. Good day, Mr. Marlowe."

I almost said something else but there was no point. I'd heard him hang up and there was only a dull hum on the line. I hung up the phone and walked back to the beer spigot in front of Eli. He must have seen something, maybe the shock in my face, because he said nothing. Not that I would have heard him. The voice in my head was too loud.

The Old Man, whom I knew to be a coldblooded murderer, had just made a threat against someone. And he'd said that someone was a person I cared for. It had to be. Otherwise the Old Man couldn't be sure I would be motivated to do as he requested.

Who was he going to make a move on—Shamrock, Dianne, my children maybe, or someone else who meant something to me? And what did he have planned?

What should I do about it? What *could* I do about it?

The floor under the rubber mat beneath my feet started to turn to quicksand. A sense of dread, as if I'd just heard a tsunami was about to slam into Hampton Beach, rolled through me. I didn't have my Xanax with me, so for the next few hours I used every trick in the book I knew to keep the anxiety from turning into a full-blown panic attack.

It was a long shift to say the least.

Chapter 39

I SPENT THE entire night endlessly rehashing what I was going to do about the threats the Old Man had made. It was a fool's errand. How could it be anything else? Number one— I had no idea what the Old Man planned to do. Number two—I didn't have an inkling which of the people close to me was going to be involved in this scheme to shut me up. I'd narrowed the list down to probably five or six possible people but that wasn't written in stone. Even I had more friends and family than that. And number three—I didn't have a goddamn clue who the Old Man was.

It wasn't until I reached the High Tide later that morning that I found out I'd wasted a lot of brain power pondering the issue all night. I could have just waited to get an answer—to the first two questions, anyway. I'd forgotten how the Old Man had said his ploy was already in motion and that I wouldn't have long to find out. Not really forgotten. I remembered almost every word he'd said. It just never dawned on me he'd move this fast.

"They've put a lien on the restaurant, Dan!" Dianne was sitting behind the desk in her office. I'd just come through the back door to start my shift when she'd called to me. I stood looking down at her. She was visibly upset.

"A lien?" I said stupidly. "Who? How much?"

"Yes, a lien." She rubbed her hand across her forehead and over her hair. "The state. And for more than I can come up with."

I sat quickly in a chair, leaned my arm on her desk. "What the hell for?"

"Failure to pay the food tax for one. With a ton of interest and penalties."

"When did you get this?"

She let out a deep sigh. "Yesterday when I got home."

"You should have called me."

"What for? So you couldn't sleep too?"

I reached out, put my hand on Dianne's which was resting on the desk. "Honey, you don't have anything to worry about. I know you. You've probably paid more than you owe."

I was sure of that. Dianne was as honest as any restaurant owner could be, maybe too honest. "Have you talked to your accountant?"

Dianne rolled her eyes. "Not yet." She looked at me with something in her eyes I didn't like seeing there. Fear. "What if he made a mistake along the line somewhere?"

I shook my head. "No, he's the best. You don't have to worry there."

Dianne took her hand from under mine and glanced away. "What about . . . you know?"

And suddenly I did know. And I also knew the reason for my queasy stomach. I used to own the High Tide. Then I'd lost it, along with my family and every dime I'd had. Dianne had bailed me out. She'd bought the business and had kept me on as a bartender. And that was the least of what she'd done to save me from myself. It had all worked out, too, so far anyway. I still had my fingers crossed.

What Dianne had alluded to though was some financial shenanigans I'd been involved in when I was at my worst. This had taken place while I'd owned the Tide, before Dianne had bought the place, and included some creative payments to the state. Anyway, that had been a long time ago, and I'd believed, or at least had hoped, that my misconduct had slid under the radar. Apparently it had. Until now.

Then it hit me like a sucker punch. Somehow the Old Man had found out about the payments I'd played free and loose with and he'd been able to get someone in the tax department interested. Or maybe he ordered them to act. Could he be that powerful? It didn't really matter how he'd done it. What was I going to do about it? That was the question.

I felt my face flush a bit as I said, "Have you talked to your lawyer? They can't hold you responsible for that? Can they?"

"I just left him. We didn't have time to talk about everything. But he did ask me if I knew if there was anything owed before I bought the business."

I felt myself becoming sicker as I looked at Dianne. I couldn't tell if she was worried or angry. It was probably both. I'd told her in a drunken moment what I'd done with the Tide's taxes. Told her after she bought the business, unfortunately. And she'd hit the roof. No surprise there. Anyone would have been upset. What was surprising was that she eventually forgave me. That was Dianne. Because of a lack of money on both our parts, and the old adages about *let sleeping dogs lie* and *opening a can of worms*, we'd decided to keep our fingers crossed and hope it had slipped through the cracks unnoticed. I had assured Dianne at the time that if there was ever a problem, I'd take care of it.

She hesitated, then continued. "I said I didn't think so. But he asked that more than once." She hesitated again, then said, "He's probably heard the stories, too."

He probably had. Almost every year-round resident in Hampton had and he was an old townie lawyer to boot. He knew if a parking space came up for lease on the beach. So I was paying again, for the umpteenth time, for my wayward past. Correction. It wasn't me who was paying this time. It was Dianne. She was paying for the asshole I used to be and felt like I still was.

I could feel the heat in my face as I said, "They can't hold you responsible for that."

She nodded slowly several times. "He hinted that they can. Especially if there's a close relationship between us. They wouldn't believe I hadn't known. That's what he implied." A little anger came into her tone as she added, "Even though I *didn't* know."

Suddenly I felt like crawling under the desk. "I never thought that would cause you trouble, Dianne." And at the time I really hadn't thought it would ever bounce back on her. Of course, I wasn't thinking straight back then. How could I have been? I'd just come off a multi-year, record-breaking run of snorting everything up my nose on Hampton Beach except the sand. And one night I actually did a tiny bit of that, too. But that's another story. Right now, somehow, I had to get Dianne out of this.

"Gregson says I'm going to have to get a Concord lawyer to fight it," Dianne said, referring to her lawyer by his last name. "One with state house connections." She scowled before she added, "He says they may want five grand as a retainer."

"Five grand?"

"Yes, five thousand dollars. And that's just for starters, he said. With no guarantees." Dianne raised her eyes to the ceiling for a moment, then looked at me. Her eyes were moist. There was a catch in her voice when she continued. "He said there could also be criminal charges."

I didn't say anything. I didn't know what to say. This was bad. Very bad.

"What about your friend James?" she asked.

I almost fell out of the chair when she said that. I could have just told her the truth—that he was among the missing. Somewhere on the seacoast with Lonnie Ellison. The two of them on a monumental cocaine tear. But if I said that word—cocaine—Dianne would probably come unglued. So instead of telling the entire truth, I spoke a half truth. "He's a criminal lawyer. You probably won't need someone like him."

Dianne sputtered. "Are you deaf? Didn't you hear what I just told you? And I didn't tell you that he said it's more than possible I'll be charged." She stopped. I could tell she was holding back tears. "I'm scared, Dan."

That was enough for me. Dianne saying those three little words hit me as if I'd just been struck by lightning while walking on the beach. It wasn't about my own legal situation. At least not yet. After all, I'd had my fair share of run-ins with the law. In fact, I was *almost* getting used to them. But Dianne? She didn't deserve this. She was as clean as Mother Theresa. It was my own jackass actions that had gotten her involved in this. Right down the line.

And what if she was charged? It could happen. Because of me. That was even worse than the money and her possibly losing the High Tide. I could work my fingers to the bone. Pay her back every penny this fiasco caused her. But I couldn't pay her for the shame she'd feel if she were arrested. Or the stress a court case and the horrible publicity would put on her. I couldn't let that happen. I couldn't let any of it happen.

I tried to remain calm. "Give me a couple of days before you hire a new lawyer or do anything else, Dianne."

She looked at me, furrowed her brows. "Why? What can you do?"

I couldn't tell her what I was thinking. She already had more than enough on her mind. Besides, it wouldn't do her any good if I told her who I thought was behind this. I had caused her to be in this position. *Me*. Not the Old Man. He'd just taken advantage of what I'd created.

I had to get her out of this jackpot any way I could. Even if what I had to do to extricate her from this situation went against the promise I'd made to myself about never backing down from anything. That was small potatoes. It was all about Dianne now.

"Just a couple of days, honey. I think I can make this right."

Her eyes narrowed. "You aren't going to do anything crazy, are you?"

"No, nothing crazy," I said to her.

But to myself, I added, *At least not as crazy as what I did to get you in this pickle. Matter of fact, it's pretty sane. It's the only thing I can do. I have no other choice. Personal promise or not.*

Chapter 40

I'D NEVER REALIZED that one man had this much power on the seacoast. But *now* I believed it. In fact, I was a True Believer. The Old Man could ruin lives and apparently get away with it. He wielded that type of power. I had to acknowledge that power and play ball with him. Not because I was afraid for myself, what with the tax people digging around in the High Tide's old financial records. I was sure there was plenty in there to incriminate me even though I couldn't really remember a lot of what I'd done back then. I had no trouble envisioning myself as a resident of the Rockingham County Jail, or worse, the state prison in Concord. It didn't scare me. Oh, maybe a little, but not much. You see I don't really have a high opinion of myself, not then or now. And when you feel that way about yourself, the thought of a stint in jail is oddly an "oh well" moment. Everything in my world had felt like a struggle for quite a while now. Maybe I could even use the vacation. Besides I deserved whatever I got, didn't I?

So I wasn't going to knuckle under to the Old Man's demands to save myself. I had to do it for Dianne. I had no doubt that she was in danger of losing the High Tide. Maybe even her condo. And there was a chance personal bankruptcy would follow. I could see all that happening easily. The authorities loved to go after assets and Dianne had them. Me? Just a mortgaged-to-the-hilt cottage, nothing more.

Beyond that was the chilling specter of criminal charges. I hadn't told her what I truly thought about the possibility of her being arrested and tried, but only because I didn't want to frighten her more than she already was.

But I *was* worried that they would tie her into my financial stupidity. After all, she was my significant other. That alone would raise eyebrows when certain illegal actions were exposed to the light of day. It would be unlikely that they'd believe she'd known nothing of my playing with the books, even though it was the truth. Even when I backed her up, which would be like Clyde Barrow claiming Bonnie Parker was innocent of all their crimes. My reputation wasn't sterling.

The night after my talk with Dianne, I sat in my easy chair drinking beer with the TV on, pretending to relax. Believe me I wasn't. I was a freaking wreck. That's when the phone rang.

"Mr. Marlowe." His voice was steady and commanding.

And even though his words hadn't been in question mode, I answered, "Yes."

"I assume by now you've been informed by someone that they have . . . let's say . . . a very vexing problem?"

I inhaled deeply through my nose and let it out. "Yes."

"Good. And have you come to a decision regarding my offer to eradicate this problem?"

"Yes."

"And?"

"You win." It was that simple.

"Fine," the Old Man said. "My research indicated that, even with your sordid past, you had some decency underneath. I'm glad to hear it was correct and that you've made the right decision."

I must have been trying to grow a little bit of spine because I said quickly, "That's if you follow through on your promises."

The Old Man chuckled, then quickly cut himself off. "Never fear, Mr. Marlowe. I am a man of my word. I will have the off-color tapes removed from your beach and your name erased from involvement. Also Ms. Dennison will find out that her troubles have acquired a knack for fixing themselves."

Even though I had no doubt of the validity of his statements, I still asked, "You can do all this?"

"Mr. Marlowe, *please*," he said. Then clearing his throat, he added, "I may not be able to put *everything* back into the bottle for Ms. Dennison. You realize that once these inquiries are begun, only so much backtracking is possible. Even for me."

"Wait a second. You said—"

He cut me off brusquely. "I know what I said, Mr. Marlowe. And I also know whatever small financial penalty may have to be levied on Ms. Dennison so my associate can close the case without arousing suspicions is an insignificant price to pay to avoid the other outcomes that could have been."

We were both silent for a long moment.

Then he said, "And it *was* your fault after all, Mr. Marlowe. Ms. Dennison could have only been put in this unpleasant situation because of your past indiscretions."

Of course he was right. And boy, did I know it. "You know all about me, don't you?"

"Mr. Marlowe," he said, his voice going up and down a bit. "My abilities and connections were, of course, necessary to put this all into motion. But your background is an open book on Hampton Beach. But you know that, don't you?"

Yes, I did.

"So, Mr. Marlowe, I hope this will be the last time I have to contact you. I've given my word as to what I will do. And you will soon see I am a man of my word. You have promised to stay out of my affairs and suspend your inquiries. I expect you to be a man of your word. Remember, anything that I have been good enough to stop, I can put back into motion at any time. And the second time around will be *much* worse. And permanent. So good night to you, Mr. Marlowe. Sleep well."

I didn't try to say anything before he hung up. There was nothing to say. It was over. My past had returned to ask for payback—again. And I had just paid. I'd probably go on paying for a long time to come. How long? Who the hell knew. It was the Old Man today. Tomorrow it would probably be someone else. And I deserved it.

All I could hope for now was that he'd keep his word, that the Old Man would make Dianne's problems disappear. Also that he'd get rid of the porn tapes on the beach and pull my name out of that mud hole. I was now certain that porn tapes on Hampton Beach were small potatoes to someone like him. Even to me, they no longer mattered much. Just a little side dish I didn't really care about. The important thing was freeing Dianne from this terrible situation. All because of me.

Chapter 41

ABOUT A WEEK after my phone conversation with the Old Man I was at Dianne's condo. We were in bed. We'd just had sex. Very nice sex. It was almost always very nice sex with Dianne. And the times it wasn't? Well, that was always my fault too. But I don't dwell on it. I'd recently started to feel a bit better about myself and I certainly had no desire to ruin that.

It was dark except for the moonlight coming through the open windows. Dianne had just opened them and turned off the air conditioning. I could smell the salt in the warm humid air drifting in along with the sound of pounding waves on the beach across Ocean Boulevard and the hum of passing cars. I leaned my bare back against the headboard, Dianne's head in the crook of my arm. The smell of some fruity shampoo in her hair mixed nicely with the salty air. It was all very relaxing.

We were going over it again. The same thing we'd been talking about for the past two days. And we seemed to agree on everything. Well, almost everything.

"For the last time, Dan, I'm not going to let you borrow the money."

And I said, just as adamantly, "Yes, I'm going to. I *have* to, Dianne. And that's final."

The Old Man had kept his end of the bargain. As fast as the state had placed a huge lien on the High Tide, they'd offered to take it off just as fast and clear the bill. For $10,000. Because of how I'd manipulated the Tide's taxes in the past, Dianne felt it was a good idea to pay the bill and be done with it. And she was right. If the offer wasn't accepted, we both knew the state would most likely continue digging around, in which case they might find all kinds of discrepancies in the back taxes. Probably enough to put the Tide out of business and maybe even enough to put both of us in prison. I shuddered at the thought. I'd probably look good in stripes. Dianne, not so much. I pulled her tight.

Dianne turned her head, looked at me. Her green eyes shone in the moonlight. "You're not going to be happy unless you do. Are you?"

I chuckled. "I have to do it. It *was* all my fault. Sometimes I feel like a loser."

She gave me an elbow. "Get off your pity-pot. I don't like it."

I didn't much either. So I lied and said, "I was kidding."

"Hmm, sure you were." Dianne snuggled her head harder against me. "You've got a lot to be happy about. Hopefully, nothing else about the Tide's books back then is going to come out now." She looked at me again and shook her head. She forced her lips thin for a moment, then turned back. "And that disgusting stuff the police thought you were involved in is gone now, or so you said."

Dianne was referring to the porn tapes. The Old Man had kept his word on that, too. The tapes had disappeared from the few beach stores that carried them within a couple of days of my conversation with him. That hadn't surprised me. What *had* surprised me was when I spoke to Steve Moore a few days after that. He'd told me that Gant had stopped his ranting and raving about my supposed porn operation. One of the very few cops that Gant confided in had told Steve that Gant had been informed that the tapes on Hampton Beach were part of a Boston-based distribution ring backed by organized crime. And they'd pulled their flicks out of Hampton because up here there wasn't enough money in it for them to bother with. Gant had also been informed that, except for the few store owners who had carried them, there were no other locals involved in the porn distribution racket. That had included me.

Who whispered all this in Gant's ear? Steve didn't know. And it really didn't matter to me. I knew who was behind it. The important part was that I was cleared of that embarrassing accusation.

"Not *all* the police believed I was involved with the porn," I offered. "Mostly just Gant."

"Asshole! You should have sued him, Dan. He hit you."

Me sue Gant? I would've loved to, but there were way too many skeletons in my closet. It would have done nothing but make my life harder than it already was. I hadn't told Dianne, but I'd decided right after the night Gant slugged me that I owed him something, all right. But it wasn't a lawsuit. It was a punch in the chops. I'd be the one to pick the time and place. Just like he had.

"That would just make a bad situation worse," I said. "A lot worse."

Dianne let it go.

We didn't speak for a couple of minutes. We were both lost in our own thoughts—until Dianne said, "Funny how everything seems to be all cleared up now." She looked at me again. "It is all cleared up, isn't it, Dan?"

"Sure, it's all cleared up," I answered, trying to reassure her.

"And . . . what about those men found murdered?"

I had to be careful. I didn't want Dianne to worry anymore. She'd worried enough. Because of me. "The guys in the dumpster? That had something to do with the Boston gang. Maybe the porn stuff. That's what Steve said the cops think anyway. It was just a coincidence that it happened when it did."

"Not just them. The Bartender and his driver? And Walter Fishbain too?"

I shrugged. Her head went up and down on my arm. "Early and his driver were in the porn business. Maybe someone wanted the competition out of the way or they could've gotten caught screwing their Boston boss. And Fishbain? You know what he was. He could've been involved in anything. Maybe he was even tied into the porn racket. Who knows?"

I'd already told Dianne all this. I'd also told her that Steve had said the police felt higher-ups in the porn racket had heard the false rumors about me in the porn trade, believed them, and had ordered Big Man and Little Guy to shut me down as unwanted competition. Maybe they had been at my cottage that night to just give me a beating, but it had escalated. Whoever they had worked for hadn't been happy. Then again, Steve had said, maybe they were killed for some other misstep and it just had been another coincidence they'd been taken out then and there. Steve had also said that the police believed what I'd told Dianne regarding the other three murder victims.

I knew the truth though and I kept it to myself. I had to. To tell Dianne or anyone else what I knew, risked Dianne's safety. So I kept tight lipped.

Still, Dianne had a sixth-sense about me. I knew she was suspicious but she was pleased with the way things were turning out so she didn't press. That was good—I couldn't have told her anyway. The Old Man had insisted on that. And I also had no idea how Dianne would react. If she reacted badly and told someone else . . . well, I couldn't take a chance on what the Old Man might do if he heard about it. His tentacles ran deep and he had eyes and ears everywhere. I knew that much for sure.

When Dianne asked me, and not for the first time either, "What about that Old Man stuff, Dan? You really don't believe he exists now?"

I let out a deep sigh. "No. He was a figment of my imagination, I guess. Just like everyone'd been telling me. Probably just too much beer and not enough sleep."

Dianne lifted her head off my arm and looked at me like I'd just told her I doubted the truth of the moon landing.

But I didn't dare ask 'What?'

I'd been so sure of the Old Man's existence. I'd told Dianne so. And she knew me very well. So the more I talked about the Old Man, the greater the chance she'd know I was lying.

She wasn't the only one I'd have to disavow my previous statements about the Old Man to. I'd have to keep backtracking on that story every time someone mentioned my

Old Man tale. Shamrock, Steve Moore, or anyone else who had picked up on it one way or another. I had no choice. It was for the best. Dianne and the High Tide were no longer in jeopardy—as soon as I borrowed the money somewhere and paid that ten grand penalty, that is. I planned to do that as quickly as possible. And my name had been cleared of any association with the porn business. That was a very big plus too. To have that accusation circulating out there indefinitely wouldn't have helped with the rehabilitation of my name.

So, yes, it was all for the best the way it had turned out.

Still, I had to ask myself why I felt so uneasy, as if it really wasn't all over? The Old Man had done what he'd said, cut loose his hold on Dianne and the High Tide, and given my name a whitewash as far as the porn business went. I wouldn't be hearing from him again as long as I stopped referring to his existence and nosing around, trying to find out information about him.

I *had* stopped and had no intention of restarting. I had too much to lose. The main thing being what was snuggled up against me right now.

So why did the annoying little voice inside my brain keep whispering that I hadn't heard the last of the Old Man yet? I didn't know.

It was then I heard what sounded like a crowd cheering out on Ocean Boulevard. We looked at each other. Dianne's face puzzled. I was puzzled too. But only for a few more seconds. That's when the curtains on the windows rustled loudly and a wave of cool sea air rolled into the room. The heat wave had broken. The wind had turned off the water. Things could change that fast on Hampton Beach.

"Thank god," Dianne said.

We just held each other and enjoyed the feel of clean cool air on our skin.

Finally, Dianne spoke. She mentioned one other thing we'd been talking about a lot recently. "I'm going to miss her, Dan."

I nodded. I knew who she meant. Skye. I was going to miss her too. In the days after her death, Dianne and I had both come to realize we had grown close to her. In funny ways. If she hadn't been from upstate New York and her burial services held there, we would have attended. But we didn't. I felt guilty about that and more so about her death, no matter how she'd really died.

I shook my head, tried to clear it of the troubling thoughts. Not much luck. There was *one* thing that could make me forget. At least for a while.

I turned toward Dianne, started to pull her face close to mine.

"Again?" she said, feigning a puzzled look.

"Sure, why not?"

"No reason. It just doesn't happen every day . . . or night that is. You must be feeling a lot better."

We both laughed and only stopped as our lips met. And yes, I did feel better. Of course Dianne had been right again. In my book, what else could she be.

About the Author

JED POWER is a Hampton Beach, NH-based writer and author of numerous published short stories. *The Boss of Hampton Beach, Hampton Beach Homicide, Blood on Hampton Beach, Honeymoon Hotel,* and *Murder on the Island* are the five previous novels in the Dan Marlowe crime series.

The Combat Zone, the first crime novel in a new series, is now out. The series follows a P.I. who hangs his hat in early 1970s Harvard Square and roams the Combat Zone, Boston's red-light district. This novel was a finalist in the St. Martin's Press/Private Eye Writers of America "Best First P. I. Novel" competition. All books are available in both paper and ebook.

Find out more at www.darkjettypublishing.com.

CPSIA information can be obtained
at www.ICGtesting.com
Printed in the USA
BVOW06s0123290118
506585BV00001B/40/P